Spoiler alert: This book is the sequel to The Involuntary Ghostwriter. Reading The Ghostwriter's Wife first will reveal events that do not occur until the later part of The Involuntary Ghostwriter.

Warning: This book contains adult themes and sexual content that may be objectionable for some readers.

This is a work of fiction. The characters and events in this book are fictional, and those roughly based on either real people or real events have been heavily twisted, bent and distorted by my imagination, until they have become fiction. Only one character in the book is closely enough based on a real person in some passages that they may have claim to being misrepresented or slandered. I've made a solemn promise not to sue myself.

This is a work of fiction. Names, characters, organizations, places, events, and incidents are either products of the author's imagination or are used fictitiously.

Text copyright © 2015 Douglas Debelak
All rights reserved.

No part of this book may be reproduced, or stored in a retrieval system, or transmitted in any form or by any means, electronic, mechanical, photocopying, recording, or otherwise, without express written permission of the publisher.

Dark Ink Press
www.darkinkpress.com

ISBN-13: 978-0998480138 (Dark Ink Press)
ISBN-10: 0998480134

Cover design by Michelle Azru

Printed in the United States of America

For
my wife
Debra

my mother
Annette

and
my son and daughter
Eric and Amber

In the beginning ...

Posted: 12/15/2014 7:57 pm

In the beginning...
I was born.
Not what most of you expected to hear, but hearing much of what I say will not be easy for those of you with long-held and cherished beliefs. You may have difficulty making any sense at all of much I tell you, because it will be so contradictory to your preconceptions and all you've been taught.
Some of you are so entrenched in your beliefs that you will continue to insist you know me better than I know myself.
I hear many of you protest, "Don't tell me what I believe!" But, who else would know that better?
Of course, many of you haven't listened for years and didn't expect to hear my voice at all. Some of you are the most surprised to hear my words. As always, most of you will continue to disbelieve, and will refuse to accept these words as mine.
None of this changes the truth of me one iota.
I did not create the Universe. I exist within it. I am not what any of your modern religions define as "God." I did, however, create the tiny part of the Universe where you exist, what you think of as everything and call the universe. If you insist on a title, of those used in the past, "Creator" is the most accurate. "Father" is a name I long to hear, but it would not be appropriate to address me so, as yet.
The Universe is far larger, older and more complex than you've yet to imagine. There are many of these tiny objects you call the universe, but these universes are all parts of one much larger Universe. Think of your universe as merely one tiny sparkle of light in a galaxy of sparkling lights. So far as I know, there is only one Universe, but even what I have come to consider the Universe may, in fact, be only one of many within a still greater UNIVERSE.

Douglas Debelak

I was born, in a universe much like your own... longer ago than you can possibly imagine. I grew up and once had a life much like your own.

I did not invent sex. I can't take credit for that. It predates me, but it is one of my favorite things.

I did not invent sin. That is entirely a creation of your own.

I hear your brains boiling over with questions. All in good time.

Intrigued – Annie Fry

7/4/2015 7:35 AM

'I was born.'

"Of course," was Annie Fry's initial reaction, reading the words, "Of course. Wasn't everyone?" Then she looked at the chapter title. 'In the beginning... I was born,' together, in the same breath, did make her pause and think; *Why would someone bother to write 'I was born,' if there wasn't some significance to the statement?* It almost sounded as though God was saying He was born. In fact, that was exactly what the statement was saying. She couldn't get her mind around that notion. She sat on the sofa in the den, focused intently on the screen of Jonathon Fry's ThinkPad, wearing only the she'd towel wrapped around herself. Her hair was still wet from her shower.

When Annie woke in her own bed and realized Jon wasn't beside her, she'd gotten up to see whether he'd fallen asleep in his chair again. He did that, more and more regularly of late, and, if she found him, she'd usually wake him as gently as possible and get him to come to bed. She hated seeing him sleeping in his chair, but not quite as much as she hated him sleeping in the back bedroom; which was the next logical place to look. But, it was the picture album laying open that took her thoughts away from both her missing husband and his computer being left out again. She'd read the words, 'Good Times,' and started to cry.

Afterward, she'd slipped out of the bed, in the back bedroom, as quietly as she could, in order not to wake her husband. She didn't think sex was dirty, but it could certainly be messy. She'd left the bathroom door open while she showered, perhaps as a subtle invitation, if Jon were to wake. When she'd stepped out and reached for a towel, she'd had a direct view back into the den, and Jon's ThinkPad caught her eye.

Not that she wanted to snoop. That wasn't something she'd ever done and she felt guilty about it; but he'd been careless lately, and he'd left his ThinkPad wide open again.

Every evening, she'd been closing it and moving it somewhere safer and out of sight. She couldn't help herself being fastidious, wanting everything in its place. Now, she couldn't help herself either. She touched the touchpad to see what happened, and the screen instantly came alive.

Jon was still logged in. Her heart rate jumped to a gallop. She really should stop right there and leave things alone before she fucked it all up again. But, he was also still logged into the administrative screen of this blog he'd been talking about. Everything he'd been working on the entire past year. She'd read the first few posts, trying to convinced herself, she wasn't snooping. She wasn't checking up on him. She was just intrigued. Still, she found herself constantly looking up to make sure Jon didn't catch her, as she continued to read. She'd decided, if he woke and walked into the den, she'd jump up and drop her towel. That would distract him enough to keep him from asking what she was doing.

Jon had been strange, it occurred to Annie, momentarily pulling her attention away from the ThinkPad's screen. It wasn't unreasonable that he'd been happy to have all she'd put him through finally come to an end. But, she hadn't expected him to cry. Then again, she really had no way of knowing what she'd put him through.

She'd been wrestling with the whole tangled mess of her own insecurities from the beginning and Jon was right; she had been unfair, and, if honest, just plain mean. She'd been intending to tell him she was sorry for several months. That she'd agree to go with him, talk with his therapist, and do whatever was necessary to get their lives back, including their sex life. But, she couldn't get herself unstuck, and days and weeks slipped past. She couldn't just admit she was wrong and he was right. And, he had also been right; he couldn't control what he dreamed.

But, no, she'd been stupid and insecure enough to mess things up, when she'd been having the best sex of her life. Who the fuck cared what got his hormones in such an uproar? Sue, her best friend, had been beating her over the head about that from the beginning, too. Jon hadn't just been fucking her brains out, which he had, but he'd been doing it while making wild passionate love to her. To her. Not some other woman. If he had been having sex with someone else, she couldn't imagine he could possibly have had that much energy left for her. But, she couldn't keep her stupid mouth shut. She had to do what she always did, and go digging for something wrong with what had been so wonderful.

What an insecure bitch she could be sometimes.

She hoped she'd started to repair things between them, if even a little, that morning. She'd certainly tried. And, if Jon's body's reactions were any indication, she'd succeeded. At the very least she'd got them unstuck. Got herself unstuck. Jon would have been unstuck the instant she asked, 'Do you want...?' She doubted she'd have had a chance to complete the sentence. He'd have happily 'stuck' her right there on the floor, where ever they happened to be. Annie chastised herself again.

What an insecure bitch she could be sometimes. What a goddamned insecure bitch!

Intersection

Posted: 6/30/2015 12:00 AM

Why tell you a story of a life that could have been any of yours?

Exactly for that reason. So, you'd understand my early life was not so different from your own. I had many of the same experiences and struggles. I did not begin as I am, and I did not begin having advantages you do not.

Why am I addressing you now?

Because you are at a pivotal point in the evolution of your species. There have been transformative events during the history of your planet before, such as the evolution of fishes into amphibians, when something first slithered out of the water and began to live part of its life on land. Humans are now poised at the precipice of another such transformative, potentially transcendent, evolutionary event, where you have the opportunity to take an immense leap toward becoming far more than you can currently imagine. But, close your eyes and try your best. Let that thought settle a moment, then try again to imagine far beyond that, then further, far, far, further. Don't be concerned your imaginations will take you beyond what is possible.

Your imaginations are what create those possibilities. Your imaginations are the driving force of you becoming... More.

You are participants in your own creation. When one of your early ancestors first held something in their hand to use as a simple tool or weapon and when one of them first stood up on their hind legs and began to walk with their head held higher than the rest, those events mark the beginning of your participation in your own evolution beyond just another animal occupying your planet. Your participation progressed in earnest when others of you learned to make more sophisticated tools, others first learned how to use fire, others to domesticate animals, to grow and raise food, rather than hunt and gather, at which point your earliest civilizations began to form, which was followed shortly by one of your most transcendent discoveries when you learned to read and write.

The Ghostwriter's Wife

Stop a moment and look back five-hundred years and try to appreciate how dramatic the changes in your world have been. Consider how the modern world, which you all accept with casual nonchalance, would seem to a person of that era. Nearly everything you do in your daily life without giving it any thought would be seen as witchcraft. Every one of you would be seen as sorcerers. Can you imagine explaining your smartphone to the Inquisition?

Now try to let your imagination look ahead five-hundred years more, then beyond. Can you imagine far enough into the future to where you would begin to perceive humans of the time as gods? Do you have the faintest concept of the possibilities ahead of you?

I can't predict your future since you are free to make your own decisions and alter your own course. But, here are some teasers:

Eventually, someone might be able to talk meaningfully about 'Global warming' because they'll have lived long enough to have experienced a span of geological time. The quick answer is, yes, the climate of your planet changes. It has been in a continuous state of flux from the very beginning, which will continue, right up until the instant the atmosphere is boiled away and your planet is absorbed into the Sun. That will certainly be 'Global warming.'

Does this mean you shouldn't concern yourselves with the ecological state of your planet? Of course not, unless you don't care whether you continue to live there. But, don't get caught up in the hype and blindly accept the words of others, many of whom have agendas other than those they admit publicly. Keep in mind: Glaciers once covered most of the planet and fossilized remains of tropical plants have also been discovered in the polar regions of your world.

Einstein will likely become a footnote in history, alongside Ptolemy. What will bring about Einstein's fall to the bottom of the page? I could write at length, of course, but few of you would have any interest, so instead I'll just throw out a few little tidbits: It is possible to travel faster than light and it does not result in traveling backward in time. Traveling backward in time is actually impossible, but the explanation is *best left for another time. Secondly, E is not equal to mc^2. As I've said, even what you think of as the universe is far larger, older and more complex than you know. Far more.*

Why do I say likely? Could he actually be right? No. There is just a very real possibility your species won't survive long enough to make the discoveries that will leave his theories no more useful than loops around the earth to track the movement of the celestial bodies.

There will also likely come a time when your current definition of Moore's law will seem like stasis. What took 18 months will occur in closer to 18 minutes, then 18 seconds. But, there will also come a time when Virtual will no longer be differentiated from reality, and Artificial will no longer be differentiated from intelligence. Nor will metaphysical be differentiated from physical... A time when mortality will become a distant memory for some and the reality of only lesser beings.

This point in my narrative marks the intersection of yesterday and tomorrow, where the story of my early years has overlain your much more recent past, and the story of my life from this point forward might well foretell of events in your future. All of the ideas and technology I've discussed to this point, already exist in your world, even if they are not commonly known. Going forward, more and more of what I tell you will resemble science fiction, and further forward still, just as your present would to those from five-hundred years earlier, it will seem like magic, perhaps more appropriately: Magick.

There is more, much more to tell you. Once again, be patient. I am a long way from the end.

Holy Shit – Annie Fry

7/4/2015 2:35 PM

"Holy Shit!" Annie repeated, for the third time. She didn't know what to think or make of everything she'd just read; but her eyes burned from staring at the computer's screen for the past six hours, she was hungry, and she had to pee. She was still sitting in the den in nothing but a towel. Her hair had dried in tangles - to which, she added another, "Shit!"

Then it struck her, as she looked at the time in the corner of the screen - Jon couldn't still be asleep, could he? She'd better check on him! "Fuck!" Adrenaline shot through her as she jumped up from the couch, instinctively holding on to her towel. Seriously, what the fuck, she thought, she was in her own damned house, and her husband had seen her naked before. Recently, in fact. It had been dark, so he probably didn't see much. But, his hands had done the seeing for him.

Jon wasn't there. How was that possible? Annie didn't think she'd been so absorbed that he could have walked past and she wouldn't have noticed, nor could she imagine that he wouldn't have asked what she was doing with his computer. So, "What the hell? Jon!"

There was no answer. She was baffled. Then it occurred to her, he must have gotten up while she was in the shower and gone downstairs. That was the only logical answer, because she didn't believe in alien abductions. She instinctively headed toward the stairs, then decided, it was one thing to run around naked on the second floor, with all the drapes pulled closed, but the front door was directly at the bottom of the stairs, and it was mostly glass with a clear view of the street and sidewalk that ran in front of their house. She wasn't technically naked, she did have a towel around her, but that still felt more than naked enough. So, she should probably throw on some clothes, rather than expose some innocent passerby to her flabby, old, towel-covered, naked self. And, she might as well run a hairbrush through her tangled rat's nest. And, pee!

Her thoughts went back to everything she'd read that morning, now afternoon, as she sat and felt an instantaneous rush of relief as her over full bladder emptied. She'd read everything Jon had posted, but all the more recent posts had been at midnight every Tuesday morning, which confused her. She supposed it was possible he was still posting them. He was almost always up late enough.

But, he'd told her earlier that he hadn't written anything in months. She'd specifically asked how his writing was going and he'd told her, it wasn't. Had he already written everything and somehow set it up to post automatically? In which case there had to be more of what he'd written somewhere on the blog site. She couldn't ask, because then she'd have to admit she'd been snooping. So, she'd just continue snooping.

After she'd dressed and brushed the tangles out of her hair, she went back to the den and sat at Jon's computer again. There were indeed over a hundred additional files in a folder titled 'unposted,' with what looked to be dates at the beginning of each file name, all future dates, and - she counted days in her head – all of them Tuesdays. So, there was a whole shitload more than what she'd already ready read. She was tempted, but she was really hungry, and she still hadn't located her missing husband.

She found him sitting on the deck, in nothing but a T-shirt and his boxer briefs, staring out into the yard.

"Hey," she said, putting her hand on his shoulder – concerned. He wasn't himself. She didn't know what was up.

"Hey," Jon said, turning to look back at her. "So…?"

"What?" Annie asked.

"So, what did you think? I came back up to ask if you wanted coffee and saw you reading. I said your name, but you were obviously engrossed, so I decided not to bother you."

"Oh…" Annie said, a flush of embarrassment reddening her face. She'd been caught. "Are you pissed?"

Jon shrugged and shook his head. "No. Why would I be? I've been leaving it out so you'd find it. I figured you'd have been curious enough that you'd have already read it. So, no. Read it all. Please. I still don't know what the fuck to think about it. I really don't know what to think about anything anymore." He grimaced and looked back out into the yard.

"Lunch?" Annie asked him. It was late for lunch, but she hadn't eaten anything that day, and she assumed Jon wouldn't have either.

"Sure, I guess," Jon answered, still staring intently at something in the yard.

Annie looked in the direction he was looking, but didn't notice anything out of the ordinary. She had a wicked thought and wondered whether a blowjob, right then and there, might not yank him back out of whatever funk he was in, but she looked around at all the windows, from any one of which, or all of them, someone could be watching. Probably not the best idea, she decided. Or, her insecurities, lack of courage and all the rules stuffed into her head her entire life, about what was acceptable behavior, had decided. She thought it was excellent idea. But, her wanton new voice had been out voted. Lunch now. Blowjob later.

Sometimes, she wished she weren't such a coward and was more adventuresome, like her friend, Sue. She was all but certain Sue would have given Jon the blowjob and thought nothing of it. And, Annie didn't mean, given the same circumstances. Given the chance, she thought Sue would probably have given her husband, Jon, a blowjob on the deck. Fuck what the neighbors thought.

Start Ups

Posted: 7/7/2015 12:00 AM

The legal firm, that helped negotiate the deal for the sale of my patent, also handled the details for the formation of a pair of corporations. The first was Magick Hat, Inc., the intended business of which was the development and marketing of the Brain Computer Interface devices Bob and I had been creating since shortly after we'd met at grad school. Of course, there would also be all the auxiliary parts and accessories required to attach these Hats to customized signal processing systems. Then, there was what would always be the star of the show: the software to analyze, and help researchers make sense of the data they collected, which by itself appeared to be nothing but thousands of senseless static wave forms.

I'd spent hours going over legal entanglements I might encounter with the University, ad nauseam, but since I was leaving the University with nothing but the contents of my own brain, the attorneys felt there was little need for concern. A photographic memory was an extremely handy complement to the binary gene with which I'd been born. I'm not sure which parent I had to thank for these. My father, I suspected, which was ironic, since he'd never had any formal education beyond elementary school. Thanks to these gifts, not only could I see the schematics for all the electronics I intended to manufacture projected on the inside of my skull as clearly as if they'd been displayed on a computer screen, but I could also scroll through line after line of computer code. I'd regularly debugged code in my dreams, waking to know exactly which lines to fix to eliminate the problems frustrating me the day before.

I planned to get patents for my Magick Hats, copyrights for the software, and take all the other steps required to legally protect my intellectual property. But I also wasn't nearly as concerned about anyone stealing from me as I was about keeping my ultimate intentions a secret.

That was the purpose of the second corporation I had the attorneys form, which I very humbly named Telepathic Collaboration, Inc. Initially, TCI would be just another customer of

Magick Hat, Inc. The world had no need to know of it, until I was ready to introduce it to them. I had a vision of a grand unveiling. I'd publicly do business through Magick Hat, Inc. until then, from which I'd funnel the proceeds to fund the research and development for Telepathic Collaboration, Inc.

I had a well-formulated master plan, which clearly went well beyond simple telepathic texting. I had dreams to share dreams. And, as much as innovation had accelerated over the past century to the present, my intention was to supercharge that creative process, accelerating it to the rate collective minds participating in Telepathic Collaboration could imagine. I believed the only limit to anything was imagination, which would accelerate as well, with what could be imagined continually building on the foundation of what already had, forever reaching out toward the infinite.

For the first time, it occurred to me, if my wife could do all she'd dreamed, my own limitation would only be my own imagination. It was my first glimpse of the possibility of becoming what I am. The thought passed through me as an adrenal jolt of fear. It was too terrifying a prospect to process and I chased it from my mind to concentrate on more immediate tasks. However fast the future seemed to be racing toward me, the truth was I was racing toward it, the only way I could; a single step, a single act, a single thought at a time. But, from that first day, my pace was far beyond pedestrian.

Douglas Debelak

Day Dreams and Lunch – Annie Fry

Annie made sandwiches for lunch, while watching her husband through the French doors off the kitchen. Something was off, but, Christ, hadn't she learned her lesson? Leave it alone!

She'd treated the poor guy as though he was unworthy of her for the past year. She'd left him questioning whether his marriage was going to survive. What did she expect? That he'd come flying back into her arms like an excited, grateful puppy at the end of a workday? Maybe if she'd pulled her head out of her ass months ago, he would have. But, she hadn't. She hadn't been able to get over herself. So, she'd procrastinated, even after she'd come to the conclusion that she was wrong, and that she needed to tell him he was right; then quit being such a neurotic bitch, and just fuck her husband. Why had that been so fucking hard, even with Sue bashing her over the head every opportunity she had? Annie thought Sue had actually taken considerable joy at all the shit she'd given her. But, she'd been right. Jon had been right. And she had to accept that she'd caused this distance between them. She'd pushed him away, even after he'd pleaded with her.

It was a wonder he hadn't left her. She'd given him every reason. Had she ever seriously thought about asking him to leave and getting a divorce? The seriousness of such thoughts had certainly hit home after her talk with Jon about the realities of taking that path. Losing the house. Everything. Because she'd been jealous of a dream. And, she knew she hadn't really wanted to lose him either. That's when she realized what a world class brain fart she'd had, and that she needed to get her shit back together before it was too late. Even scared into that realization, she'd dragged her feet. Susie had a field day with her, every time they'd talked of late. She dreaded the thought of the conversations ahead of her with her mother and sister.

She was going to make it up to Jon, and thinking about how she'd make it up to him had her own hormones going. Images of their bodies flowed through her thoughts and sensations flowed through her body. She wanted to taste him. That thought, complete with visuals, popped into her head with crystal clarity. She wanted to taste him. She wanted to feel his body respond when she took him into her mouth. And, she wanted to look up and see that look he always got in his eyes when he lost himself in passion and pleasure. She wanted to hear his words, or just the sounds he'd make. She wanted to see, feel, hear and taste his pleasure. Smell was in the mix too, but at such a deep, visceral level it escaped her conscious thoughts, but her most primal self wanted to smell him too.

She thought about him making love to her afterward, because he'd want to. She loved the way he kissed her. Loved how he made love to her ears. How he worked his way down her neck, wet and firm enough, it was like he wanted to pull her blood through her skin, but still never so hard he left a mark. Something about that always sent lightning bolts straight through her body to her vagina. She'd be wet before he ran his tongue across her left nipple, almost always her left nipple first, then sucked it into his mouth hard enough that it was like he wanted milk. That bowed her back just thinking about it, just as it always arched her back up from the bed when they were making love. Then he'd work his way down her body, the same way he had her neck, each pull on her flesh sending electric shocks through her, which she swore went all the way from her scalp to her feet.

He was predictable, but not in a bad, boring way. He always headed straight down, to make her the same offer, every time, if she'd let him. If she had the patience not to push him away, not to rush things along because she wanted to feel him inside her. If she let him, he'd make her explode over and over until she was limp, soaked in sweat, the sheets sticking to her back. And, then when she thought she couldn't possibly have another orgasm left in her body, he'd slide up, while his fingers took over, wiping her juices from his face with his forearm, kissing and sucking back up along her stomach, taking a quick pull on each nipple, until they were eye to eye, and he'd stare intently into her eyes, while the pressure built within her, then he'd dip and take her breast into his mouth again, just when she'd reached the edge, pushing her over into more convulsions of pleasure.

Only then would he finally roll on top of her, or, more often, gently roll her onto her side, spooning behind her, and ease his way into her, moving slowly inside her while his grip on her body gradually tightened. He made soft sounds of pleasure that sounded the same as if he was in pain, involuntary little groans, like when his back was bothering him. Then, at last, he let out a sighing groan, like when he... did something she did not want to associate with sex in any way, but it was the sound she'd heard him make when was on the toilet. She'd only heard it a few times, never intentionally, when she'd been standing outside of the bathroom door, about to ask whether she could come in; since they gave one another privacy for certain personal activities. It was a sound of release and relief, following a brief but intense physical effort.

She knew that he had more intense orgasms than those when he'd focused his attention on her. The best, oddly enough to her way of thinking, was just the simple old handjob, like they'd have done in the back seat of a car, if they'd known one another as teenagers; because he wasn't holding back, either trying to make intercourse last longer for her or still having some reluctance, after all their years together, to let go and come in her mouth. But, even though these orgasms, after being so attentive to her needs, weren't as intense, he seemed much more satisfied because he'd brought her pleasure. And the more pleasure he brought her the happier he seemed.

She was stupid not to let him do what he wanted. She'd needed to resist the urge to feel him pounding into her, with the slap of his body slamming into her ass. She loved that, but she couldn't expect him to last long enough for her to come. But, to be fair, even if he could have gone like a jackhammer for half an hour, she wasn't sure she could get there from that alone, still... it felt so goddamned good while it lasted. But, his orgasms seemed somewhat muted then as well, from his trying so hard to hold back and make it last for her. Always for her. What more could she ask? What the hell had she been thinking?

For the past year, she'd been damping down her sexual urges, nipping them before they got started, telling herself she didn't need that anymore. She was past menopause. Wasn't it natural for desire to weaken before it went away? Or, did it ever go away? Regardless, she'd been trying to suppress her urges, like when she used to get migraines, and she'd recognize the signs the instant they appeared. She'd taught herself to relax and let everything go, and her migraines gradually lessened in severity until she no longer got them at all. She'd thought she could suppress her desire the same way, except it wasn't by relaxing and letting it go, she'd pounded it back down, at the first little sign of it raising its head. Like some idiotic game of whack-a-mole.

She'd only allowed herself to masturbate twice in the past year- refusing herself, out of her stupid insistence on refusing him, when all he really wanted was to give her pleasure. He had his pleasure too, of course, but he was clearly less satisfied with a quick fuck, handjob or blowjob. He was never a "hey honey, how 'bout you get me off," kind of guy. He'd asked her for that, yes, several times, out of frustration this past year, but she knew, if she'd relented, he wouldn't have been satisfied with a quick handjob alone. He'd have been kissing her neck, trying to entice her, reminding her how he could make her body sing. He was quite a musician when she relaxed and let him play.

And, he really was a good man. He hadn't meant to hurt her, and why it had hurt her as much as it did was impossible for her to explain even to herself. Mostly her own insecurity that he'd want someone younger, as she grew visibly older and less happy with her own body; thinking, she'd want someone younger; if she was looking at what she saw in the mirror. She might have kicked herself to the curb and gone after someone younger and prettier.

And, he'd have found someone. No kidding herself there. He was a handsome man, even if he didn't think so. He was successful, and now he'd written a book - which ought to have some groupie allure. And, the ace of aces, he had that beautiful red Porsche, which, irrational as it was, she knew firsthand what that fucking car did to her own hormones. Just that car would have gotten him laid or blown in a heartbeat. But, he hadn't. Or, at least she thought he hadn't. But, she could hardly have blamed him – especially when she flat out told him to do it. She couldn't blame him, but she also wasn't sure she could have forgiven him, or forgotten that it had happened. She'd have lain awake thinking about it, visualizing what had taken place, torturing herself with jealousy and insecurity. So... she really didn't want to know. She really needed to flush that possibility from her thoughts. And, if she had an ounce of sense, she ought to make damn sure she kept his balls so drained he'd never have a drop for anyone else.

Annie looked down, surprised to find that her fingers had slipped into her jeans and had been busy while she'd stared through the French doors at her husband. She was close enough, she could have come, right there standing in her kitchen. Should she knock on the glass so he could watch? Would that turn him on? She knew it would. But, she'd save this one and let him have the pleasure of coaxing it from her body. She should knock on the glass, unfastening her jeans, and shove his hand into her panties as soon as he walked through the door. Let him feel how wet she was, then release the orgasm that was hanging there like a boulder at the edge of a cliff ready to fall.

Then, she'd drop to her knees and suck the juice from him in an ambush that would catch him so off guard he'd never have a chance to think, let alone hold back. Yes. Lunch could wait. It was just sandwiches. They wouldn't get cold. And, who cared if they did? She was going to have him the instant he stepped inside. She was like an animal ready to pounce. But, he still sat where he'd been since she came down and found him there. She should drop her clothes on the kitchen floor and walk out onto the goddamned deck butt naked. Channel her inner Sue. Screw the neighbors! She wanted to see the look in his eyes. What would he think about that? But, she knew she could never let herself, no matter how tempting...

Instead, she opened the door and told him, "Lunch is ready. Come on in." She felt all the energy that had built inside her drain away, as the words left her mouth. Must be like a guy losing a hard on, she thought. Damn!

A New Beginning

Posted: 7/14/2015 12:00 AM

It had been my intention, while my wife attended her interviews, to find a place for us to live and some space to house my new ventures. We'd headed out with a few suitcases, a couple of notebook computers, one guitar and a portfolio of legal documents that said I was the sole stockholder of two companies not yet worth a dime; but with more money in the bank than I'd ever dreamed possible. We went fully committed to stay. We'd given up our apartment, sold the furniture we'd accumulated over the past few years. My wife wanted to know what we'd do if she didn't get an offer. We didn't have any place to return to. We'd even sold our cars.

Despite her determination to achieve what most would tell her was ludicrous, just like myself, my wife was often filled with doubt and her own worst critic. Fortunately, when the self-confidence of either of us wavered, we were also the most confident believers in one another. She was genuinely surprised when the offers came one after another before the end of the week. I told her, these companies wouldn't have made such an effort to recruit her, if they hadn't already been prepared to make her an offer. These meetings weren't as much for her to convince them, as they were a face to face opportunity for them to convince her. By the end of the week, she had official offers from her first three interviews and another two came over the weekend. I was sure the documents had been on someone's hard drive, complete, but for a signature and date.

I also knew, my wife's decision had been made well before our trip, and she immediately called to accept the offer from her first interview. They were thrilled to have her. The others were disappointed when they learned she'd been won by another company. Was there anything they could do to change her mind? More money? They could increase her starting salary, if that was the issue. No, the company she'd chosen was doing research she wanted to do, or close enough to what she intended to do. No one was openly researching what she wanted to do. If they had, she'd have been there for half the pay. If there'd been no funds to pay her at all, she'd have looked at me, and I'd have told her we'd figure it out.

My wife wouldn't be starting her new job for several weeks. They'd assumed she'd need time to get herself relocated and settled in, and weren't prepared for her to start that Monday. So, her first objective out of the way, she had time to help me look for an apartment. I'd been looking through listings and had located a few possibilities, but my wife's new company provided relocation services that included assistance finding housing. The morning after my wife had accepted their offer, a real-estate agent picked us up at our hotel, and chauffeured us around to show us apartments near the facility where my wife would be working.

The apartments were all in trendy high-rise buildings, with a security desk in the lobby, staffed twenty-four seven; the elevators required a keycard, all had secure indoor parking, and there were fitness facilities in each of the buildings. There was an onsite laundry - in the one instance where a washer and dryer weren't provided in the apartment - but all also offered laundry services for tenants too busy to do their own. One building had an indoor pool and hot tub on the top floor, and all the others had outdoor pools. Most of the apartments had balconies with nice views. They were all nice. Very modern. And, all very small. One bedroom. One bath. A living area and small kitchen separated by a breakfast bar. They were also all expensive.

We both had a moment's sticker shock when we heard what the rent would be for the first apartment we were shown, before it registered that we could afford it, easily. Her new company wouldn't have sent us to see places we couldn't comfortably afford on my wife's new salary alone. We nearly took the last apartment we were shown, just to be done with it. We agreed they each had all the basics we needed, they were all nicer than any place I'd lived prior to that, but neither of us was sold on any of them. I could tell, from my wife's body language, she was anxious to get back to our hotel, and fuck the frustration of the day out of our bodies and minds. I was looking forward to that, as well.

The real-estate agent asked, if we'd mind her making a quick stop on the way, before returning us to our hotel. There was a property that she'd just agreed to list through her agency. She had to put out the 'For Sale' sign and set up a lockbox for the house keys. It would only take a few minutes and would save her another trip clear back across town. She'd buy us dinner in exchange. My wife and I exchanged a quick glance. Fuck! But, since it would only take a few minutes, we agreed to stop. I suspected, we'd be skipping dinner.

We pulled into the driveway of a huge old house, in a run-down neighborhood, with rows of what had once been very stately homes. To be more accurate, 'huge old house' didn't do this house justice; it was a mansion. The real-estate agent explained, this wasn't the sort of listing she normally handled, she strictly handled apartments and condos, but this was part of the estate of the mother of one of her largest clients. In fact, the client owned all the high rises we'd visited that day. He'd wanted his mother to move to one of his apartments, but she'd refused. She'd wanted to stay where she was. The house had been her home since she was a girl. This was also where the son had grown up, but he had no sentimentality for either the house or the neighborhood. By the time he'd lived there, the neighborhood was already well into its decline. Her client was in his early seventies. His mother must have been in her mid-nineties and only recently passed away.

She explained all of this, while my wife and I took turns complaining about what bothered us most about each of the apartments she'd shown us. Mostly, they were stark little vanilla boxes that made us both feel claustrophobic. My wife told me she couldn't make up her mind whether they reminded her more of one of her college labs or her old dorm room-nicer, of course, but bland and antiseptic.

We had intended to wait in the car, but, when my wife gave the house a glance and it immediately caught her eye. It was a lot bigger, but it reminded her of her grandmother's old house. She got out of the car to look closer, so I followed. The window frames needed to be painted and the lawn needed cut, but the house was built out of stone and looked like a fortress that would last forever.

The real-estate agent asked if we wanted to do a quick walk through since we were already there. I told her, I didn't think either of us was in that much of a hurry. My wife gave me a look and a poke in the ribs, as a reminder that there were things she wanted to do, back at our hotel. I reminded her, she was the one who got out of the car to look at the house. She agreed; she was intrigued, if torn, and, finally agreed to see the house, since we were there.

In the front, there was a huge stone porch, the entire width of the house, with all the heavy wooden porch furniture still in place. The entry way was easily the size of the apartments we'd just seen. The real-estate agent said it was the grand foyer. We looked up three stories to where a huge crystal chandelier hung down from the ceiling. There was a beautiful set of stairs in the middle of the room that split and continued up along both sides of the railed balcony which surrounded the foyer from above. The ceilings on the first floor had to be at least sixteen feet high. The house was still completely furnished. The real-estate agent said she'd have to arrange an estate sale to clear the place out. It was going to be a royal pain in her behind. She had no idea how she was ever going to move the place, even though the property prices were still extremely depressed, while the area was showing signs of resurgence.

Our hotel room was forgotten for the moment, while we followed the real-estate agent through the entire house. There was a library, with shelves on each wall still filled with expensive leather-bound books, old leather furniture, and a library ladder that rolled around the entire room. There was a huge wood burning fireplace, with all the tools and a stack of firewood ready. There were decanters, still partially filled with various shades of brown liquid. A table, that would easily seat two dozen people, filled the dining room. The china cabinets were full. The silver was still in the sideboard. Another huge fireplace was ready for use. A butler's pantry separated the dining room from the kitchen. Serving pieces filled the shelves.

My wife said it was like walking through a museum. The furniture reminded her of her grandmother's, too. I could tell she was feeling nostalgic, which I'd never seen her do.

The kitchen was industrial, a place servants once prepared meals for huge dinner parties of formally dressed guests, not the center of entertainment kitchens had become. Pots and pans hung from hooks, all the other cooking utensils were stored beneath long metal-topped work areas. There was a commercial-sized stove which looked like it should have been in a restaurant kitchen.

Since there were stairs from the kitchen to the basement, we had a look there, next. The basement reminded me of a medieval dungeon, with the old coal furnace still in place beside its modern replacement. The ceilings in the basement were high as well, not quite as high as the first floor, but a good ten feet. It was enormous, the footprint of the entire house. There were several rooms off the central basement, including the laundry, which had the same industrial scale as the kitchen. A storage area for canned goods that looked to be stocked for an apocalypse. Then there was a wine cellar with easily a thousand dusty bottles still on the racks.

On the second floor, an elegant banister ringed the balcony overlooking the foyer. Hallways to both wings of the house each lead to two huge suites. The suites had separate rooms for sleeping, dressing, and sitting. Each had huge marble-floored bathrooms, with a tub and shower with plenty of room for two, a double sink and a mirror filling one entire wall. The toilet, bidet and another small sink were in an alcove with a door for additional privacy. There were walk-in closets the size of the bedroom in our old apartment.

The closets in several of the suites were still filled with clothes and racks of shoes; women's in one, and men's in another. The old woman and her late husband had evidently stayed in separate suites, and she'd never cleaned out his closet or disposed of his clothes when he'd passed away. The closet in a third suite also still contained men's clothes, significantly smaller in size. The husband had obviously been a large man in his later years. The smaller clothes must have been what the son left behind when he moved out on his own, which would have been nearly fifty years earlier. It was an uncomfortably intimate look into the history of this family. The beds were still made. Dressers and armoires were still filled with clothes. Brushes, combs, perfume, cologne and makeup were where they'd been left. The bathrooms were all fully stocked with monogrammed towels and washcloths. There were closets full of linens in both hallways.

A third hallway ran toward the back of the house, to more stairs. The real estate agent explained those had been used by the servants. There were another eight rooms on the third floor with four more bathrooms – not as grand as the en suite bathrooms on the second floor, but nicer than any I'd ever used to that point in my life. Six of the third-floor rooms were furnished as bedrooms, another as a sewing room, and the last as an office, which appeared to have once been the husband's. There was a huge attic above the third floor. I laughed, when I saw how expansive it was, and said we could have play tennis, except for the trunks, boxes, and pieces of old furniture in the way.

Behind the house was a detached carriage house, with an apartment above it, and a larger garage further back, both of which we both decided we didn't need to see. We were back in the grand foyer, tired from the day, from before we'd spent the past hour walking and climbing all the stairs in the house. The real-estate agent told us, the sad thing was, if we bought the house, the mortgage payment and utilities would be less than the rent for any of the apartments we'd seen.

There'd never been any expectation or expression of interest in our buying the house, so I laughed at the real-estate agent's choice of words, then my wife unexpectedly asked, "Just out of curiosity, what does the guy want for the place?"

The real-estate agent told her, "We haven't completely settled on a price, which I ought to do before I put out a sign and start getting phone calls. If you'll excuse me a moment…" She stepped into the library to make her call. "One-hundred-thousand," she informed us when she returned, and added, "It would easily be worth two million in any other part of the city. That is just sad."

My wife made a sweeping gesture and asked, "What about with all the stuff?"

The real-estate agent, laughed, "Seriously?" She didn't bother to wait for a response, just excused herself again, then came back and told us, "One-fifty, all in." She was shaking her head, laughing, and getting a little entertainment for her day.

My wife looked at me and whispered, "I want it." She turned back to the real-estate agent and told her, "One-twenty, for everything."

The Ghostwriter's Wife

The real-estate agent and I both stopped laughing.

My wife hadn't been laughing - or smiling.

"Okay," I told her, "I guess, if you're serious, which you obviously are; hard as it still is to believe, we can afford it."

The real-estate agent was looking back and forth between us, like we really were playing tennis, and finally said, "If you aren't fucking with me, excuse my French, you just freed me up from a colossal pain in my ass. I'll not only take you out to eat, I'll take you to the best place in town."

My wife and I both nodded that we wanted the house, but at the same time waving off the necessity of dinner. We had other plans. The real-estate agent smiled and held out her hand to my wife, who took it, while asking, "Don't you have to call your client?"

The real-estate agent told her, "I only made the first call. My client authorized me to dump it for one-hundred, everything included." Then she asked, "What are you going to do with this place? It is cool, I guess, but you hardly need all this room. Or, all this stuff."

My wife told her, "Naked hide and seek. Maybe we'll make a place down in the basement for the winner to tie up the loser."

The real-estate agent roared, laughing and told me, "Your wife has a wicked dry wit."

I figured we'd be playing naked hide and seek, as soon as we got the keys, and my wife just might want to give tying one another up a try. I wasn't sure how you kept score at naked hide and seek, but there were certainly enough rooms and pieces of furniture I assumed she'd want to try out as soon as possible. I immediately envisioned her sprawled naked on the dining room table, or hanging on, two rungs up the library ladder, one leg thrown over my shoulder, with my face buried between them. I was aroused by those possibilities and wished the real-estate agent would give us some time alone to play.

When the real-estate agent was off the phone, informing her client of the sale, she asked, "When do you want to close? I'm sure you'll need some time to get all the financial arrangements together?"

My wife shook her head. "As soon as possible. I'll write you a check." Then she looked at me and laughed. "I like that. It's only a hundred-twenty-thousand. I'll write you a check."

When were back in our hotel room, my wife immediately started dancing around the room, clapping her hands, acting weirdly, even for her, and wanted a high five. Again, not one of the things I'd come to expect of her.

I asked, "What got into you?"

"Nothing yet, but that is a great idea," she told me, taking off her clothes as she danced and laughed.

I asked again, "What is so funny?"

She started singing, "Free house, free house... we just got a free house..."

I'd have thought she must have been smoking something, if I didn't know that would have been an absurdity. I told her, "It was one-hundred-twenty thousand, which is probably a great deal, but hardly free. You're evidently adjusting to our new financial circumstances a lot quicker than I am."

She stopped and asked, "What do you think all the stuff in the house is worth?"

"Oh! You want to sell the furniture? I think we can afford to keep it. Plus, we'd just have to buy more to replace it."

"No! I don't want to sell the furniture. But, did you see that wine cellar? There must be thousands of bottles, and I'd guess most of them are expensive. And, I'm betting the garage and carriage house aren't empty either."

"We get to keep all that?" I asked.

My wife said, "I said, 'All the stuff,' and once we sign the papers, all of it is ours."

A Blessing to Continue – Annie Fry

"So, you really don't mind that I was reading your stuff?" Annie watched her husband's reaction, still concerned he might be angry. "You really aren't pissed about it?"

Jon looked up long enough to make the briefest eye contact, as he continued thoughtfully chewing a mouthful of sandwich. When he'd swallowed, he told her again, "No. At least someone will have read it, other than me." He waved off her concern. "Please, read it, read it all. I'm happy you're reading it. I can't imagine anyone spends the time it took to write what I did, hoping no one else will ever read it. Diaries, I guess. I'm not sure what this is, but it isn't a diary. And, I'm interested in what you think."

"Really?" Annie asked, surprised. "Why?"

"Why not? You're my wife. And, like I said, no one else will care."

"Why do you think that?"

"Why would they?"

"But, you're wrong," Annie told him, "People are interested."

"How would you know that?" Jon laughed.

Annie looked at her husband perplexed. "You really haven't looked at your blog since you created it and posted everything?"

"No. Why? I've only logged on in the hope you'd eventually look at it."

"Oh, so you were baiting a trap for me?" Annie gave Jon a knowing look. "Huh! Well I'll have you know there's this little hit counter thingy, and it is way up there in the tens of thousands, maybe over one hundred thousand by now. What do you think of that?"

"No fucking way! How would they even find it?"

"They did a Google search; how do you think?" Annie gave him her 'you're the village idiot' look. "Just like anyone finds anything. Not only that. There are questions and comments." Annie got a wicked smile on her face, and asked, "Want to respond to some of them?"

Jon paused a moment, then told her, "I don't, no. But, go ahead if you want."

"Okay. I think I just might," Annie told him, nodding. "Yeah, maybe I will."

"What are you going to do, write whatever comes into your head?" Jon asked, then answered his own question, admitting, "But, I guess that's what I did. I don't know where it came from."

He wrote the administrator username and password on the notepad they used for grocery lists, tore off the bottom half of the sheet and handed it to her. "With my blessing."

"Thanks," Annie told him, looking at the scrap of paper a moment, then back up to Jon, adding, "A little scary though, once I start thinking about it."

"Tell me about it," Jon agreed, looking off at whatever he saw within his own head again.

New Digs – Naked Hide and Seek

Posted: 7/21/2015 12:00 AM

My wife wrote the check, looking at it with awe, then a satisfied little grin, before handing it to the real-estate agent. "That was fun!" she said. "I don't think I could ever have imagined writing a check that big in my life. That was pretty exciting."

"But, you expected us to be rich," I reminded her.

"I expected you to be rich and writing big checks," she told me, with her, 'you-know-what-I mean-don't- correct-me' expression. But, it was the happy version. So, no acts of sexual contrition would be required, unless that was the happy part for her. But, it was something I enjoyed as well. So, I'd be happy to be contrite.

The real-estate agent handed her the keys, with a flourish. "Enjoy your naked hide and seek."

"Oh, we will," my wife assured her, pointing to our luggage. "I brought my naked hide and seek clothes."

The real-estate agent looked back at her, pausing an instant to contemplate my wife's words, before bursting into laughter. She looked to me and said, "Oh, lord, you have a live one. Lucky you." Looking back at my wife, she said, "Happens, I brought mine too. Can I play?"

I have no idea what level of seriousness was behind that question, and I awaited my wife's response with a little trepidation. I just never knew. She'd wanted to give me a blowjob in contrition behind a dumpster, once. It was not beyond the realm of possibility that she'd suddenly find a three-way of naked hide and seek intriguing. And, since we'd never played naked hide and seek before, I had no idea whether it was strictly a two-person game or what any of the rules were. As usual, I'd wait, while my wife made the rules.

My wife looked back at the real-estate agent, in contemplation, long enough it would have made anyone nervous. But, to give her credit, the real-estate agent didn't crack and say she'd only been kidding. She held her ground, and I was beginning to imagine this woman running through our new house in her naked hide and seek clothes. I had no idea what was in store for me.

"Let us try it out just the two of us first," my wife finally decided, holding up the real-estate agent's business card. "I know how to find you, if we decide to expand the game."

The real-estate agent burst into laughter again, I think at least partially in relief, not knowing what she might have just gotten herself into, but she looked to me again and said, "A live one, I'm telling you. Wow, I'd love to hear the stories you could tell. But, I need to get moving, before I find myself running naked through an old house, and late for my next appointment."

We'd brought everything we owned, ready to take occupancy our new mansion as soon as we had the keys. We hauled it all up the grand staircase, and I followed my wife, assuming she'd already decided which of the suites we'd occupy. Then we went exploring. I was surprised we still had clothes on, until we went out our back door for the first time. My wife was right, there were several old cars in the carriage house garage that looked nearly new. The apartment above was also completely furnished and had once been occupied, by evidence of an ancient pack of cigarettes on the coffee table, along with a glass with some sort of evaporated brown residue. My wife, of course, picked up the cigarettes, debated what to do with them, then finally stuffed them in the back pocket of her jeans. She took the glass into the kitchen, washed it, then looked through the cabinets to find where it belonged. She told me, she wanted to have sex in our new bed the first time. Then we'd try all the other interesting spots we'd find. So, I knew she'd at least contemplated having sex somewhere in the carriage house and probably in the back seat of one of those old cars.

There were more old cars in the other garage. I assumed my wife was right again. We could have covered the cost of the house by auctioning off a few of those old cars. Or the wine in the basement. But, we had other priorities, and we could get back to the cars and wine, if we ever found ourselves more strapped for cash than time.

We did play our first game of naked hide and seek the next morning, after having properly familiarized ourselves with our new bed and bathroom our first night. I caught her the first time starting up the library ladder and realized my earlier vision of her on the library ladder. My vision of the dining room table took place a while later, only it was me sprawled on my back, after my wife came flying out of the butler's pantry to tackle me.

I wasn't sure at what point it should have ceased to be considered naked hide and seek, as opposed to us just being nudist sex maniacs in our new house, because we never put on any clothes that first week, unless you count wrapping myself in a bedsheet to take delivery of the pizzas we ordered every evening, or my wife modeling very naughty nighties and lingerie. I decided, it was obvious, we weren't playing naked hide and seek, if we weren't hiding and seeking, even if we were naked.

When my wife wanted me to come with her to the basement a few days after we'd moved in, I flashed back to her talking about us tying one another up, but she just wanted us to pick out a bottle of wine.

"It's our anniversary," she reminded me. "I want champagne. I hope there are a few bottles. Otherwise, we are going to have to go out, and I'd much prefer to stay home, drink champagne and play naked hide and seek."

"No, I didn't forget," I told her. "I already found a couple of bottles and have them chilling."

I touched her shoulder and said, "You're it. Count to one hundred." Then I turned and ran. I will point out, one of the inconveniences of naked hide and seek, which will be obvious to any man, was the rules precluded wearing an athletic support. So, running, bending and turning had its occasional unpleasant surprises. But, my wife, finding me bent over in pain, would always insist, she'd kiss it and make it better. It always did, even if it took a while at times.

As I suspected, my wife not only wanted to see how many different bedrooms we could have sex in, but also in or on how many different pieces of furniture. Once she started her new job, she'd be back to working eighty to a hundred hours a week again. She figured I wouldn't be too far behind, getting my companies up and running. She wanted to have as much fun as we could until then. Not that we wouldn't still have our fun. Just not a solid week of naked hide and seek and general debauchery.

Questions and Stupid Comments – Annie Fry

Annie read awhile, then drifted off into her own thoughts, before returning to read some more. All the questions, most of which were just plain stupid, or a repeat of those already answered in anticipation of what would be asked. The stupid included: "Is my husband cheating on me?" Annie gave that a brief thought, then reminded herself again not to be stupid and invite trouble that was unlikely to be there, for herself or anyone else, since she'd considered answering, 'If you're asking, you probably know the answer.'

"Who the hell is this? Really?" That question gave her a chuckle. That wasn't one of those explicitly answered in the Q & A, but if, who ever asked the question had read the first page of the blog the question had been answered. At least it claimed to be God, or not God, but our Creator. But, then she knew who wrote it, and was tempted to respond, "My husband. You stupid twit." Her hands had reached for the keys, several times, then she pulled them back. No, she had a sudden profound sense rush through her that she had to give serious thought to anything she wrote, and not just be flippant; like part of her believed this might have come from God, in which case, how dare she write anything? But then Jon had… He wrote it all. So…

Q: Are we alone in the universe?

Q: How do you create a universe?

Q: How did you become God?

Q: Why a blog? Why don't you just communicate with us directly?

Q: Have intelligent forms of life developed on other planets?

Q: Are there intelligent beings that are nothing like anything on our planet?

Q: Have you had similar conversations with intelligent life forms on other planets?

Q: Is your mother the Virgin Mary?

Q: What kind of impact did your direct communication have on your narrator?

"Good fucking question," Annie said out loud. Jon hadn't really been the same since... It must have been before he'd told her about his dreams. Which reminded her again how stupid and insecure she'd been. Stupid fucking bitch! She had these moments when she was truly exasperated with herself.

Q: Were you proud of your dad for pulling the guy through the screen door?

Q: So, you think your dad can beat my dad?

Q: Are you still proud of breaking that kid's nose?

Q: Were you once a human being, or is that just some sort of metaphor?

Q: Since you were born, could you still die? What will happen to us?

Q: Aren't you already dead? Wasn't that reported in The New York Times years ago?

Q: When did you realize you were God and no longer just a man? Are you a man, or a woman, or neither?

Q: You said, 'Sex is one of your favorite things.' Do you like boys or girls?

Annie wanted to write, "Read the fucking blog. Twit!" He obviously likes girls.

Q: Can you time travel?

Q: Did you exist before the Big Bang or not? Or, was that you making all that noise?

Q: Can you be two places at the same time?

Q: Can I have a pony for Christmas?

"Christ!" Annie thought. "Someone let their child read this. There are definitely some parts not for children." Or, it was just some moron who thought they had a phenomenal sense of humor. Hopefully the later.

Q: Do you still have a body?

Q: Do you have a girlfriend?

Q: Can I be your girlfriend?

Q: Are you married?

Q: Do you have any children, or are we your children?

Q: Are you alone, or are there others like you?

Q: What do you and your friends do on Friday night?

Q: What is your favorite beer?

Q: Do you make mistakes?

The Ghostwriter's Wife

Q: What is the exact right temperature to serve red wine?

Q: What's the best bottle of wine you ever had?

Q: Do you still have sex?

Q: Are you a wanker?

Q: Is our universe just some aquarium or terrarium that you sit and watch when you are bored?

Q: Do you ever get bored?

Q: What is your proudest accomplishment?

Q: What is your saddest moment?

Q: Are you interested in selling your URLs?

Q: Would you write my history report, since you've been there for it all, and know what really happened?

Q: Can you make two plus two equal three?

Q: Can you make Pi R round?

Q: Can you make Pi equal three or four, instead of what it is?

Q: Is there such a thing as anti-matter? Is there such a thing as dark energy?

Q: How far can you hit a golf ball? What's your handicap?

Q: Are spirits real? Are there such a thing as ghosts?

Q: Are vampires and shapeshifters real? Are there any on other planets?

Q: Are there forms of life on Earth we don't know about yet?

Q: Are we the smartest animal on our planet?

Q: Did Paul Bunyan really have a blue ox?

Q: Is Santa Claus real?

Q: Are you Santa Claus?

Q: Is the Easter Bunny real?

Q: Can pigs fly?

Annie thought that if there is any possibility there is a God, or Creator, and this is real, some of these assholes shouldn't be able to sleep at night. She envisioned a huge hand reaching from the sky to flick them in the back of their heads.

Q: Do you pick your nose and eat your boogers?

Q: Did my brother steal my guitar?

Q: Do you know where I can find Eric Clapton's Les Paul? The one on the Beano album cover that got stolen. It's got to be worth a million bucks by now.

Q: Is there really a lost chord?

Q: Did Atlantis really exist?

Q: Is Jimmy Hendrix still the greatest guitar player who ever existed?

Q: Would he have beat the devil at the cross roads?

Q: Are you fucking kidding? Is this some sick joke?

Q: Do you believe in yourself?

Yep. Big hand reaching down from the sky. Pop! Right in the back of the head.

Q: Is evolution real, or did you do this all by yourself?

Q: Did your mommy tell you how?

Q: Did your dad buy you an erector set? Or, the 'Build a Universe' set of Legos?

Q: Do you fart?

Q: Do you ever get sick?

Q: Do you ever get depressed?

Q: Do you ever think about ending it all?

Q: Is it really worth it?

Annie suddenly wished there was a hotline she could reach out to. She hoped whoever wrote that was okay.

Then she noticed the time in the lower right hand corner of her computer screen. Hours had passed. It was getting time for dinner. She wondered again where Jon was. She still owed him that blowjob, even if he didn't know it. She owed him like thirty-thousand, or at least… she counted on her fingers… one a week, for the past, what… eighteen months. So, she should be doubling up for a while. God, her jaw was going to be sore. She smiled at the thought of leaning into the shower. She knew what he did in there sometimes. "Can I help with that?"

Hi Bob!

Posted: 7/28/2015 12:00 AM

The plan from the start had been to invite Bob to come west and join us as soon as we were settled. I'd assumed we'd let him stay in one of the second-floor suites, which he did for a couple of days. But, the evening he arrived, he was barely through the front door, when my wife yelled down from the balcony.

"Naked hide and seek! You're it!"

She was standing there in her naked hide and seek clothes. Bob looked up at her in shock, then quickly turned away.

"Bob! Hi!" She started around the balcony toward the stairs, then stopped, "Sorry, Bob. I'll put on some clothes."

Once Bob got his bearings, he asked if it might not be better if he stayed in the mother-in-law apartment above the garage in the carriage house. "In case you spontaneously want to play naked hide and seek again in the future. I don't want to ruin your fun."

I laughed. The last was a bold remark for Bob.

I offered Bob an equal share of both Telepathic Collaboration, Inc. and Magick Hat, Inc. He told me half wasn't fair. The ideas were mine. The software was mine. The seed money was mine. Plus, he had no living expenses and was going to be completely unfettered to do exactly what he wanted. He had some money put away and, since he expected us to feed him, he didn't even need a salary for a while. He'd be plenty rich, plenty soon enough. He agreed to take twenty-five percent, no more, two-hundred-fifty-thousand shares, and he insisted on paying me five-thousand dollars for them. He knew it wasn't near enough, but he wanted to contribute something to the startup costs and that was all he had.

Bob had been making a joke about us feeding him, a Bob joke; but a joke none the less. But, we did feed him, just as we fed ourselves. We had menus from dozens of places. Every time we decided to try something new, we acquired another. One of us made a phone call and food was delivered.

Bob and I spent several weeks setting up our lab in the basement. I bought enough computers and other hardware to reproduce what we'd had back at the university, only newer and better. I had our electrical service completely upgraded, and had internet service installed. The agent for the internet service provider was a bit taken aback by the bandwidth of the connection I requested. "For a home service?" I didn't bother to explain. I was the customer; that was what I wanted, so he suggested I contact a commercial provider. We did, and even they wanted to argue about the service I'd requested. Right from the start, I knew lag would be our second biggest issue, right behind RF interference.

We ordered all the electronic components we needed, began building Magick Hat prototypes and fleshing out software modules enough to provide demos. My wife promised Bob we wouldn't play naked hide and seek in the basement, or the carriage house, or the yard. Anywhere else, he might want to announce himself if he didn't want to chance seeing naked bodies running past- or, worse, I'd added, and Bob had blushed.

I didn't know whether my wife would have ever considered the yard as in-bounds for naked hide and seek or not. A quick naked dash across the yard to the carriage house for some variety- I could see that happening, absolutely. Angry sex with a handful of her hair and her face pressed against the glass of a dormer window in the attic had happened. That's where I caught her, and she'd insisted I pull her hair. I could date that moment, because her hair hadn't come off in my hand. And, the attic had still been unoccupied.

Trepidation and Replies – Annie Fry

Annie perused the list of questions several times, anxiety building in her chest, concerned a panic attack was heading her way.

Q: Are we alone in the universe?

Her hands shook as she typed.

A: No.

She paused, thinking she should add something more. Then, she decided that simple answer was sufficient. She didn't want to over-extend herself by adding anything she wasn't profoundly convinced was true.

Q: What kind of impact did your direct communication have on your narrator?

Without hesitation, Annie typed.

A: He is forever changed.

Wigs and Things

Posted: 8/4/2015 12:00 AM

My wife came home late one evening to find Bob and me wearing our Magick Hats, with several empty bottles of wine on the floor around us. At some point, we'd had the brilliant idea that the Magick Hats would get better results if we shaved our heads, which we did, and, even though we'd told ourselves it was a brilliant idea, we were still surprised when we did get much cleaner signals. Bob was amazed that hair caused that much deflection of the signals. I speculated, it was more likely the static electricity.

My wife didn't say a word about it at the time, but several days later, it was getting late and I was talking to Bob in the foyer, before he headed for the carriage house for the night. I realized she was looking down at me from the balcony, stark naked, not a hair on her body, head or hoo-hah. I hadn't been aware she'd returned from work, so I'd have been surprised to see her even fully dressed. The sight of her at that moment caused me to suck in a deep breath.

She was gone by the time Bob turned to see where I'd been looking. I told him I had to go and went upstairs to our suite to find a redhead in our bed: a red wig and matching tuft of red pubic hair below. It took me immediately back to my adolescence. I'd told her about my first wet dream, and she was doing her best to make that wet dream a reality for me. She even had green eyes, which I assumed were contact lenses.

She looked down, following my eyes and said, "It's a little wig for my hoo-hah. I thought you might like me to switch things up, now that we've passed into seven-year itch territory. How'd I do? Is this close to what you remember?"

"I loved your hair," I told her, slow to appreciate my wife's generous gesture.

She swept her hands down the length of her body. "Don't you like the new me?"

Yeah, as a matter of fact, I did. "Obviously," I told her, looking down at the front of my jeans.

The Ghostwriter's Wife

She told me, "My hair will be back in a couple of days. I know you love it, so I'm having it made into a wig. Plus, it will grow back, if you really want me to do that. But, now we'll have my old hair and some variety too. Did you see anything else you like?" She pointed around the room.

The dresser had a lineup of a dozen or more wigs, in a variety of colors, including bright blue and emerald green, in different styles. There had to be twice that many little tufts of fake pubic hair in colors matching the wigs, trimmed in several different styles for each color. I noticed that even her eyebrows matched the color of her wig. She explained, she'd had her eyebrows bleached white and she could brush colored wax through them so their color matched the rest.

After that, I never knew how she'd look from one day to the next. If she wasn't so tall, I doubt I'd have been able to find her in a crowd. But, we never went anywhere there'd be a crowd, so that wasn't an issue. And, she never wore her wigs and things outside our suite, unless we were playing naked hide and seek. I wasn't sure Bob would have survived a flash of naked ass and emerald green pubes. Fortunately, we never had to find out. For a long time, he wouldn't venture anywhere in the house other than the basement, unless I invited him, and then he'd knock on the door and cover his eyes until I assured him naked hide and seek was not in progress.

Douglas Debelak

Dream a Little Dream – Annie Fry

Annie stared down at the man beneath her. She didn't recognize him and had no idea who he was. She felt a horrid sense of guilt. She wasn't with her husband. It wasn't Jon. She shouldn't be doing this. But, the pleasure she felt was so intense. The pressure was building through her entire body. And, she couldn't help herself. She just rode him, whoever he was, as hard as she could as she got ever so close, watching her sweat fly from her hair and face and splash on his chest. His chest was smeared with emerald green paint and when she looked down her body she saw that it had come from her. The body wasn't her own. Still, she felt as though she was there, within it, feeling and experiencing every sensation. And, soon, those thoughts flew from her mind, as wave after wave of a spectacular orgasm exploded through her.

Annie blinked a few times, disoriented. She found herself in her own bed, no longer naked and covered in green body paint; instead, her nightgown clung to her skin, soaked in her sweat. She was on her knees on her own bed, with no man beneath her, shock waves of her orgasm still rolling through her; she continued to shudder and let out a soft, nearly silent groan in reaction to each. What the fuck?

Jon was awake, next to her in bed, staring up at her with an expression of amusement on his face. "That was a quite a show."

Annie swallowed, mortified and afraid. "What the fuck just happened?"

"I have no idea," Jon told her, "But, I'd say you just had one hell of a dream."

"Jesus Christ! I think I was her."

"Her who?" Jon asked, frowning in confusion.

"Her, her, the woman you told me you dreamt about. Her. I think I was just her." Annie lowered herself onto the bed, rolling on her back, holding a hand on her chest, still breathing hard. "Holy fuck!"

Jon chuckled. "Was it as good for you as it looked?"

Annie reached out and slapped his chest. "Shut up. I'm embarrassed." Then the expression on her face changed and she turned to him. "I get it now. I'm so sorry." She rolled closer to him, sliding her hand down his chest into his boxer briefs. His body jerked in response, as she closed her fingers around him, and he took a hard breath. She continued, rolling part way on top of him, kissing his lips and mouth with a frantic passion. "I get it," she breathed out. "I owe you a whole hell of a lot of sex. Angry sex, and acts of contrition. Lots of contrition. And, I want it too. God, do I want it." She pulled him out of his boxer briefs, as she slid down his body, pausing to say, "I'm so, so, sorry. I'm going to make it up to you. I promise." He was already hard in her hand, as she let go to take him far enough into her mouth that he hit the back of her throat. His entire body went rigid and began to shake – with pleasure she presumed, then she stopped thinking about anything but giving him pleasure as intense as she possibly could. This wasn't her first act of sexual contrition, but the first since she'd realized how contrite she should be. She swore to herself, it wouldn't be the last. Not for a long time.

Hats for sale

Posted: 8/11/2015 12:00 AM

It was nowhere near what I ultimately hoped to do, but, for the first couple of years Bob and I were in business, I became a hat salesman: of Magick Hats. Our Magick Hats were not the sleek, edgy looking devices targeting the recreational market. In fact, there was no getting around it, they were big, ugly, clunky, homemade-looking things.

What set our Magick Hats apart enough from any other such devices that our clients would pay a significant premium over anything else in the market?

None of our competitors' Hats had near the variety of sensors, nor were their sensors bundled as densely. We'd also come up with some clever solutions for connecting and bundling the sensors in different combinations, which made our Magick Hats easily and endlessly reconfigurable. So, a lab didn't need to order a new, custom made device anytime they wanted to run a different experiment.

Our competitors' signal processing systems didn't provide half the simultaneous inputs, nor near as high a sampling rate. So, if they were using our Magick Hats, they were also buying our hardware. But our biggest competitive edge was, and always would be, software. We provided a standard signal analysis package that we bundled with our systems, and I wrote customized software to any of our clients' specifications – in my spare time, when I wasn't selling hats. That was during evenings in hotel rooms and weekends during the day, since my wife nearly never took a day off. Only our holidays – birthdays and anniversaries. She did take off a few extra hours most Sundays. We were still devotees of our Pagan Rites.

The market for our Magick Hats and signal analysis systems was limited: mostly universities and private labs doing BCI research. For various reasons, I tried to steer clear of the military, even though I knew they were by far our largest potential client. I didn't want to entangle myself in their bureaucracy. I didn't want their scrutiny. And, I didn't want to think about what uses they'd have for the technology I developed. I didn't want to think about

The Ghostwriter's Wife

them monitoring what went through people's minds. I didn't want to think about them injecting thoughts into people's minds. Talk about invasion of privacy. I also didn't want them ultimately taking it all via some variant of eminent domain, the interest of National Security, or anything of that ilk.

I attended BCI conventions. I networked, made cold calls, and visited universities and labs around the world. And, our Magick Hat business did exactly what I had intended it to do, which was to raise money for Telepathic Collaboration, without us having to borrow or seek out venture capital, which would have necessarily tipped our hand in the process. We could hardly expect to have investors without sharing our plans.

The sale of my patent for the smartphone security device got us started, but, as I'd told my wife, that wouldn't be enough to keep us going for more than a year or so. That first year, I was able to sell three Magick Hats and signal analysis systems, with two of the purchases requiring customized software. That was in a partial year, less than six months from the time we moved west until the end of that year. The next year I sold two dozen Magick Hats and systems, along with our standard bundled analysis software, and half a dozen customized software packages.

At a half a million a pop for a standard Hat package, I brought in twelve million that second year, and that didn't include the customized software modules I developed for various clients. I have no idea what gave me the audacity to name that price the first time I was asked. It was a totally spontaneous decision. Bob and I had debated whether we'd sell any at fifty thousand. I may have been thinking fifty thousand and five hundred thousand came out of my mouth, instead.

I'd been about to say I'd misspoke, when the head of the team I'd provided the demo of our system told me, it was a no brainer, if our systems could do anywhere near what I claimed... and if not, he'd sue to get his money back. Flash back to the dance club where my buddy had told me to shut the fuck up and let the girls talk. I nodded, shook hands and assured the man they wouldn't be disappointed.

I didn't know when I'd grown such a pair, but then I had once said 'Hello' to my wife, then asked her to marry me less than a year later. She'd said yes, and now she came home, wore kinky outfits and played naked hide and seek. So, obviously, I could sell anything to anyone.

My wife reminded me again, she'd known I would make us rich. And, once again, she let me know she was right. At the rate I was going, who knows, I might just wind up the richest man in the world. Everything was certainly falling into place, as it had for those who'd preceded me with that title, because Magick Hats were just the very tip of the iceberg and my wife knew the entirety of my plans nearly as well as I did myself. How could I doubt myself, when she believed in me with so little doubt?

I was hardly richest man in the world, yet, but the profits from Hat sales allowed me to hire a handful of sharp young software and electrical engineers, and each Hat I sold meant we could bring several additional engineers on board.

For what I ultimately had in mind, Magick Hats wouldn't need to be near as elaborate or reconfigurable as those for BCI research, but they would need to be a lot smaller and prettier; much more like the recreational headsets, but with a whole lot more horsepower and accuracy. They would have to target specific brainwaves from much more specific areas of the brain. We had several young engineers dedicated to designs for prototypes. Issues with RF (Radio Frequency) interference remained our biggest challenge. We'd worked hard to create an environment that eliminated all external RF interference, but we knew that our new, trimmed down and fashionable Magick Hats would need to work out in the real world, where we had no control over their RF environment. And, what I ultimately envisioned would be no more intrusive than blue-tooth ear pieces. I woke at night dreaming about solutions for shielding my Magick Hats from RF interference, when I slept deeply enough to dream. When I didn't, I'd lay awake for hours thinking about the same.

Love and Hate – Annie Fry

Q: How do you create a universe?

Contemplating the question, Annie felt a wave of nausea roll through her. Was she out of her mind? Her hands shook as she reached for the keyboard, but she settled her fingers on the keys and waited for them to be still.

She'd woken sometime after she and Jon had made love, unsure how long she'd slept, because she hadn't been aware of the time when she'd woken the first time, from her crazy, intense, embarrassing dream. She'd been too busy to check the clock afterward. She'd extricated herself carefully from beneath one arm, pulling one leg from between his, and slowly slid out of bed trying not to wake him. She'd taken a shower, as she'd always liked to after sex, and was sitting at Jon's computer, once again, wearing only a towel.

She hadn't expected Jon to be up for a second round, especially after the blowjob she'd given him, but had been pleasantly surprised when he'd reached out for her. Her eyes had been closed. She'd been smiling up at the ceiling, happy that she'd pleased him. She'd been about to drift off into a continuation of her earlier dream, when she'd felt his touch. She'd taken his hand and pulled him toward her. Then he'd made love to her. He'd done all the things he liked to do, and she'd let him. It really had been her pleasure.

Maybe things would be okay. Maybe she hadn't fucked things up beyond repair; amazing, the restorative power of a blowjob. She chuckled, and then had another flashback to her dream - talk about power. She shivered in her towel, as the memory rushed through her, and not because she was cold.

Wow! No wonder Jon had been all over her after his dreams. Talk about an aphrodisiac. It sure beat the hell out of porn, which they hadn't watched together in quite a while, now that she thought about it. But, they hadn't been doing anything for quite a while. She'd ask if he'd like that. No, better if she'd just slide into bed naked, clear over to his side, snuggle against him and make sure his hands found her naked flesh, as she turned on the TV and started clicking through the adult channels. Whatever he wanted to watch. Whatever he wanted to do. Whatever he wanted her to do.

Q: How do you create a universe?

How the hell should she know? But, somehow the answer seemed obvious.

A: With love.

Q: And, how do you explain the hate? Where did that come from?

Annie jumped away from Jon's computer, instinctively grabbing her towel to keep it closed. She'd barely finished typing and hadn't even thought about a possible response. Certainly, nothing that immediate. It felt intrusive, as if someone was watching her. And, standing there, holding on to her towel, she had an instant of feeling naked and that she should put on some clothes. She knew there was a camera built into Jon's computer. She'd have to ask him to make sure it was disabled. But, then she thought, as many hits as the site was getting, she should have anticipated that someone would be online, watching, waiting, without the need for a camera. She shouldn't have been that surprised. But, she'd been startled, on top of already being stirred up by the recurring flashbacks of her dream. Camera or not, she still felt like someone was watching her.

Annie snapped back to the present and took a deep breath. No, she was in her own fucking house. She defiantly threw her towel on the floor. Fine! She was naked. Let them watch. Then she smiled and sat, the tension leaving her, as she remembered that the question in front of her had already been answered. She just needed to read back a bit. There!

"A: I've already answered this question."

She paused. She wanted to type those words so badly, followed by: "If you'd been paying attention." But, no... she shouldn't let herself get pulled into that kind of pettiness. God wouldn't be petty. Would He? She wasn't sure why she felt compelled to maintain that pretense; she hadn't been any more of a believer than Jon, but she couldn't allow herself anything else.

A: To do otherwise would take away your freedom to choose, to think and act according to your own will. If I prevent hate and evil, I prevent love and goodness, as well. If I prevent any of your choices, none of them matter because they are no longer yours to make. I allow hate and evil, but they are not my creations. They are ours.

Annie had kept her eyes on the earlier post as she'd typed, word for word, then realized her mistake. Crap! She hoped no one would spot and jump all over that. But, it was only a matter of time. Had she meant to say that? Or, was it only a typo, and she'd missed typing the 'y' in 'yours?' Crap! Crap! Crap! What the fuck was she going to say? What should she do? What the hell did she think she was doing anyway?

Telepathy

Posted: 8/18/2015 12:00 AM

At Telepathic Collaboration Inc., a team of software engineers was tasked to securely piggyback telepathic texting onto existing internet protocols. The team lead believed it should be as simple as creating standard encrypted texts that could be transmitted through the normal channels. We could reliably send texts telepathically and receive them on our phones, so long as the sender was sitting in our basement wearing a Magick Hat that was sufficiently shielded from any external RF interference. The software guys continually harassed the design team, waiting on the smaller, prettier, but more robust Magick Hats. The design team was the hold up; otherwise sending telepathic texts was ready for prime time. Telepathic delivery was still a work in progress, even though Bob and I had succeeded in a limited manner back at the university lab where we'd met.

"I can read your mind," I remembered telling Bob.

"I can read yours too, and I wish you wouldn't think about your wife that way when I'm doing it," had been his response.

"Really?" I'd looked at him in alarm. Bob wasn't one for practical jokes, so when he pulled one, he'd catch me flat. "Hey! Now who's thinking dirty thoughts about my wife?"

"Sorry, you're right," Bob had snickered. "I apologize. That was very naughty of me." Then his expression changed, "Please don't tell her. I don't want her to think I think that way about her."

I'd waved off his concern. "She likes you. Relax." Then I'd added, "Besides, I don't know many men who don't think of her 'that' way, and I can't blame them. How lucky am I?"

"I know," Bob had answered, clearly not getting the full implication of my permission for him to lust for my wife. He'd continued, "Women usually don't like me. I don't want her to change her mind. I don't want frostbite, like Ed."

We'd had a long, hard laugh together remembering Ed's first interaction with my wife, then again, when Bob recalled the first and only time Ed had made a suggestive remark about my wife in my presence. I'd reminded him of her reaction, then added, "She not only doesn't like you, she thinks you must have a small dick."

The Ghostwriter's Wife

The smile had fallen from Ed's face. "Really?" I'd shrugged and let him think what he would. My wife couldn't have cared less about the size of his dick. It was his brain she thought must have shriveled to the size of a raisin.

I'd reminded our software engineering team that their time would be better spent ensuring we had a rigorously secure delivery protocol for both sending and receiving. We needed to be ready to go the moment we had those pretty Hats that would function in RF hostile environments. I had concerns about privacy and preventing anyone from filling other people's minds full of random crap. There was a lot of work to do before any of it was ready for prime time. Don't wait for the damn hats. Get serious. Get creative. Rah, rah, rah.

My wife had rolled her eyes. She had pom-poms and little cheerleader outfit when I went to bed several nights later. But, no panties. Naughty girl.

Within a year we had a basement full of really smart young people and a backyard full of fuel efficient, hybrid and alternative fuel cars and bicycles.

We couldn't afford to pay as much as other companies who'd have gladly hired most of our new employees, but we engaged a company to create a stock incentive plan. Once an employee was with us a year, we issued them one-hundred-thousand shares of stock, which would vest over four years. This was a very small fraction of what Bob and I owned, and the stock still wasn't worth anything, but it sounded like a lot. They were each issued more shares every year on the anniversary of their hire date, which also vested over four years. So, by the end of their second year, every one of them owned a piece of the company.

Far more than any present or future monetary rewards, most were motivated more by getting to hang out with other really smart, cool people – all of them nerds to the rest of the world. They played with really cool stuff. And, they were part of something that was going to really be something. They were all excited about our vision of the future.

In addition, we fed them. Pizzas were delivered almost hourly, there were coolers full of energy drinks and there were coffee makers that they could use to make any coffee drink they desired.

There were workmen present continually, first putting bathrooms with showers in the basement, then doing I didn't know what else. I was away most of the time, so Bob worked all that out with my wife, who'd just given him carte blanche to what he wanted, so long as it wouldn't interfere with naked hide and seek. The big garage in the back became a shop, filled with injection molding machines, and any other equipment required to fabricate prototypes of our new Magick Hats. I'd transferred most of the money I'd made from the sale of my patent into an account and handed Bob the checkbook.

My hair grew back, but there were still a lot of bald heads in our basement, including Bob's, and some, I became aware, belonged to young women. My wife continued to be hairless, head and hoo-hah, wearing her expanding collection of wigs and merkins.

Those were happy days. Everyone was engaged and fulfilled, playing with Magick. And, my wife was happy, working one hundred hour weeks, then coming home to play with her wigs and things, even though naked hide and seek did become impossible as more brilliant kids continued to fill the house.

Carrion Birds – Annie Fry

"No, mom," Annie spoke into her cellphone. She was on her back deck, nervously pacing back and forth, one hand on her hip. She listened a moment, then said, "I know you don't. I know you never have." She gestured with her free while she talked, as though her mother was there to see it. Jon always teased her about talking with her hands while she was on the phone. She knew it was silly and pointless, but it was instinctual and now too ingrained a habit to worry about correcting. He could laugh. She didn't care. She was too old to try and reinvent herself because someone else found her habits odd.

...

"But, that isn't what happened."

...

"I know I did. But, I don't think that anymore."

...

"I don't know. I just did. But, I was wrong. I just got the wrong idea and got things twisted up in my head."

...

"No mother!" Annie said, in exasperation. Stomping one foot and nearly smacking her hand against the railing of the deck.

...

"I just do, okay..." *God, mother!*

...

"Well, because he couldn't have..." Annie said, thinking, at least Jon couldn't have done what she'd thought he had and with whom, when he'd told her about his dreams. *They were just fucking dreams!*

...

"Because she wasn't real, she isn't real. It was just a stupid dream." She was the one who'd been stupid. She should never have reacted the way she did, certainly not to the extreme she did. She should have cooled off and apologized, but instead, in her usual fashion, she'd had to run to the phone, run her stupid fucking mouth, and make a complete mess of it all by telling her mother and sister that she thought her husband was having an affair.

...

"Mom, I just know." And, since having her own dreams. *Christ! How could Jon have helped reacting the way he did?* She'd had one of the orgasms of her life, dreaming she was fucking some other man, while her husband watched her bounce on their bed, coming her brains out. That had to have been quite a scene. Jon said, he was okay, but she couldn't image what had gone through his mind at the time.

...

"I just do." *But, Jon wasn't flipping out. He might actually be happy for her.*

...

"For Christ sake mom, would you please let it go. I was wrong. I just was."

...

"No, I don't. I haven't followed him around, checking up on him every minute of the day."

...

"Because I had, and have, no reason to." Annie's head tilted back as she rolled her eyes at the sky and her free arm pleaded for an end to this ridiculous... *Christ! Mother!*

...

"Because he never gave me any..." *At some level, she ought to have known that.*

...

"Christ, Mom, you're as bad as my sister. Not all men cheat." *She had to accept anything that might have happened since was at least half her own damn fault, and she really needed to leave that the hell alone.*

...

"I can't help that. That's her husband, not mine. And, please don't start talking about Daddy. He's dead. The past is the past, and I love him and miss him." Tears began rolling down Annie's cheeks as she continued to listen to her mother's chatter.

...

Annie finally said, "Mom. Mom! Mom I'm going to hang up

now. Bye." She clicked her cellphone ending the call and took a couple of deep breaths, determined stop her tears and not completely break down crying. *Jesus Christ, that woman could still get under her skin. She loved her mom, she did, but sometimes...*

Annie turned to head back into the house, when her cellphone played a different ringtone than her mother's, so she immediately knew who it was and didn't bother to look. *Typical.* "What!" she shouted into her phone, making no effort to keep the edge from her tone.

...

"Of course I did, and you damn well know I did! You two always tag team me."

...

"I DO NOT FUCKING CARE!"

...

"Look... just because your asshole husband couldn't keep his dick in his pants doesn't mean..."

...

"Oh please, give me a fucking break..."

...

"No, no... look, I can't do this right now. I'm going to go." She ended the call, not bothering to say good-bye. *She just needed to end that conversation before it grew real legs and every second was just more opportunity for it to pick up momentum.* "Fuck!" she spat out in the direction of her garden. The two of them... "Fuck!" And, if her sister called any of her friends to get them into the action, she'd have her fucking head.

God, this was all her own fault. Why couldn't she just keep her mouth shut? But, that had been the root of the whole problem, hadn't it? She just couldn't shut the fuck up.

Annie paced back and forth on her deck, agitated enough that if she'd smoked, she'd have needed a cigarette right then. *Thank God she'd never picked up that habit. And, thank God she didn't drink, except for a social glass of wine, because Jon's Scotch would have been pretty tempting right then. Fuck the glass.* She envisioned herself drinking straight from the bottle. She looked at her cellphone just long enough to shut it off. She didn't need any more aggravation right now. *All the Goddamn cawing carrion birds could leave voice mails. Her marriage was not dead. And, she was not going to let it die. Not if she could help it.*

Birthday - Not a Happy Day

Posted: 8/25/2015 12:00 AM

When my wife turned thirty, she did not have a happy birthday, despite spending the day in bed, drinking champagne and making love, as was our agreement.

She'd had the bedroom furniture removed, from the second suite across the hall in our wing of the house, replaced it with a couple of couches and other living room pieces, and had a door installed at the end of the hall between them to create one huge apartment. I hadn't been sure why at first. We didn't need near that much space. We'd hardly ever use the living room area of our single suite before the expansion. We didn't entertain or have visitors. We were at work, asleep or having sex. But, she wanted more space for her growing collection of lingerie, shoes, wigs and accessories, for which she took over the entire living room and dressing area in our original suite.

Every time my wife changed her wig or merkin on her birthday, she stood naked in front of a mirror again, looking for evidence that she was aging. On a day to day basis, other than dressing up for sex, she hardly fretted about her appearance at all. She showered, put on a wig that looked just like her old hair, jeans, a sweater, comfortable shoes and was out the door. She wore a lab coat all day. She'd told me no one at her lab had ever noticed that she was wearing a wig now. But, she didn't wear different wigs to work. Those were for my viewing pleasure, only. She also didn't wear the wig she'd had made from her own hair to work, for fear it would be damaged. The copy was also real hair, just not hers, and was virtually identical. If anyone noticed anything, they thought she might have had it trimmed a bit. The wig from her own hair was just for me, too.

I told her she looked better than ever, which was the truth. I thought a woman's appearance was usually at its peak in their mid-thirties or early forties. I thought of all the actresses that were pretty and cute in their twenties, but are suddenly in a whole new league when they get into their thirties.

Rather than the compliment I intended it to be, she took it as confirmation of her eventual expiration date, after which I'd be looking at younger women. She hated the thought of us living forever, with me being attracted to younger women. She did not have a happy thirtieth birthday at all. We had angry sex as many times as I could manage and I did everything else I could to make her happy while I recovered in between. She even masturbated a couple of times when I went to the bathroom. I could hear her. Then she changed wigs, merkins, drank champagne and looked in the mirror again.

She should have been drunk on her ass, but she was too charged up for the alcohol to have its way. Nothing I said helped. So I shut up and did what she asked as best I could. In the morning she went to work, pissed off and determined. She'd gone out the door once, still bald headed, and had to come back for her hair. She had to turn around before she reached the door again, to bring back the wig made from her own hair and leave again with the copy.

The next week, my wife told me she needed samples of my blood, bone marrow, and tissue from several other areas of my body, including my testicles, and of course, sperm. I thought it might have been fueled by her being upset with me over some inadvertent thing I'd said on her birthday, but when I asked her if she was angry with me, she looked surprised.

"Why should I be?"

I told her, "You've seemed angry since your birthday. I wanted to make sure it wasn't something I'd said or done."

"No, I'm not angry with you. I'm angry that years are passing and I'm still so far from what I wanted to accomplish. The samples are for my research."

"Aren't there a lot of other potential victims who could provide you samples?"

"Plenty," she told me, then she confessed, "The samples aren't specifically for any research I'm doing at the moment. I have no plans to do any testing on these samples until much further down the line. I'm just going to freeze them. I'm doing this myself, too, so I'm not just picking on you."

I asked her, "If you aren't going to use them now, why not wait until you're ready?"

"Just a hunch. My gut told me, get samples now, while we're still young."

Giving the blood samples was no big deal. I wasn't particularly afraid of needles, at least not the one they stuck in my arm. The needle they stuck into my right testicle, to be honest, was scarier than it was painful. Not that it didn't hurt, it did and I was sore for a few days, but I'd felt worse from several other causes, including accidents during angry sex.

The bone marrow was the worst. They took it from two places, my left hip, and left femur. When the local anesthetic wore off, it felt like someone had just drilled holes in my bones, which they had. I limped for several days and had to be careful not to roll over onto my left side in my sleep. Between my left hip and my right testicle, there wasn't really a position I could find to sleep that didn't hurt.

The sperm sample, my wife was kind enough to help me with herself, so I didn't have to go through the humiliation of going into a little room at the doctor's office, where everyone knew I would be watching porn and masturbating into the little sample cup they'd handed me.

She told me later that she'd also had her eggs harvested and frozen. Just in case we changed our minds about children someday.

One night shortly afterward, I saw a flash of something shiny, when she took off her panties. "What is that?" I asked.

"Clit ring," she replied, nonchalantly. "Technically, clit hood. I read about them the summer we were married when I had all that time to fill. I've been curious ever since and decided, what the fuck, you only live once." She laughed at her joke. "Even if it is forever."

"Okay, so what's the…" I began.

She finished my thought for me, like she so often did. "Benefit."

I nodded.

"Well if what I read is true, I might be able to come with you inside me, without either of us having to…" She made a little rubbing motion, which was unnecessary. I knew what she meant.

"So, what do you…" I began, but again she answered me before I could finish my question.

"I want to know how it feels when you flick it with your tongue."

"Okay, I can do that. Right now?"

She gave me her village idiot look. She didn't have her panties off for nothing.

Annie, Annie, Annie – Annie Fry

Annie Fry sat at her kitchen island, chin on her hand, in deep concentration, pensively tapping the fingers of her free hand on the marble counter top.

"Annie, Annie, Annie," she said out loud, to herself, since no one else was in the room. But, her husband, Jonathon happened to come through the door at that moment.

He asked her, "What's up? What's wrong?"

Annie's response was an instinctive, "Nothing." Shaking her head, no, as well, "Why?"

Jon gave her a knowing look. "I call bullshit."

"No, seriously, nothing."

"Oh, come on Annie, we've been together too long for me not to know something is bothering you. What's going on?"

She considered, then quickly decided not to get into the conversations with her mother and sister, which in truth was what she'd been mulling over and over like playing back a recording. No, that discussion would just stir up exactly what she did not want to stir up. Instead, she told him about her typo – which was, in truth, causing her some angst as well, but all the shit with her mother and sister had temporarily pushed that to the back of her mind. She told him about typing 'our' instead of 'your,' shaking her head at her stupidity. "I can't believe I did that. I panicked the instant I posted it. I should have just left things alone. I've been afraid to go back on to the site to see the fallout."

Jon sat down on another of the stools surrounding the island, smiling at her and chuckling softly. Annie felt a flood of relief seeing him smile and hearing him laugh, even if at her expense. He'd done little of either, recently. If making a fool of herself was all it took, then… but she thought she'd done more than just make a fool of herself. She'd really screwed up, for which she seemed to be developing a talent. "Why are you laughing? This is really bothering me."

"Why didn't you just delete the post?"

"What?!"

"Why didn't you just delete it?"

"I can do that...?" she didn't complete her question. "Shit! I'm the administrator. Of course I can do that. Fuck! I just wasn't thinking. Uhh Ahh!" she groaned in exasperation. "Idiot!" Which also earned her a self-administered slap on her forehead. Then she looked back at her husband, "But, now the damage is done. It's been out there since early, early, this morning. I don't even want to look at the comments that has to have inspired."

Jon shrugged, "Yeah, I suppose, but, who cares?"

Annie sat up straighter, "I care! I don't want to write stupid things that I know are wrong... and neither did you, I'm sure, because I know you, too." Then she glumly acknowledged, "But, I have no business writing anything at all. So, that's what I get."

Jon frowned, his brow wrinkling in concentration, admitting, "I've got about a dozen questions that all want to be first."

"Like: Why am I doing this at all?"

"Okay, let's start there."

"I don't know. Did you?"

Jon leaned back to chew on that question a moment, then acknowledged, "Nope. Still don't. So that's fair. And, I still have no idea where it all came from. My imagination I suppose, or at least part of me wants to believe that's the case. But, it was honestly like it was just there, like it was already written and I found the manuscript and all I did was re-type it. During which, by the way, I made plenty of typos and I'm sure I didn't catch them all. So, don't stress yourself."

"God makes typos? Because at some level that's who you really believe this came from, right?"

Jon shook his head and looked off into a corner of the kitchen ceiling. "I don't know what I think. You know, I haven't believed in God since I was in my early twenties, but... it didn't feel like it was just me, like it did when I first started. Even then, it felt as though the words were just there. But, they felt like my own words. But, then it felt like someone else's words were mixed in there, too. So, it was difficult not pick up the wrong words, the ones that weren't mine. Pictures of places, people and things that I've never seen. Memories – at least they felt like memories - that weren't my own. Events I've never experienced. And, the words to describe them were just there. One after another. My fingers moved – sometimes not fast enough and I skipped words or letters

– then the words were on the screen. It wasn't like I struggled, trying to figure out what I was going to write next. I hardly ever stopped typing. My hands were sore as hell some evenings when I finally had to stop."

Annie nodded in agreement. "I could hear you when you were still trying to write in the basement. It sounded like a machine gun, or a string of firecrackers going off. Bang, bang, bang, bang, bang… I never heard you pause, now that you mention it. So, I knew you were really working at it, which helped me a lot, if I'm honest. Because, when you told me you were going to write, I was afraid you'd just sit around and do nothing. But, you didn't. You did what…"

Jon laughed in self-deprecation, "Go on. I did what? Because I sure as fuck don't know."

Annie shook her head, "I don't know, either. But, you did what you said you'd do. You wrote, and I have a sense what you wrote is important, somehow. So, that's why I don't want to screw it up and shouldn't have touched it in the first place."

"But you did. And, you don't know why any more than I did."

Annie continued to shake her head.

Jon told her, "I did my part. I typed whatever came into my head and I thought I was supposed to type, whether it was just my own imagination, or… but even then, even if it was just my own imagination, what was the inspiration? I don't know. I don't know that I can ever know. My mind hurts from trying. Now I'm done. Do what you want, or feel you need to do, which I think is what's happening. Wherever your words are coming from, you or from some other place, you, a human being, are the one typing. We make typos. I'd toss that fact out there for all the thirty-year-old morons, living in their mother's basement, with nothing better to do. Let them play their brainless mind hockey with that."

Annie nodded, grateful, "Yeah, that's what I'll do. Thank you. And, thank you for reminding me I could have just deleted it. I swear, sometimes I think they must put the 'dumb' in the bottles of blonde hair color. Maybe I should go back to my original color. What do you think?"

Jon shook his head, "Blonde, definitely blonde," he told her in his poorly rendered Dustin Hoffman Rain Man impersonation.

"And...?" Annie asked, leaning back and looking down the length of her body.

"And, what?" Jon shook his head, obviously not getting her meaning at all.

"And – remember the part where our dream woman asks dream man, or whoever the man with her is, whether he had a preference?" Annie tapped the front on her jeans with a finger, so he couldn't help but get the reference.

"Oh, yeah...," Jon said, quizzically, "And...?"

"Jesus Christ, don't make this so hard. Do you have a preference? Did I ever ask you that? I don't remember."

Jon gave the question a moment's serious thought and told her, "When I see you naked, across the room, I love seeing that little patch of hair. It does something powerful to me. Maybe because that's how I grew up expecting a woman to look. And, when I first saw 'dirty' pictures of naked women that aroused me; that was how the women looked. But, when I'm tasting you..."

Annie held his eyes, even though she wanted to look away in embarrassment. Why? She asked herself. Why the hell should she still be embarrassed when her husband talked about going down on her and giving her pleasure. So, she held his eyes in determination. "Yes...?"

"Well... getting a hair in my mouth is not my favorite part of that experience. And, not just because I feel like I need to spit it out. It's that I have to stop to spit it out and I can feel what's building inside you start to slip away."

"So, what do you suggest?" Annie asked, then snorted to herself. It was like they were talking about some household project, not her pubic hair. This was not a conversation she could imagine herself ever having before, so she couldn't possibly have ever asked him before.

"Maybe... enough to see and enjoy when I look at you, but not down where it gets in the way, when..."

Annie didn't wait for Jon to finish. She just agreed. "Alright. That's what I'm going to do. Right now, in fact." She jumped from her stool, grabbed his hand and pulled him along with her on her way out of the kitchen. "Come on," she told him, looking with a smile, and laughed. "You'll have to take this bad girl for a test ride, when I'm done, right? Isn't that what she said?"

Jon gave her a look, his mouth moving, like he was trying to get out words stuck in his throat, but instead, agreed with his wife, "Yeah, something like that," and let her guide him upstairs.

"Do you want to watch?" Annie asked, feeling much bolder – wanton in fact – than did her normal self, but somehow she knew, she was forever changed as well. And, she was just going to roll with these new feelings. She'd never thought so much about sex in her entire life – especially not before her dream. "Would that be a turn on? Or, not so much?"

Jon told her, "Only one way to know, right?"

Annie nodded in agreement, suddenly feeling excited about her husband watching her do something she'd always felt was one of the most private things she did. "Yes, only one way to know."

She hoped he'd get excited enough he'd want to masturbate while he watched. She thought about asking him if he would do that for her, then they'd both be doing something very private together, and she wouldn't feel so self-conscious. And, again, she thought, why should she feel self-conscious? It wasn't like he hadn't seen her up close and personal before. In fact, that seemed to be one of his favorite things, and she needed to let go and let him do those things. Then, a thought occurred to her, she wished she had some flavored, edible, shaving cream. Then he could go down on her while she was trimming her bush. She'd have to stop shaving while he did, but... She pulled him into the bathroom with her and began tearing off her clothes, buzzing with arousal. God, what got her hormones in such an uproar?

… Douglas Debelak

A House Full of Children Becomes a Real Company

Posted: 9/1/2015 12:00 AM

Every time I returned from a business trip, it seemed something had changed, even if I was only away a few days. Since my wife had created a larger apartment for us, from two adjoining suites, the business had overrun the rest of the house. No more naked hide and seek.

There were brainstorming sessions in the library. The whiteboards had been replaced by a dozen sophisticated mobile smart boards, which some of the wiz-kids in the basement had outfitted with motorized controls, so they would deliver themselves where needed, using smartphone apps to be requested.

Small formal meetings were held in the dining room. We'd grown enough that any all-hands meetings could only be accommodated in the basement. What had been the formal living room became a common area for employees, where I'd increasingly find young people I didn't know, talking about almost anything, from the physics of low power electromagnetic fields to the metaphysics of virtual reality. What had been the informal dining area off the kitchen was designated as the employee lunch room, although most lunches, snacks and other meals were still eaten in the basement. The den had become our sales office. We planned for the two remaining suites on the second floor to become our corporate offices.

The third floor had unofficially become a dormitory. We discovered that some of the kids never went home, but wandered up to the third floor to crash on one of the empty beds instead, when they couldn't stay awake any longer. A few now used the house as their official residence, sharing one of the third-floor bedrooms with a roommate. A couple of the bedrooms had bunk beds, which were new, for non-residents to continue to have somewhere to crash. The attic was being cleaned out and remodeled into a bunch of smaller rooms, surrounding a common area in the middle. Several additional bathrooms were being added in the attic as well. The back of the house had been expanded to install an elevator from the basement to the third floor. Anyone

The Ghostwriter's Wife

going to the attic would still need to use the stairs. Those plans had come after the elevator had already been installed.

The bathrooms in the basement had been expanded into locker rooms, with multiple toilet stalls, private changing booths, and what had, when I'd seen the original plans, been a large open shower area in each. I followed a bald head into what I assumed to be the men's locker, looking for a urinal, only to find that there were none. I hurried back out, assuming I had to have been in error thinking I'd followed a young man. I walked across the basement to the other locker room and there were no urinals there either, and, when I went out to look, there were also no signs indicating whether either of the facilities were for men or women. At that point, I had no idea whether I'd followed a young man or woman into the first locker room. I tracked down Bob for an explanation.

Bob told me, when we still only had the two single stalled bathrooms, some of the young women started using the men's restroom when the women's was occupied, and, shortly after, some of the young men decided fair was fair and they'd had the men's and women's signs removed. When Bob brought the contractors in to build the locker rooms to accommodate our growing number of employees, he'd assumed they'd want to go back to separate men's and women's areas, especially since the plans were to include a common shower area in each.

He had ordered urinals for the men's, and then ordered shower stalls for the women's, assuming the women would want more privacy than the men. But, since the locker rooms were in opposite corners of the basement, everyone just went to whichever was closest. He'd had the employees form a committee to decide what they wanted to do. They decided to make them both unisex, take out the urinals, put in extra toilet stalls in their place and add shower separators with shower curtains to both shower areas. He said a lot of the kids tended to be very casual about their nudity in the showers. He'd made the wrong assumption several times about the sex of a naked bald-headed person coming out of a shower stall; until he looked down and quickly realized he needed to look away.

I asked whether everyone was okay with this arrangement. He said he'd had a company meeting and asked for a show of hands if anyone had any objections. He'd followed up with each employee to make sure there weren't any who hadn't wanted to object in a public forum. Everyone claimed they were fine.

It became a common sight to find bald-headed kids sitting together, wearing Magick Hats, laughing, smiling, even blushing at one another, with no one saying a word. Since some of these were R&D sessions, we logged and analyzed all the texts being exchanged, and some of the content our young men and women were sending one another was pretty ribald and graphic in nature. A lot of the young people, who were shy by nature, were a good deal less so when they didn't have to say what was on their minds, when they didn't have to hear themselves say the words.

I heard rumors, there were some sessions at night, when there weren't as many people around to watch, that were the natural evolution of phone sex. They called it 'thought sex.' It was also the driving force behind some of our young, sexually repressed, engineers working on modules that would allow them to telepathically share images: now officially the 'What I See' R&D project, it began with a couple who were too shy to be naked in one another's presence, but not too shy to share the images of them looking at themselves naked in the mirror. Not the first time people had naked video chats, but it was the first time there were no cameras. Once again, sex was driving technology. Another discovery was that images were images. They weren't limited to what the participants were seeing through their eyes at the time. The images could originate in their imaginations as well. So, they could share explicit images of their fantasies.

The technology didn't specifically differentiate, although Bob wanted to know how the brain differentiated. We knew the difference between fantasy and reality, even if the line was becoming ever more blurred, didn't we? If there was an inherent difference, it was rapidly disappearing.

One of my young employees, not fixated on sex for a moment, had the insight to recognize the implications for art, when people could transmit the exact images they saw in their imagination. Hadn't that been the principal thing many artists struggled with the most? To capture and share what they saw in their own minds? Wouldn't this free creative people who'd never had the talent to

The Ghostwriter's Wife

paint, or sculpt... Oh! Yes! There was no reason these imagined images wouldn't be three dimensional, and we had several three-dimensional printers in our shop.

Of course, the fixation on sex didn't wane for long. Several days later, after much experimentation with how to capture and communicate three dimensional objects from their brains to the printer, the young woman who'd had the insight, and a young man who'd volunteered to assist her, each brought lewd miniature nudes of one another to show off to the other engineers. Apparently, even though they'd begun their experimentation both clothed, what they began to imagine and communicate to the printer was each other progressively less so. And, one thing led to another. They claimed they'd re-cycled the plastic of several that were too pornographic to share.

A few of our engineers saw past the sexuality of the miniature nudes and realized this would be perfect for designing new Magick Hats.

In addition to all Bob's purely curiosity-driven research, he led our growing team of neuroscientists, physicists, and electrical and software engineers, in scrubbing through terabytes of data to narrow in on the data acquisition channels which captured the specific brainwaves necessary to support our initial offering of services. He also then began reducing the number and types of sensors required for what would become the first generation of our mass market Magick Hats. Design engineers were working on prototypes that would accommodate those requirements in as small a package as possible. The newest prototypes in the office reminded me of tiaras from beauty pageants. The young man who'd imagined the tiaras into the three-dimensional printer had to tolerate a fair amount of harassment.

The hair styles of our engineers evolved during the development of various prototypes, as the areas of the scalp necessary to contact the sensor bundles steadily decreased in size. It made for some interesting, if unintended, fashion statements during those phases. It eventually became unnecessary to bare much of the scalp at all. At most, a depilatory jell was applied to the ends of a template of the new hats to remove hair in the tiny areas necessary, after which our testers glued their Hats in place, since they had no reason to remove them, until the next prototype became available.

Very cool stuff. I was always excited to discover what new things we'd invented, then contribute my own ideas for the direction of further development and research. Although I missed being present and hands on every day, and was looking forward to the day I could be again, I was still the boss. I was still the foundation and center post for all this innovation. None of it would have happened without my ideas, my ingenuity, and it continued to grow in the directions I steered it.

When I got back from a trip shortly thereafter, I took notice of a car parked in front of our carriage house, which had been there three weekends in a row. I was curious. I doubted it was Bob's because I was fairly sure he didn't know how to drive. He rarely went anywhere. There were a few lights on in the carriage house as well, when it had usually been dark. Bob wasn't down in the basement. I thought it unlikely, but I went up to see whether he'd decided to occupy our proposed corporate offices. He wasn't there either. The doors were still locked and both were still furnished as a bedroom suites.

I don't know why I bothered. I knew Bob well enough to know he'd never want to work anywhere but the basement, at least not until we ran out of space, which appeared to be occurring rapidly. I mentioned the car and Bob's absence to my wife when she got home several hours later. She laughed and said, Bob was getting lucky. She'd introduced him to one of her co-workers. They'd gone on a couple of dates and hit it off. Now she was there most nights on weekends, and an evening or two between. She thought they were in love.

"A date? Bob?"

My wife laughed and told me, "Well, according to my co-worker, the dates had consisted of sitting in the lab, with a couple of Magick Hats, sharing dirty thoughts, until she suggested they share more than thoughts. I'd have loved to have seen the expression on poor Bob's face when she propositioned him. It would surprise me if he'd ever seen a woman naked, let alone touch one."

The Ghostwriter's Wife

Good for Bob.

My wife agreed. She liked Bob. She'd have liked him even if she knew he'd had dirty thoughts about her, which I wasn't sure had ever been the case, but I'd promised him I'd never say anything, and hadn't.

When it was my turn to turn thirty, I was beginning to feel like an old man compared to all the kids working for me. Since I'd had a bit of a delayed start, even Bob turned out to be two years younger than me. A couple of our earliest employees were twenty-five by then. The rest were within a year or two either side of twenty. A growing inbox of resumes was waiting for me when I returned every weekend, from students in a wide range of fields, looking to leave school early for what they called 'the educational opportunity of a lifetime.' Our employees tended to gush about their experiences on social media, and a steady flood of the smartest of the smart were being encouraged to come join in the Magick.

Contributing to my feeling old, was the realization that these young people had significantly different attitudes about sex and relationships, especially among the young women. Most didn't feel they needed to ever get married. If they eventually wanted kids, which most didn't, then they'd have kids. Most weren't even interested in permanent relationships. They were interested in their work, in which I recognized the mindset of my wife. They worked really hard and when they were ready to play, they wanted to play, and they didn't want to answer to anyone. I'd have said, when they wanted to let their hair down, except for a time most of them didn't have hair. I don't think any of them had wigs and things, but that's an assumption with no empirical foundation.

Bob told me, there were some couples, and at least one set of gay roommates, but he thought half the kids living in the house were having sex with one another pretty indiscriminately. No one seemed to be passing any judgment on the orientation, preferences or morals of any of their co-workers. Mostly, they were too busy working, but having such a great time doing it that they didn't feel like it was work.

I learned we had several datasets captured when a couple decided to put on Magick Hats and have sex. I wasn't sure when they would have found a time that they could have been alone in the basement. But, again, I still tended to make such assumptions. There may well have been an audience, many of whom would have been every bit as interested in the data being generated as they were in the couple having sex in front of them. Then, again, that's an assumption. I also had no idea whether the data came from a couple or just a couple of co-workers who were curious enough about digitized orgasms they decided to take off their clothes to capture a few.

Bob also informed me about the rumors that orgies were occasionally taking place in the attic. He hadn't gone up to confirm these reports. He was still largely his shy self and wasn't sure what excuse he'd use to explain why he was up there. And, he'd be embarrassed if he went up and found the rumors were true.

I figured it was my house. I didn't need an excuse. Plus, I was the boss. I told my wife I was going up for a look when she got home one night. She said she'd go with me. There was a gleam in her eye that should have frightened me, if I hadn't been preoccupied.

We hadn't quite reached the top of the attic stairs before we saw a naked young woman walk across the common area from one of the bedrooms to another. When we got to the top, we saw a couple having sex in one of the bedrooms with the door still half open. There was a couple having sex on some cushions off in a far corner of the common area, and there was a young woman riding one young man, giving a hand job to another and a blowjob to a third. No one seemed to be taking particular notice that this was going on. They were busy with their own activities. There were beer cans and wine bottles lying about. I did not notice any condoms, either discarded or in use.

Several of these young employees of mine spotted us. They stopped and waited nervously to see what we'd do. I assumed they knew who we were. The girl riding the young man was brazen enough to wave us in and ask if we wanted to join the party. I believe my wife might have stayed, not by herself, but I wouldn't have put it past her to want to hang out a while for the two of us to have sex while others were doing the same all around us. She did take my hand and give it a squeeze, but she could tell I was uncomfortable. I thought staying would be a bad idea.

Other than still being my mother's son, I was worried this would become a legal problem; if someone claimed it wasn't consensual, or that they suffered some sort of emotional distress from their exposure to this highly sexualized environment. None were using condoms. I was concerned about having a house full of kids with STDs, pregnant young women, or young women needing a ride to the abortion clinic.

I'd always been uptight, and, despite the efforts of my wife, I still hadn't completely rid myself of feeling that way. Now I was uptight and had liability.

My wife saw my point. What was I going to do?

I postponed my next trip out of town and called the head of the local legal firm we'd been using. He arrived at the house the next day with several younger associates and we spent the next couple of weeks talking to every employee individually. There were several of the young people, two women and one young man, who weren't in agreement with the things they'd heard were going on upstairs, but they didn't live at the house. Nothing objectionable was going on in any part of the house where they needed to be, at least none they'd observed.

I wondered how the digitized orgasm session had escaped their attention, or if they'd just considered that legitimate research. A couple of people who lived in the house said, they knew what went on in the attic. They just didn't go up there. None of this was important in comparison to the work they were getting to do. They had no interest in rocking any boats.

I asked if there was anyone who lived in the attic, or if that was strictly the orgy area? It turned out that people had claimed rooms in the attic as their own.

Did any of the people living in the attic have a problem with the activities there?

One young man said he wasn't into that scene. He and his girlfriend closed the door, but it was still far from quiet and they had to walk around naked people having sex to use the bathroom. And, of course, there were people having sex in the attic bathrooms as well, so they occasion had use one on the third floor.

How often did these orgies take place?

They were fairly random. It wasn't like they were scheduled or invitations were sent out. Everyone worked almost non-stop until they couldn't work an instant longer, and some of them needed to fatigue their bodies enough to offset the fatigue of their brains, otherwise they'd never be able to sleep.

It might start with a couple, not necessarily an actual couple, but two or so people who broke away from work and found their way to the attic at the same time, hoping to find someone, just about anyone. And, when more than two happened to be in the attic at the same time, it wasn't uncommon for an orgy to spontaneously combust.

Were any of the orgy participants living on the third floor, rather than in the attic? Would they be willing to swap rooms?

The third-floor rooms were bigger than those in the attic, so there were several participants who were reluctant to move for that reason. The attic rooms were tighter quarters for two people, but the girlfriend of one guy in the attic lived with her roommate on the third floor, and the roommate regularly participated in the attic orgies. The roommate said that she'd happily swap rooms with the third-floor boyfriend and save herself climbing up the stairs an extra time to get laid. She'd laughed, she could just roll out of bed, or kick open the door and someone would recognize that as an invitation. With the move of the boyfriend from the third-floor, the couple was thrilled to be able to stay together and not continue to step around naked bodies to use the restroom. I had flashbacks to my wife's dorm when I'd needed to use the restroom. Even then that seemed a long time ago.

I asked Bob, how these kids were living in the house in the first place? He said, some of them just started staying. They all worked such long hours that it didn't make sense for them to waste the time for the round-trip home and they were usually too tired to be safe for them to drive. When they were ready to drop, there was a place to sleep and a place to shower. Some had come from other parts of the country to work for us, spent their first night and never looked for any other place to live.

The Ghostwriter's Wife

Bob apologized. This was mostly his fault. He wasn't the most authoritarian person to start with, and he'd been a bit distracted, too. He and his girlfriend were talking about getting married. He was hoping my wife and I would stand for them. I told him we'd both be thrilled.

But, we still had the situation in the attic.

The attorneys agreed, it was a bit of a wicked problem. The company was doing so well. We didn't want to get sued. But, we also didn't want to start letting people go who were a key part of our success. They suggested that the first thing we needed to do was start looking for work space outside of our house, then no employees would be living on the premises, and we would separate work activity from these other activities.

Bob agreed, It was time, anyhow. There was no more room for anyone else to live in the house. We were running out of work space in the basement. Several months later, we began relocating to an office park on the other side of town. It meant a drive for Bob and me. But, it also meant a drive for everyone else, and as the lawyer predicted, our house began to empty of kids.

I only had occasional contact with my family. As it was, I barely had time for my wife, and everyone else had become a lesser priority. There was: my wife, Bob, and the businesses, in that order. I did call or email my mother periodically. So, my brother, son number two, was surprised to hear from me when I reached out to him. We'd never been close, but it became apparent we needed a chief financial officer. He had an MBA and a CPA and had been working as the CFO for a mid-sized company on the East coast. He had always been focused on money, even as a little kid. He agreed to come on board and get things tidied up financially, especially as we'd soon be inviting other investors.

A year later, we launched phase one. We were selling subscriptions for telepathic texting services, along with pretty little Magick Hats. We were mostly still a novelty, but people were signing up. Especially young people. We were trendy. And, money started pouring in from more than just the sales of

Magick Hats. There were people out in the world, telling jokes and others laughing, without anyone saying a word. As anticipated, everything was transmitted through existing texting services or email accounts.

The first generations of our new Magick Hats initially communicated through a Smartphone as I'd originally proposed, so we could leverage their connectivity with the existing wireless infrastructure and the internet. We developed apps for all the popular models of phones. There were dozens of different models of Magick Hats, in different colors and styles, with far more to come. Since Hats were becoming a fashion accessory, we built a fashion design team. We were even paying several celebrities to wear them.

I heard rumors that some of our employees still held orgies, but they were not on company property, nor in our home. Some of them were also starting to become adults. The queen of our orgies was now a mom, nervous to have rumors of her wanton past left behind. Parent-teacher organizations were not where you wanted to be asked what it was like having sex with ten guys the same evening, sometimes several at a time.

Bob and I soon found ourselves featured in several online financial and news magazines. Telepathic Collaboration, Inc. was the buzz. We grew to have several million clients. The texting was becoming more robust. We were extending our services. We had personal accounts, and corporate accounts that were more secure, offering encrypted texting and management tools for corporate contact lists, guaranteeing telepathic texts could not be transmitted to any unapproved parties. There were devices that blocked unauthorized or private telepathic texting within corporate offices.

The next phase: We were working on turning our 'What I See' research into an extension of our telepathic services, offering to 'Turn users' eyes into video cameras,' so they could send streaming images of what they saw to their friends and family.' Of course, there'd be a new wave of online sex. We were working on streaming audio of whatever we heard. That wasn't far off. The possibility of sharing tastes, smells and the sensations of touch were still speculation, but none of the things we were doing had been more than speculation a few short years before.

Telepathically delivered entertainment was on its way. Telepathic VR games were on their way. Virtual reality was on its way to becoming very real.

True telepathy was still tantalizingly just beyond our reach, but we were closing in on the ability to share thoughts, not just words and images. So, we no longer had to use the excuse that the name of the company was just a product of my offbeat sense of humor. Telepathic collaboration would soon be a reality.

I'd never doubted it would and it was only a small part of all that I'd imagined.

We were certainly no longer a secret flying below the radar. The rumors were flying fast and furious that we would soon be filing for an initial public offering.

Tell Me Only This – Annie Fry

Annie and Jon rolled apart, their legs still entangled. Annie was still buzzing from her last orgasm. She thought it was unfair that she could only give Jon one, two on rare occasions, while she could have them until her body and mind both screamed, 'Uncle.'

"We really should..." Jon began, before Annie cut him off, covering his mouth with her hand, to keep him silent while she thought very carefully about the words she would say next. A rarity, which she knew she should practice more often, but she was going to try.

"Stop! No!" she began, shaking her head, "Please don't. I know you've been wanting to tell me something, but I told you I didn't want to know. Those were my own words. And, now, I think the best path forward is to stick to them. So, unless you were about to say something about plans for later today... the past is the past. Tell me only this: Is there anyone else?"

Good job Annie. Why? Wouldn't she want to win him back if there were? Stupid! Her mouth had no brakes. She couldn't stop it. It just kept flapping, until she'd finally get an answer to a question she couldn't live with.

Jon hesitated, thinking a moment.

"Shit!" Annie said, pounding her free hand on the bed.

"No!" Jon spat out quickly. "No, there is no one else! I swear!"

"You hesitated, like you had to think about your answer."

Jon's face and words pleaded, "No. Annie. There is no one else. You know I always a pause when I answer a question, because that's the way my brain works. I have to chew things and make sure what comes out of my mouth is really what I want to come out of my mouth."

"Unlike me, where everything comes flying out of my mouth unfiltered." Annie smiled, admitting this about herself, then she asked, "You're sure?"

Annie immediately cursed herself again, after she'd just pleaded with herself to be more careful and selective, but, no, she had to head down a path that had disaster as one of the only two possible outcomes. Shut up, shut up, shut up! She told herself.

Why do you do this? Just stop. But, now you've opened your stupid mouth and can't take back your words. Again! Plus, what a stupid question.

"If I'm not, who would be?" Jon answered, echoing back the very words her thoughts were screaming in her head.

"Sorry, sorry," Annie said, rolling back toward him and stroking her fingers across his chest.

"Why are you sorry?" Jon asked her, pulling her naked body closer with the arm that was still beneath her.

"Because that was a stupid question, this is all my fault and I'm sorry," Annie said, burying her face against his chest and wetting it with a sudden flood of tears. "I'm so stupid. I don't know why I..."

"Stop, stop, stop," Jon whispered softly into her hair. "Don't do that to yourself. These past few days have been..."

"Wonderful," Annie continued, sobbing.

"Yes, wonderful," he told her, kissing her hair, pulling her even tighter against him. "The most wonderful since..."

"I was a stupid bitch," Annie finished, as she began laughing in self-deprecation, through her tears, "Since I was a stupid bitch who couldn't keep her mouth shut. Yes, that was wonderful too, and I don't know why I couldn't just let myself enjoy it. But, that's what I always do. Like a goddamn chicken looking for a spot on another chicken to peck, until I draw blood and the whole world goes to shit when the other chickens smell it.

"Only I'm the only fucking chicken, going nuts over the blood I drew myself. I managed to create this whole mess this last year all by myself because something inside made me go looking for a problem where there wasn't one. So, now I should just shut up, before I keep talking until I do it again. Annie, please just shut the fuck up!" she finished, then lifted her head to look up at him. "Sorry, please forgive me?"

Jon lifted her chin so he could kiss her. He told her, "Yes, Annie, please, shut the fuck up." But, he said the words with tenderness.

They lay together, silently, until they both dozed off. Annie woke after a few minutes, talking again, always talking. "What parts are true?" She asked.

"Parts of what?" She knew Jon must have been asleep too, because he jerked as if he'd been startled awake.

"The blog, when everything starts to blur. You told me it was mostly true, then it started to change…"

"My head hurts when I try to think about it all. Ask me something specific."

"What's the first thing that was different? Anything before you met your ex?"

"Yeah," he told her, "Computers. Personal computers didn't exist when we were kids. Cell phones."

"Of course," Annie agreed, "I should have thought of that. What else? You were good at chess, right?"

She felt the bed move the slightest bit, and looked over to see him nodding.

"You got picked on. That's true too? And, you really broke that kid's nose?"

"Yep," Jon agreed, continuing to nod.

"And, your dad really pulled his dad through a screen door?"

Jon stopped nodding and frowned. "No. Not quite. I did see him pull some guy through a screen door. But, not that kid's dad."

"The kid's dad never came to your house?"

"He did," Jon told her, "but my dad didn't pull him through the screen door. He threw him off the porch. Literally. So, it was just as good. He went out like he was going to talk to the guy, then grabbed him and heaved him over the porch railing, head first. My dad told me to stay inside, so I was watching through the screen door. The other kid's dad landed with a thump in the grass in our front yard. I heard it. Then, when my dad started walking down the stairs, the guy got up and ran like hell to his car."

Jon chuckled to himself, remembering. "So, that's different. The guy he pulled through the screen door lived across the alley. He had a little brother who was a few years older than me and was always picking on us. Not just me. My younger brothers and sister too. And, my dad caught him tormenting one of us and went after him and the kid ran home."

Jon pulled himself up onto his elbow. "My dad walked over, pounded on the back door and this kid's big brother answered the door. He was a lot older than me. Twenty, maybe twenty-five. He was a big, muscular, weight lifting guy, who always acted tough.

He said, 'What!' like he was going to intimidate my dad, but my dad just asked, 'Where's that little piece of shit brother of yours?' The guy laughed and said, 'You want him, you'll have to go through me.' He barely got the sentence out of his mouth, and he was halfway through the screen door, with his nose pressed against my father's. My father was really scary, because he didn't yell, he just asked in a regular voice, 'Is that far enough through you? Or do you need further demonstration?' I'm pretty sure the answer was 'Yes, sir. No, sir.' Then he yelled, 'Eddie! Get your ass out here and talk to this man!' That was the end of Eddie picking on us. He didn't even insult us anymore."

"Would your dad have hit him?"

"Who? Eddie? No. Maybe, but I don't think so," Jon laughed, "My dad never even talked to Eddie. I don't think he even looked at him. He told the big brother, to tell that little piece of shit brother of his that it better never happen again, because he didn't want to have to come over and 'go through him' again. Next time he might lose his temper."

"What else?" Annie asked, "I know you told me your dad was really strong."

"Shortly after I married Carol, we needed a refrigerator. My dad repaired them and said he had one he'd sell us cheap, but we had to come down and get it. We couldn't afford to rent a truck, so my father said he'd lend us his. My brother and I went to his house, and almost killed ourselves getting this huge side-by-side refrigerator onto the back of our dad's pickup truck. My dad said we could borrow his dolly too, then decided he didn't trust us to drive his truck. Instead, he grabbed a six-pack of beer from another refrigerator in his garage, popped one open, hopped into the truck and drove us back to my apartment."

"He drank a can of beer?" Annie asked, skeptically. "While he was driving?"

"Two, I think, maybe three," Jon told her. "I remember that he reached out the window and tossed at least one empty can over the top of the truck onto the side of the road. He told me to hold the wheel while he popped open another can. But, he always did these outlandish things. Sometimes I thought he was trying to impress us. Other times, I thought he just didn't give a shit."

Jon continued, "My brother and I got the refrigerator onto the dolly and off the pickup, without either of us getting hurt, which was a miracle. Our dad was laughing like crazy, watching us struggle. The apartment was on the second floor and there were outside stairs we'd have to haul the refrigerator up, then another set of stairs inside. First, there were two or three steps to a small landing. We managed to get the refrigerator up the first couple of stairs, but the landing was too small for us to get the refrigerator and dolly turned, toward the outside stairs. I don't remember how long we tried, but we just couldn't do it, Apparently, our efforts were quite humorous, because both Carol and my father were laughing at us."

Annie had her hand in front of her mouth, laughing at the image Jon's words were painting. She had tears in her eyes.

"Now you're laughing too," Jon said, then laughed himself. "My father told us, 'I can't believe the two of you sprang from my loins.' I think the word 'pussies' might have been somewhere in that statement."

"He did not," Annie laughed, having a difficult time getting out her words. "You're making this stuff up."

"No. I remember those exact words, except I don't remember whether he called us 'pussies.' Let me correct that. He called us pussies, but I don't remember whether it was part of the statement about his loins." Jon paused, shaking his head at the memory, then told her, "The six-pack had those plastic rings that held the cans together. Remember?"

Annie nodded. "Don't they still?"

Jon shook his head, "I have no idea. When was the last time I bought a six-pack?"

"Never," Annie said, "Not since we've known one another."

"My dad chugged what must have been his third beer, because I think there were still three cans in the rings, hanging from his hand. He'd never set them down. He told us we were an embarrassment to our Polish heritage, or something like that, then told us to get the hell out of his way. I'm sure 'pussies' was part of that statement."

"Stop!" Annie told him, laughing hard, "I'm going pee the bed."

Jon shook his head, then said, "One hard jerk and he turned the dolly so it faced the yard, and I couldn't figure out what he was doing, because my brother and I had damn killed ourselves to get that damned refrigerator turned halfway toward the stairs. Then he reached down, released the straps and threw the dolly into the grass."

"What? No…" Annie began.

Jon held up a finger, "Wait, because you'll think I'm totally full of shit after I tell you the rest. Remember, he was only using one hand because his beer was still hanging from the other one, like a stringer of trout. He had the refrigerator, one side stuck out a few inches over the edge of the landing. He was standing one stair below. He grabbed the top of the refrigerator and tipped it toward him, stepping down one stair, so the refrigerator was leaning against his back, then he bent and grabbed the bottom, where it was sticking over the edge of the landing." Jon stopped, for emphasis, nodding and smiling, then added, "With one hand."

Annie looked back, her face wearing her 'Yes, you really are full of shit' expression.

"I told you, he never set his beer down." Jon continued, "Never. It was still hanging from this left hand. He grunted, straightened his legs, and the damn refrigerator was on his back. He turned around, then marched up those stairs with that refrigerator oh his back, grunting every step, yet somehow managing to continue belittling my brother and me between grunts. He turned when he reached the second landing, then grunted his way up the inside stairs. I followed him, hoping he didn't drop the refrigerator and have it crash down the stairs on top of me. He turned again when he reached the top and carried the refrigerator into the kitchen, and slid it down a wall to the floor. He pulled another beer from the rings, popped it open and asked, 'You two pussies think you can handle it from here?' At least he was sweating and a little out of breath. I was too stunned to answer him."

"I don't believe you," Annie told him. "That can't be true. It's funny, but it can't be true. Nobody can carry a refrigerator up two flights of stairs by themselves. Maybe a big, strong guy could pull it up two flights of stairs by himself, on a dolly, using both hands."

"I don't blame you," Jon told her, "I can hardly believe it myself and I was there. My youngest brother is strong like that, too. Not the one who was helping me. That gene bypassed the rest of us somehow."

"Why isn't that in the story you wrote?" Annie asked.

"It probably would have been in the story I started," Jon said, "but I never got that far. I was already married a couple of years when this episode with the refrigerator happened. Almost nothing from my life was part of the story by then."

"Your ex saw this, right?" Annie asked, "If I call and ask her, what's she going to say?"

Jon laughed, "Probably, 'You fucking bitch! You stole my husband!'"

"I did not!" Annie protested. "The two of you were already separated when I met you."

"I know that," Jon agreed, "But, I'm still not sure she believes that's true."

"So, I'll just have to take your word it's true?" Annie asked, then her face brightened. "When was the last time you talked to your brother, the one who helped, or tried to?"

"I don't remember," Jon answered, "Why?"

"Because I'm calling him tomorrow, to see what he has to say about this story."

"I know what he's going to say, because we've talked about it quite a few times since. He still has a hard time believing it too. But, we were both there."

Booty Calls and Billions

Posted: 9/8/2015 12:00 AM

In a single day, a Monday, shortly after my thirty-fifth birthday, I became a billionaire several times over, and by the end of the week, our stock price had tripled. Bob was also a multi-billionaire. Telepathic Collaboration, Inc. had gone public and raised over ten billion dollars in capital, and somehow, through the magic of finance and investment, I found myself with a net worth of over ten billion dollars. I'd asked my brother to explain the math of how that had happened, but I found I wasn't really all that interested in the answer. I was richer than was comprehensible to me. It was stunning, numbing, surreal and would never feel real.

We also had dozens of rich, happy, multi-millionaire kids working for us, and within a month we had a parking lot full of very expensive new cars. I didn't know much about cars, but it was easy enough to tell which were 'go fast,' luxury, or what my wife referred to as 'small penis' cars (huge pickup trucks or SUVs). Then there were the environmentally friendly, weird and quirky, and finally the dull and practical. I spent a few days looking out the window of my office, seeing who got into or out of which. I was continually surprised. I also realized there were a lot of cars which never seemed to move.

The other instant billionaire was my brother. He'd only been with the company a comparatively short time, while others, who had been with us from the beginning, hadn't become near as wealthy. As with any time large amounts of money are distributed, some are bound to feel it is done unfairly. No one had any issue with Bob or me becoming super wealthy, but there was some grumbling about how rich my brother became in such a short period, and that he hadn't contributed anything, creatively. He wasn't one of our star geniuses who'd risen higher in less time than most.

I asked the few who were bold enough to raise the issue to me directly, firstly, were they not now wealthy? And, I pointed out, if it hadn't been for my brother's focus on how to maximize the perceived value of our company, none of this would have happened. Or, it would have happened, but not the way it did. If we had made any noise at all, it would have been that slight little hiss a bottle of champagne makes, when opened by someone who eases the cork out, as opposed to the pop that it makes when someone intends for the cork to fly across the room. In our case, my little brother intended to make as loud a noise and for the cork to fly across the room as far as possible. Without which, none of us would be near as wealthy.

My brother pushed me into doing interviews, photo shoots, and podcasts. I had wardrobe people dressing me, hair stylists, image consultants. I'd wanted to kill him multiple times long before the end. But, he'd told me to grow the fuck up and get rich like a man. I'd told him, I could still kick the shit out of him, and the parking lot wasn't that far away, so he should tread softly. He didn't, I managed to resist kicking the shit out of him, and we all became disgustingly rich, as he'd predicted. I had to swallow my pride and thank my smirking shit of a little brother. But, I told him he should thank me too. And, he did. He acknowledged that all the credit should go to me. He couldn't have made what he had happen with anyone else. But, I was the richest son of a bitch in the valley, so, in his way of thinking, I was more than fairly acknowledged. We both shared a few laughs and remembrances of our father, who'd be calling, my brother assured me- our step-father too.

Following our IPO, one of our biggest challenges was retaining these rich young kids. The reality was that in many cases we couldn't. Every one of our employees who'd started those first few years, when the company was in the mansion, were worth upward of ten million dollars. A few of our earliest employees and a handful of superstars, were worth several multiples of that amount.

For many, the choice between sunny beaches, anywhere in the world, and continuing to work sixty to one-hundred hour weeks, was simple. They'd reached the finish line and were burnt out. Some of our young multi-millionaires, with an entrepreneurial bent or just more gas still left in their tanks, wanted to take their money and start companies of their own. A few of these, for whatever reason that drives such people, just wanted to be even richer than they already were, but most of them had their own ideas they'd been wanting to explore. So long as they weren't looking to be our

The Ghostwriter's Wife

direct competitors, my brother suggested we help as many as we could start the pursuit of these dreams by partnering with them. They had enough money to get started, but we had far more, and we had resources it would take them years to develop, so our offers were very enticing.

Fortunately, there were also a handful of our best and brightest who had never been there for the money. Being rich only meant numbers in a spreadsheet to them. What they wanted was what they had: the opportunity to continue creating the coolest, craziest stuff mankind had ever known.

One of the consequences of our success, which in hindsight I should have thought to anticipate, was the onslaught of beautiful women who suddenly found a number of our nerdy young men irresistibly attractive and willingly took them to bed. The same was the case for a few of our unattached young women as well. Men too handsome and attentive to ignore began to see them and pay attention for the first time in their lives. I knew for a fact, a few of our shy young men lost their virginity to models they'd seen on magazine covers or porn stars they'd been masturbating to for years, because they hadn't been able to believe their good fortune and sought me out to thank me, and maybe brag a bit. "Can you believe who I slept with? Can you? Me?" I told them I knew exactly how they felt. None of them believed me. They'd seen my wife. I'd laughed and told them, yeah, exactly my point.

None of the young women came to brag. They were too lost in their haze of lust and love. A few of them married these men of their dreams, and as had a few of our young men. Unlike my own experience, most of these dream men and women proceeded to take their money and make their lives a living hell. One of our distraught young men shot himself when his centerfold wife left him and walked out the door with half his fortune. It wasn't enough for her to take his money. She'd felt the need to mock and belittle him beforehand until he fell into a blackness he couldn't endure. Then, since they weren't yet divorced, she got all his money.

When I heard, I told my wife, "I wish he'd at least shot her first."

With no hesitation, my wife asked, "Aren't you rich enough to have her disappeared?"

Not surprisingly, we'd been having this conversation in bed. I immediately lost my erection, and laid looking at her in silence for a moment, until she smiled and said, "Sorry. I was joking. It was tragic and not funny at all, except the look on your face was priceless." She pointed at my limp penis, and apologized again. "Sorry. Let me fix that." That became one of the most memorable acts of contrition I'd ever received. So, she really was sorry. Or, just wanted me to forget anything that had been troubling me. Or, reward me for my success.

My wife was happy for my success, but frustrated that, rich as we were, we still didn't seem to be quite rich enough to buy her freedom to focus her research on the only thing that interested her. We did discuss this at length. We had more than enough money to finance starting her own company. We could even have hired away a good many of her current colleagues. But she couldn't bring the data from all the research she'd been doing for the past ten years. She couldn't bring her work in progress with her. She would have to start again, almost from the beginning.

She wasn't going to be forty forever, she told me, that was pretty much assured. I'd be fortunate if she got to be fifty forever at the rate she was progressing. She was worried that forever might not happen, if she didn't start having some breakthroughs soon.

I'd tried to encourage her. She'd made far more progress than she wanted to give herself credit. She'd had five-year-old mice, the products of genetic modification, but, so far, they'd still eventually aged and died. But, she had identified at least some of the genes that impacted aging in humans. She had also found several more that identified the propensity for Alzheimer's and some other forms of dementia. Having a longer life, just to have a longer decline in the quality of life, wasn't what she was looking to do, so she was happy with those discoveries, but… they were just incidental findings along the path of her dreams for us to live forever, which with every passing year became more her obsession.

Since she had manipulated those genes in mice, in theory, she could have performed procedures that would allow people to live significantly longer and healthier, too. She thought, with what she'd already discovered, people could live as long as one hundred and fifty years, but there would be years of testing and approval processes to go through that would require her time and take her from the research she still needed to do. Living one-hundred-and-fifty years was not her goal, and she'd come to realize that manipulating a few genes was never going to get people to live a thousand years, probably not two-hundred, and nowhere near her ultimate goal. She could slow the process down significantly, but eventually DNA became damaged enough that it no longer replicated healthy cells, with aging and eventual death still the result. She needed to find some other answers, and she was exploring something called Telomeres. She tried to be stoic, when she told me about them, but I could hear the excitement in her voice when she said the word.

My wife and I still had all the same personal agreements in place that she'd established the first year of our marriage. There'd been others added periodically, none had ever been removed, and most of them I'd forgotten, since the only ones I needed to remember were that we'd agreed to be monogamous and have sex with one another as often as possible. Everything else took care of itself. I still enjoyed acts of contrition, giving and receiving. I still enjoyed angry sex, which seemed to be increasingly the norm for my wife. I felt bad for her frustration, but I couldn't help enjoying the act. I loved watching her at it. Hair and sweat flying through the air.

But, even long before becoming one of the wealthiest men in the world, I was young, well off enough financially, not too bad looking, and away a lot on business. So, there were opportunities and temptations. Some I'd assumed were professional opportunities. The women weren't dressed like they were also traveling for business. But, I'd never allowed myself to have a conversation long enough to find out whether it was flirtation or solicitation. I played defense against such temptations. I'd been asked once by a friend, if I could honestly say no to a naked woman in my hotel room. I'd answered, truthfully, that I doubted I could. That's why, other than my wife, I didn't allow clothed women into my hotel room, and I was very careful having conversations with them elsewhere. I didn't want to be so much as tempted by a flirtatious conversation.

I'd found myself running into some of the same guys at the hotels where I regularly stayed. Some of them took the same flights I did. We'd get together occasionally for a drink or dinner, usually at the bars or restaurants at the hotels, and a few times they'd invited me to come with them to explore the town a little. Usually, that exploration meant looking for a strip club, which I'd always declined; the one exception being, when one of them asked me to come with him because it was his birthday.

I didn't feel I could refuse the invitation, so I went with him and spent most of the evening with beautiful naked young women gyrating on my lap, his treat. He said he was doing his best to corrupt me. Of course having a beautiful naked woman on my lap turned me on. I was a man. And, as was obviously the case, I was not impotent. I nearly came during one of my lap dances, which reinforced my belief that being there was a bad idea. I didn't need the temptation of being away from my wife and spending time with naked women grinding on my erect penis. Even though it was supposedly against the club rules, I knew for a fact that some of the girls would come to the hotel after they got off work, or on their nights off, which my friend told me he could arrange. No, I was already well past the line of my defenses and needed to get back to safety.

My friend, as well as several the guys I met traveling, felt that whatever he'd "agreed" at home didn't travel with him. He told me, "I need to let my bad self out to play, so I can go home and be my good self, a good husband, and dad. If I don't let my bad self out to play, I don't think I can do that." One of the better rationalizations I'd ever heard to be sure. He told me he didn't think blow jobs were cheating. I asked if his wife would have agreed. Of course, she wouldn't. How about her giving blowjobs to someone else while he was out of town? That brought silence and what I believe was at least a private recognition, if not admission, of his hypocrisy.

I felt that coming during a lap dance would have been cheating. A blow job was totally out of the question. My wife agreed, although she said she'd have forgiven me under the circumstances, since I'd only gone to the club as a favor for a friend, and I was honest with her about it. That is, she'd have forgiven me that one time for coming during the lap dance, not a blow job. And, to be forgiven for just having the lap dances, even though I was honest and didn't come, was going to cost me multiple acts of contrition. In addition, my wife said she might need to go to a club where they had male strippers to even the score. But, I doubted she took the time to keep score or that she'd ever spend the time to follow through on that threat. She said she didn't mind me going, if I was only looking, but agreed it was a bad idea, since more than looking was involved. No more lap dances.

My friend teased me about my travel morality, but I watched him finally get caught and screw up the life he had. He'd ordered stuffed animals for Valentine's Day, one each for both his wife and a stripper girlfriend. His wife got the credit card statement, of course, and he found her stuffed animal in the front seat of his sports car, with a steak knife through its red Valentine's Day heart. I told him, I thought he was fortunate she didn't slash the seats and tires.

Instead of letting my bad self out to play, my alternative was to take advantage of another the agreements my wife had put in place. I'd seen no point in this agreement when she'd made it, but I understood its wisdom when I began spending so much time away from her traveling. I could watch porn. And, since she wasn't there for me to turn to when it made me horny, the second part of the agreement was moot. Watching porn, and reverting to my adolescent days, was a lot better than a stuffed animal with a steak knife in its heart. My wife agreed. But, to my surprise, she also suggested we could have phone sex while I watched porn and masturbated. Even if she was still at the lab, she could take a few minutes to slip into a restroom and talk me through an orgasm, and maybe herself as well. Much better than a steak knife.

There were no travel or strip joints involved, but my wife said extracurricular activities also went on where she worked. There were a lot of people working twelve to sixteen hour days in fairly close proximity. People met somewhere private; stairwells, utility closets, and the bathrooms in parts of the building were always empty at night. It wasn't all illicit. There were couples who met at work because they never went anywhere else to meet someone. Some got married, then had affairs and broke up because of them.

But, they still had to work in close proximity and it was often ugly.

A few quit to find a job elsewhere. Several were fired because their behavior became so unprofessional and disruptive. There was a suicide at her lab as well. Then there was the woman who met and married one of her co-workers and they had a child together. Several years later, she informed her husband she was divorcing him because she was pregnant to another one of their co-workers. She was very unemotional, matter of fact, and unapologetic. She'd wanted sex. Her husband was too busy. The co-worker wasn't. It was the co-worker's child she was carrying. She wasn't quitting her job and didn't understand why anyone else had a problem.

Neither of us wanted to be these people. So, we worked out new agreements. The core of the new agreements was the same as it had always been - make time for sex with one another. Another of the agreements, which I thought silly at the time, was that we'd have sex a minimum of five times a week. But it was a minimum we found ourselves now failing to meet more and more regularly. That would have been unthinkable at the time she'd made the agreement, considering that we'd had sex every day for the entire first year of our marriage.

As our technology improved, we could put on our Magick Hats and have "thought sex," which was a significant improvement over masturbating alone, even if I was watching porn with my wife on the phone. It was an incentive for me to develop better software, so we could share more. As it was, before long, I could see what she saw, as she looked down her naked body. I watched her hand moving between her legs. I could hear the sounds of her pleasure. And, she could see and hear the same. But, I wanted to feel her pleasure. I wanted to feel her touching her own body, as though her hands were mine. I wanted to feel her come. She wanted to feel the same.

We could put on our Magick Hats and mind fuck one another any place on earth. But, I still couldn't touch, taste or smell her. We still needed to make more time for real sex. The biggest obstacle, in addition to my travel, was that our overlapping waking hours away from work had been steadily decreasing, mostly because my wife was feeling increasing pressure to spend more and more time in the lab.

She suggested booty calls. To start, we'd each get two booty calls a month. If either of us "booty called," the other would do whatever was necessary to drop everything and meet somewhere for sex. We needed to be reasonable about it; for instance, if I was out of town, I could hardly be expected to meet her somewhere in fifteen minutes, and my wife had experiments that were time sensitive and she couldn't leave in the middle. So, we also got an equal number of rain checks. We both understood how important our work was, so we respected the rain checks, but we also tried very hard to honor the booty call.

Probably the most extreme example was when my wife couldn't get away from her lab. The best she could manage was fifteen minutes, if I was there. It wasn't like no one ever had sex in a closet or a bathroom there. But, security at her facility was impossible. She'd use up more than fifteen minutes, just arranging to get me access. In jest, she suggested, I could pick her up in a helicopter. We could join the mile-high club in less than fifteen minutes, right?

I told her that was brilliant. I called her back half an hour later and told her to be in the east parking lot of her facility in twenty minutes. She told me, she'd been joking. Security would freak if a helicopter landed in their parking lot without advanced clearance. For all she knew the idiots would try to shoot me down. Was I serious about the chopper? I was joking, right?

Then she heard the sound of the blades spinning up, as I began strapping myself in. She yelled into the phone, so I could hear her over the noise. There was a mall immediately across the road from her building. Find an empty spot in the parking lot to land. She'd find me. She hung up and I knew she was sprinting through her building. Money wasn't everything - unlike my brother, I'd never thought it was - but, I'd discovered, sometimes it was good to be rich.

Tea and Tales – Annie Fry

"Tell me again." Annie's best friend, Sue, asked, eyes gleaming with vicarious lust. "Tell me the whole dream again. Don't leave anything out."

Annie lowered her cup and set it on a coaster, looking across her living room at her friend. "I'm sure you can quote it back to me word by word." She blew out a big breath. "I woke up, still jumping around like I'd just grabbed a live wire, with Jon looking up at me with this smirk on his face. I was so embarrassed, but I was also so sexually charged up that I couldn't help but jump his bones."

Her friend laughed, "So, you got the benefits from his dreams – until you fucked that up - and now he benefits from yours, but you still feel like a total shit for how you reacted to his?"

Annie nodded, her face wearing a series of expressions that as much as said, 'Yeah, how dumb of me ,and how sad for what I put him through, but I hope now everything will be okay.'

Sue told her, "Hey, I told you from the beginning you were being a stupid bitch, because that's what friends do, when their stupid bitch friends are truly being stupid bitches. I'm glad you finally got the message. Go fuck your husband. Who cares why his hormones are in an uproar? Just thank God it happens. Especially at our age. At least your husband still has hormones. Christ, I used to lay awake in the morning, waiting for my husband to get his morning wood. Absolutely no reason to waste a perfectly good hard on. I quit when I reached the point I no longer wanted to talk to the miserable bastard."

"When was that?" Annie asked.

"Probably a month before our wedding," Sue told Annie, laughing.

"Then, why did you marry him?" Annie asked, then immediately realized the stupidity of her question. She'd been there. "Right… you thought you were pregnant, but weren't."

"Oops. Shit happens." Sue shrugged, "No home pregnancy tests back then. I missed two months, that was good enough for me."

"Then, why don't you just divorce him?" Annie asked. "You've been bitching about the man for almost forty years."

"I've thought about it often enough. But, then what?" Sue told her, "I'm not interested in falling in love with some other jerk and starting all over. Plus, you've seen my house. You've seen the little sports car I drive around. I'm not giving that up. He may be useless in bed, but he's still useful in a lot of other ways. So, I just decided, I'm not giving up anything. If I want a man between my thighs, I'll go out and find one. There is a world full of willing participants. Another great part of being a woman."

Annie laughed at her friend, "You talk like this was a decision you've struggled with for years. You've fucked anything that walks since junior high. You've had how many affairs now? Can you even count them?"

"Hell no, because they aren't affairs. They're just... hey, sometimes a buzzing piece of plastic doesn't cut it, and I need to augment my routine with something real."

"Your routine?"

"Three mornings a week, 10 am, like clockwork, on goes the porn and out comes the magic wand. I get myself off as many times as I can until 10:45, then it's time for a shower and to figure out the rest of my day, including whether to go hunting in the afternoon. Usually that's just my off days, but I'll do it any day the urge strikes me. Amazing what you can find in a grocery store if you flash just a little tit."

Annie stared back at her friend Sue in amazement for a moment. "Let me get this straight. After coming for a solid forty-five minutes in the morning?"

Sue shook her head, "Sure, some days, and isn't that another wonderful part of being a woman. There's an unlimited supply." She laughed too hard for a moment to get her next words out. She finally sputtered, "They just keep coming."

Annie joined her laughter, until she managed, "I think I just wet myself. Susie, you are truly awful. But, I'd never get to experience the wild side of life, if I didn't do it vicariously through you."

"Right back at you," Sue told her. "I live vicariously through you too. This dream of yours. Plus, you have a man in the real world who will do anything to please you in bed. Do you know how many women would kill for that? You've told me he's a good lover. Not that he does anything for me... oh, shit that's a lie. I'd do him in a heartbeat if I didn't love you so much. What is it that he does that's so special?"

Annie thought for a moment, then told Sue, "Nothing specific, it's not like he knows a bunch of little tricks that are guaranteed to get me off. It's... remember when you told me, your husband thinks you having an orgasm is a happy accident?"

Sue twisted her face in disgust. "Can't remember the last time it was even an accident." She added, "Can't remember the last time there was any possibility of an accident for that matter."

"Jon knows it's not an accident. And, he pays attention to how he can make it better. I guess that's what it comes down to. He pays attention and he wants to please me."

"And, he doesn't have any issues with your dream? Like some stupid bitch I know, who got all bent out shape because of a dream he had."

"I told him every detail, just like he did. I've told him, again and again, how sorry I was. And, yes, I know. I even agree. Stupid bitch. I could tell he was struggling not to give me a little shit, like I deserve. But, he hasn't been smug, or acted vindicated. He's just distant and quiet. I keep hoping one of these blowjobs will shatter whatever shell he's been in. I want him back, laughing and engaged. I'm doing everything I can think. I even started cooking again. I've been looking through recipes to make him some special meals. The old saying, 'The way to a man's heart...' and if it isn't his dick, then maybe it really is his stomach. Although, I'm still betting on the dick."

Susie laughed, "Hell with his heart. I'm all about the dick."

Annie thought to herself, maybe he was keeping score and waiting until she made up for the sex he felt he'd been denied the past year. She was doing her best to catch up, and at least he wasn't pushing her away or turning his back to her when they were in bed. Like someone else she could name. And, he was coming to bed with her, rather than staying up hours later – even if he did get back up to read or watch TV once she was asleep.

"Where did you go off to?" Sue asked. "I asked whether you'd got it out of your thick head that he might have been cheating."

"God, that dream," Annie told her, changing the subject back to something where she knew Sue would gladly jump with her. "I have no idea what to think. Whether it was just power of suggestion, from what had Jon told me, or reading his blog. Or, maybe this woman has decided to haunt my dreams too. At least she lets me be her. I don't know what I'd do if she showed up naked in my bed." She held up her hand and clarified, "In my dreams."

Sue laughed and shrugged, "What are you going to do? It's a dream. You'll have wild, hot, lesbian sex and wake up coming your brains out. I wonder what Jon will think of that. Maybe you can convince him that counts as a three-some."

"Fuck you," Annie told her friend, laughing and waving her hand trying to make the images in her head go away, except they did kind of turn her on, even if she was trying to deny it to herself. She'd never been into women. She'd never even thought about it. And she'd never, ever, actually do anything like that. But it did make her wonder, just a little, what it would be like. Then she needed to change the topic again, "You didn't happen to fuck my husband this past year, did you?"

Sue laughed, "No! Why? Can I? I do keep asking if he's interested, just so you know. So far you have no worries." She stood and announced. "Hey, gotta go. But, I have dream envy. You're a lucky bitch."

Annie stood to kiss her friend good-bye.

"Careful," Sue told her, "Right now I might go for some hot, lesbian sex. It would have to be better than nothing, right? Which reminds me. I've got to stop and pick up batteries. One of these days I'm going to break down and buy the one that plugs into the wall." Over her shoulder, on her way out the door, Sue told her, "Bye, lucky bitch. Love you."

Annie caught the 'better than nothing' remark, which struck her as odd, and inconsistent with all the shit Sue told her. 'What about all these guys she always talks about?' It wasn't the first time she'd wondered whether the things Sue told her were true. Sometimes she doubted any of what Sue said was true. Maybe she was just trying to deal with the emptiness in her life with her stories. Annie believed 'the routine' was true. She had no doubt her friend masturbated her brains out. As much as she talked about sex, she had to be horny most of the time. But, maybe she'd never been the slut she'd always claimed to be. Even back in school, Annie would have thought there would have been a lot more guys hanging around. There would had to have been, if Sue had fucked half the guys she claimed.

But Annie did agree she was lucky and not just because of sex. She really did count her blessings, including that she still had a husband. She'd joined a gym and started going every day at lunch. She'd taken a good honest look at herself in the mirror, naked, turning around and evaluating herself from every angle, and decided she definitely needed a tune up. Not that she looked horrible for her age, nor did she believe, if she didn't shape up, Jon's eyes would wander and he'd follow them. If he hadn't the past year, it didn't seem likely he ever would. But, she did want him to be happy with how she looked. And, she wanted to feel better about herself.

Things she hadn't considered for a long time were now jumping up and down in front of her, yelling, 'hey, hey, you'd better pay attention!' So, in addition to the gym, she'd made an appointment with her beautician to color and style her hair, rather than just getting a cut and coloring it herself, and she'd had it cut in a shorter, sassy, new style. The waxing place she passed each day on her way to work had also caught her eye. But, she couldn't convince herself to let some other woman play around with her hoo-hah... plus it hurt! 'Hoo-hah?' She had no idea how that word had tumbled into her thoughts. She couldn't remember ever using it before. She said, 'Va-jay-jay,' which she considered a great addition to the vernacular of the English language, and a better choice than any of her other options.

Living Rich

Posted: 9/15/2015 12:00 AM

With the primary intention of eliminating my wife's commute, we bought a penthouse that occupied the top two floors of a beautifully architected high-rise building in the city, which was only a few minutes' walk from her lab. The views of the city at night were breathtaking. Occasionally, we even took a moment to appreciate them.

About the same time, I also bought an extensive piece of property along the coast, north of the city. In the literature, I received, from the same real estate agent who'd sold us the mansion – now a real estate broker for the rich and famous – the property was referred to as the 'Ocean Front Estate.' Even though we could afford nearly anything - a private island or a small country for that matter - certain expenditures still seemed extravagant to us. But I decided I wanted this property and was determined to get it. Something about it spoke to me and said this would be my home for many years to come: a truly prophetic intuition. Someone else wanted it too, and we got into a bidding war. I decided I wanted it more.

As with the old mansion we'd bought ten years earlier, the Ocean Front Estate was also – in the legal use of the word - part of the estate of a family matriarch who'd recently passed. Unlike the old mansion, the Ocean Front Estate was not in a depressed real estate market. There were two miles of ocean front and all the land inland to a road that ran anywhere from a mile to two from the shore. The property map looked like the blade of a guillotine. The relatives wanted to keep the property in the family. It had hosted many family functions, weddings, birthdays, anniversaries, and reunions. Some family members had grown up there. But, the value of land along the coast had multiplied many times since the property had first been purchased by their family patriarch – whose birthday was still celebrated as the date of their family reunions. None of the heirs could afford to buy the property from the others, nor could they have afforded the property taxes.

Douglas Debelak

Only part of the shoreline of the Ocean Front Estate was accessible or walkable. The house was atop a cliff that was a sheer drop to foaming rocks several hundred feet below, just far enough back from the edge that there was no immediate danger of erosion tumbling it in the sea. A gazebo nearer the edge provided a spectacular view out over the ocean, directly toward the setting sun. There was a path not far from the gazebo that wound its way down to a beach.

I loved the place. My wife agreed it was beautiful, but also thought it was a waste of money- to which I'd thrown up my hands and reminded her how little that mattered anymore. Of course, anything other than the purchase of her own lab was a waste of money at the time. And, from a practical perspective, it was over twenty miles from our offices, which, given the hours we both worked, was further than either of us was willing to drive each day. I argued we could still commute, but my wife refused the use of a helicopter, especially since she was now only had a few minutes' walk from our penthouse. But, when I insisted I was buying the property, just because I wanted it, she did agree to spend some weekends there. Mostly, we spent those days logged into our office networks, connected through dedicated, high-speed, fiber optic cables I had installed. But, in the evenings, she would sit in the gazebo at the edge of the cliff with me, listening to the surf pound the rocks below us, watching the sun set out over the ocean, while we had tantric sex.

Bob and his girlfriend had married several years earlier. My wife and I did stand for them. They were still living in the carriage house. But, Bob's wife was expecting their first child and they were looking for a bigger place. I told them just move into the mansion, there was plenty of space. I doubted they ever played naked hide and seek, but people were full of surprises, and, Bob had managed to get her pregnant, so I couldn't rule it out.

The new corporate campus, which was well under way, was also within walking distance of our penthouse, on property adjacent to my wife's lab. Our new research facility was functional, if not complete, but the executive offices were still across town, in the office building where we'd relocated the business from the old mansion. I was not near as frugally constrained as my wife. I had a helicopter take me to the executive offices in the morning, then to the new research facility in the evening. My concession was that I walked home to the penthouse. On rare occasions, my wife and I both decided we couldn't work a moment longer at the same time and walked home together.

I had been seriously considering stepping down as CEO and moving back to the innovative side of the business, while I still had innovative brain cells. I didn't feel I'd done anything creative for a long time. Although, my brother would argue that building a company worth nearly seventy-five billion dollars, and creating billions of dollars of personal wealth, was pretty damn creative. That was not the inherent orientation of my mind. But it was his, which was why I was considering offering him the position of CEO, and moving back over to research. I'd remain chairman of the board.

The company had become a monster of a money-making machine. It would require true ineptitude to stop it or even slow it down. My brother was not likely to do either. If there was anything he knew, it was how to make money. I figured he'd do a far better job than I could at that point. He would be in his element. He would be loving life. He was currently our Chief Operating Officer, and second in command, a title Bob had gladly handed over years earlier.

In addition to our own money making machine, our monster had dozens of offspring; conceived by our former employees, who'd cashed out, but hadn't been ready to check out. There were some very interesting ventures with our technology as their foundation. One I found particularly interesting was a virtual sports training facility. It provided its clients the telepathic extension of visualization. Athletes could see what they wanted to do, how to perfect their strokes or throwing motions and practice them in virtual reality. Although all found their play greatly improved in the 'Real,' it remained imperfect. None could completely overcome the limitations of their physical bodies. Old injuries. Old age. Ergonomic flaws in their frames, for which they could thank their ancestors. And, some decided to give up playing in the 'Real,' and give themselves the luxury of what they'd always strove to experience: Playing as well as they could in their own minds. Some took the experience to the pinnacle, competing against old rivals, both playing as well as they could imagine. So, even when they lost, they could take satisfaction in knowing they couldn't have played any better.

A Bitch with a Whole Lot of Balls – Annie Fry

'Sue's Song,' which she called her friend's ringtone, began playing on Annie's phone. She set her cup back on the coaster, taking a quick look to see how much tea she had left, before she answered.

"Miss me already?" Annie asked her phone.

...

"I'm listening, Sue. What's your brilliant idea?"

Annie took another sip of tea from her cup, then immediately spat it out, some of which made it back into the cup, the rest went down the front of her blouse and her jeans. "Fuck!" she cried out, in response to making a mess of herself, then laughed into her phone, "I just spit tea all over myself, you silly bitch. No, I'm not fucking sharing."

...

"I know. You've already said that. I'm a lucky bitch."

...

"Okay, maybe a greedy bitch too, but you're a bitch with a whole lot of balls. I love you too, but I'm not sharing. Go buy your batteries."

...

"Good Byiiiie, hanging up now."

Annie shook her head, tears coming to her eyes, laughing, *No, there was not enough to go around*, she thought, *I am going to be a greedy bitch. I'm not leaving a drop for anyone else.* She went upstairs to change her blouse and jeans. When she heard the shower running, she smiled wickedly to herself, and began shedding her clothes in the hallway. *Starting right now. A much better surprise than flushing the toilet.*

Forty

Posted: 9/22/2015 12:00 AM

When my wife turned forty, it was far worse than when she'd turned thirty. Thirty-nine had been worse just in anticipation of forty.

I wasn't the richest man in the world, but I was listed in the top twenty and was on the rise. If nothing else, the people above me were dying off and their wealth was split and redistributed to multiple heirs or trusts; either way, the money was either diluted or moved somewhere it no longer counted as a personal fortune, and there was no one coming close to gaining on me. The closest were my brother and Bob, who surfed along on my wake.

You'd think it'd be easy, being one of the richest men in the world, to pick out a birthday present. I could afford almost anything, but, for quite a while, I had no idea what to get my wife for her fortieth birthday. And, I was terrified in anticipation of her fortieth birthday. In truth, I'd been dreading that day since she'd turned thirty. That annual milestone reminded her of the passing of time and the still finite amount left. She was increasingly terrified she would run out. I needed to do something that would offer her encouragement, otherwise, I had to be prepared for a day from hell and have nothing to assuage her despair. I thought I might have to lock her in a room and let her sip champagne from a straw through the keyhole. Except, part of the deal for birthdays was making love all day. For that, I'd have to be in the same room. But, I finally came up with a surprise that I hoped would be sufficient to offer her some encouragement.

It was one of those pieces of information that slip out between the cracks in conversations, when rich businessmen rub elbows with other rich businessmen. I was attending a charitable event, which I would never have attended, except that my brother insisted it was part of my duties of maintaining our corporate image. I stood at the edge of a group, like I had when I'd gone to the club the night I met my wife, as had always been my inclination. I wasn't unfriendly. I rarely discouraged social interaction. I just felt no need to dive into it head first the moment another person entered the room. But, I was close enough to the bar to overhear a conversation which suddenly had my attention. A small group of men were talking, and one of them mentioned he was looking to divest himself of an investment in which he'd lost interest. He'd like to free up the cash for other ventures.

Everyone else in the group agreed, they could see why he wanted out. Good luck with that. None of them were interested. They thought he'd have a difficult time finding a buyer and freeing up his cash anytime soon. The investment he was talking about was a privately held company, so he couldn't just call his broker and tell him to sell his shares. He'd have to hire a different kind of broker to find him a buyer and negotiate a deal, which would take far more time than he'd like. Opportunities were passing him by.

I wanted to seem as marginally interested as possible. But, he held a controlling interest and it was all I could do not to offer to buy him out without even asking the price. I tried to take a deep breath and channel my little brother. I went to the bar for another drink and casually followed up on the conversation. I apologized for listening in, but told him I was familiar with the company he was discussing. There were a couple of areas they were researching that would be of interest to my company. It might be worth further discussion.

Even with the knowledge that we were negotiating with a motivated seller, I paid more than I'd have liked; certainly a lot more than my little brother liked. He kept telling me, we were in the driver's seat, and could have made a much better deal, if I hadn't been in such a fucking hurry to sign the goddamned papers. But, I explained I was under a significant time constraint. He still didn't want to give in even when I told why I was in such a hurry. He didn't care that it was my wife's fortieth birthday. She'd get over it. This was money we were talking about!

The seller also sensed that I was willing to pay more than someone looking to break the company up for parts. I'd slipped and made it clear that wasn't my intent. That, and my insistence on an expedited due diligence and closing showed my hand.

My little brother told me I was throwing away a hundred million dollars. One hundred million fucking dollars. I didn't care. Somethings are more important than money. He couldn't grasp that concept and thought I was losing my grip on reality.

I could have pushed the deal through against his objections, but I needed his help with the financial end of the transaction. I wasn't paying cash. I was swapping publicly traded stock for a controlling interest in a privately held entity. I had no idea what type of origami paperwork that entailed, and I didn't want to know. I just wanted it done.

Offering to step aside for my brother to become CEO was what finally persuaded him to acquiesce: Something I had already made up my mind to do anyway. So, that was free capital so far as I was concerned - a kind of capital with which he was less familiar. He didn't need to know. What I didn't realize until later was that I'd totally overcomplicated the transaction. All I had to do was sell enough shares of my own stock and pay cash, which it turns out was exactly what my brother did, so who was laughing at who? He was just trying to get me a better price.

The morning of my wife's fortieth birthday, I didn't have to make any effort to get her to start expressing her frustrations again. I asked her, what, specifically, was standing in the way of her research? Her response was a total meltdown, screaming at me for being so insensitive, for defending the assholes frustrating her, and for being another asshole who was frustrating her, when I had to know how frustrated she was.

Who was frustrating her efforts? If she could change anything, what would she do? I asked, would she want to be CEO of her company?

That incited further meltdown, but between the vituperative outbursts, I did get an answer. No, why would she want to do that? She'd never want all the hassle of running the company. Wasn't that exactly what I was trying to get away from by turning the reins of my company over to my brother? She just wanted to do what she wanted to do, without having to hide secret side projects, or to come up with some creative lie to justify them if they came to light. Mostly, she wanted the money she needed for projects, without writing proposal after proposal, just to be refused.

I told her, "I didn't expect you would want to be CEO. So, I worked that out too."

She stood staring at me a moment in a silent rage. She looked like she might spring at me and physically assault me. "What the fuck are you talking about?"

I explained, "The reason I've been locked in meetings for the past few months, used my rain checks for the entire year, and ignored a couple additional booty calls, is that I've been tied up in negotiations for an acquisition."

"Aren't you always? Isn't that what you do now? Buy up companies just to get more brilliant people to work for you?" She paused to watch the effect of those words, before continuing. "I was only kidding about you being the richest man in the world. You are close enough! You can ease off now! I never thought you'd take me seriously, and it's not like we are gaining anything of value, just being richer. We can't take it with us and I'm scared shitless that's exactly what's going to happen. Then what has it all been about?"

My wife raged around the penthouse, before adding, "You aren't getting any more rain checks. I overheard some asshole at work, telling what he thought was a joke, but what I thought was one of the most offensive things I've ever heard. If it wouldn't have been such a disruption to my work, I would have filed a complaint. He said, 'Show me a beautiful woman, and I'll show you a guy who is tired of fucking her.'" She crossed her arms, nodding, and told me, "That particularly bothered me, because you are always telling me I'm beautiful, but I'm starting to think maybe you are tired of fucking me."

"Not even close," I told her, reaching out for her. She pulled away and looked like she was giving serious thought to slapping me.

I picked up a heavy leather portfolio, wrapped in a ribbon with a bow, and handed to her. "Happy birthday."

She looked at the portfolio and back at me; like she was about to throw it at me. "What the fuck is this?"

"It is your birthday present. Go ahead and open it."

She did and said, "It is a pile of legal documents. Thank you so much. How did you know?"

She wasn't just being sarcastic, there was a viciousness in her tone. She was clearly in no mood to leaf through the pile of documents and determine what they were herself. So, I told her, "Yes, they are legal documents; contracts and stock certificates. Want to know what they really are?"

She was in no more a mood for twenty questions than she was for anything else. She stared at me.

"Carte Blanche," I told her, "I just bought you Carte Blanche for your birthday. Isn't that what you've wanted more than anything in the world? Isn't that why you wanted me to get rich?"

"Fuck you and your riddles. What the hell are you talking about? Just fucking tell me!"

So, I did. I told her, "I bought your company. It is yours. Nothing should ever interfere with anything you want to do again. You have your lab. You can do whatever you want, however you want, without asking or justifying it to anyone. You are now the de facto boss of your company, you own it outright, along with the data and your old mice. The current CEO and I had a long talk. He knows that for all intents and purposes, you are now his boss, but he has agreed to stay on through the transition. I'm still hoping I can convince him to stay longer, but if not, I'll take over until we can find someone else. Please, just go do what you want and let me know if there is anything else you need. If you need more money, we have more money. This is the only reason I've pushed so hard. I want you to have whatever you want. I want you to have your dreams and the means to make them come true. If you give me forever, I promise I will never get tired of fucking you."

She stood looking at me, then the portfolio, absorbing what I'd just told her. She was standing naked in front of the windows of our penthouse. Even knowing that the glass was tinted and we were currently on the hundredth floor, I'd never quite gotten used to that idea. She walked past me. Dropped the portfolio on the bed, and started getting dressed in her usual jeans and sweater she wore to work.

I asked, "What are you doing?"

She told me, "I want to go see my present, not just a binder full of fucking papers. If I own the fucking place, I want to walk through fucking security, like I own the fucking place! I want to walk into every area of the fucking company my security badge has ever denied me. If the fucking CEO is in, I'm telling him he'll have to step out, so I can fuck my husband on my new fucking desk!"

I laughed. "You don't believe me, do you?"

"I don't know. But, I also don't think you could possibly be fucking with me that badly." She stopped by the wine storage unit on our first floor and grabbed a bottle of champagne and popped the cork. She told me, "I expect this is a valid exception to me going to work on my birthday, and I'm going to drink on the job."

We did walk through security, like we owned the place; because I'd called ahead and told them to expect us and to please clear the path for my wife to go wherever and do whatever she damn well pleased. Overhearing that phone call got something of a smile from her, although I didn't think she believed there was anyone on the other end of the call. But, when we drove through security with the gates open, were directed to the executive parking area beneath the building and guided to an empty parking spot that said: CEO, she started to perk up, still radiating a dangerous form of energy.

"Why isn't that my name?" she asked, pointing to the wall in front of the car. "I don't care if he's staying or not, this is my fucking parking spot."

"You don't drive anywhere," I reminded her. She wasn't listening. "Fine, I'm sure we can find him another parking spot. I'll have them change the plaque and you'll have your own empty parking spot you'll never use."

There were several security people at the elevator, but they were already used to seeing my face over the past few weeks and understood I was the new boss. They were wrong about that; but they did wave us through with no need to show ID, which was good enough for the moment. She'd set them straight if necessary.

My wife fired three people on her way to the CEO's office, including her immediate supervisor, telling him he was a moronic fucking cretin and she guaranteed someone was tired of fucking him, if he ever had managed to get laid. He called security, unnecessarily, because they were already on their way and arrived before he'd hung up the phone. He looked at the security officers in confusion when they just stood beside him as he pointed at us walking away. In her hurry, leaving the penthouse, my wife had forgotten to put on a wig. She was a six-foot-two, furious, bald headed woman, walking through the office carrying her half empty bottle of champagne. He didn't understand why they weren't going after us. I'm not entirely sure he even recognized my wife, given her appearance and demeanor.

I had the foresight to know she generally wasn't kidding when she expressed her intentions to do something sexual. The CEO's office was unlocked and empty. She walked in, pulled off her jeans and hopped up on the desk. She said, "I'm about to be fucked, or fired. Either way: I'm going to get fucked and I'm going to have my own lab, because I either own this one, or you'd better fucking buy another one fast." She pointed to my pants and gestured for me to get them off. Even if she was going to get fired, she'd still really like me to fuck her on the CEO's desk, preferably before security caught up with us. She reached for her wig because something didn't feel right and realized for the first time that she hadn't taken the time to put one on.

She laughed. "That explains at least part of the reason my supervisor looked at me like I was crazy when I fired his miserable ass." Then she lifted herself up a bit, threw her panties on the floor, pulled her top and bra up above her breasts, and looked at me, like what was I waiting for, I already had my invitation.

Afterward, bald headed, still drinking champagne from the bottle, she walked through every department and corner of the facility, asking questions about the projects people were working on. I would not have been totally shocked on that day if she'd done so without bothering to put her pants back on. None of them knew who she was, but they recognized me from pictures in the online news and magazines, and, of course, they recognized the (hopefully not) outgoing CEO, who'd caught up to escort us. He explained the research projects as best he could and instructed that any questions we had were to be answered in full. I was expecting my wife to announce another booty-call at any moment, but apparently having sex on the CEO's desk was sufficient until we got home.

I really had no idea what to expect her to do. I don't think she had any idea what she might do, herself. I think the whole day was surreal for her. And, it wouldn't all sink in for weeks. But, she kept getting these quirky grins on her face, evidently thinking of the

The Ghostwriter's Wife

possibilities, and frowning at the realization she no longer had any excuses. It was on her and no one else, to get her ass busy and make it happen. But, there was a giggle or two that slipped out by the time we were leaving, and I expected her to pounce on me in the car and force me to pull over to the side of the street, so I didn't kill us both. Wouldn't that have the irony of all ironies?

We managed to get home, just barely, before she began pawing and molesting me all the way up the elevator. I thought we were about to have sex in front of the security cameras. When we finally did reach our penthouse, I got what was absolutely the best blowjob I'd ever had, even though I was scared to death I was going to fall backward one-hundred stories to my death, because she'd pushed me flat up against one of our penthouse windows, before yanking my pants to my knees and inhaling my penis. Maybe the fear of the window giving way behind me added something to the experience because my knees nearly gave way beneath me and I felt like I was freefalling through space with lightning bolts shooting through my body. She said, "Thank you," when she was done. I thought I should be the one thanking her, if I could have managed coherent speech at that moment. I didn't think I'd ever manage another erection in my life, because what was the point of the disappointment in comparison to what I'd just experienced? Wrong. She persisted in levitating me again, and again, then damn near fracturing my pelvis, until she finally collapsed, sweat glistening, hugging the leather portfolio to her breasts.

Best fucking birthday ever!

Douglas Debelak

Talk to Me Please – Annie Fry

"Talk to me, please," Annie pleaded.

Jon laid beside her, still idly stroking the nipple of her left breast, which had finally become sensitive enough she pushed his hand away, and told him, "Stop, please. My nerve endings need a break."

"About?" Jon asked, looking up at her.

It took Annie a moment to reorient herself back to her original question, then she asked, "What is going on with you? What's the matter? Something is." Then she silently cursed herself; a terrified part of her mind screaming, 'Leave it alone! You promised to leave it alone. Why do you have to pick at every scab? Do you really want to know? Goddamn it Annie, you won't quit until you totally fuck this up, will you?' But, she had to know. She was enjoying the sex. She loved the way he made her body feel, when she let him. But, she needed to connect. And, that wasn't there. He wasn't there. Not really. Just glimpses.

Jon let out a long sigh, then looked away. He shook his head, "Nothing really. You know how I've always been after I've finished something big. I get all hollow, like everything has been pulled out of me. And, you're always telling me to let myself enjoy a sense of accomplishment, but that's not how I'm wired. It's not like I'm down exactly, more that I'm just empty. But, it will get better. It always does. Sorry. It isn't your fault. Mine either. I've had to learn not to beat myself up about feeling down. It just is."

"Jon," Annie asked, reaching out to turn his face up toward hers, "You aren't thinking of doing anything are you?"

"Like?"

"Like hurting yourself. I know this past year, but... please don't do anything like that. I'm sorry. I do love you, and I'm trying." Tears ran down Annie's face. "Please, promise me you won't. That you'll talk to someone."

"I've been talking to someone," he reminded her. "Every week. You know that."

"Yeah," she nodded, "I guess I wasn't thinking about that. It's just... you have me worried."

The Ghostwriter's Wife

"I promise," Jon told her, looking at her sincerely. "Ups and downs have been part of my life as long as I can remember. And, I decided a long time ago that Nietzsche had it figured out." He laughed, "Even if it is a pretty morbid way of getting through it."

"What?" Annie asked, still looking concerned and now confused. "I don't know this guy. Should I?"

Jon made a dismissive gesture. "No, there's no reason you should. He was an 1800s existential philosopher. Some of his writing became popular with the Nazis. But, one of the things he wrote, which stuck with me, was 'I can always kill myself tomorrow.' And, my spin was, since tomorrow never comes, if I stuck to that plan, I'd never kill myself, no matter how depressed I got. And, I'm still here, so it must have worked."

"Don't talk like that, Jon. And, don't joke about this." Annie told him, upset, both at his comments and herself for not being able to shut her mouth.

"I'm not joking," Jon insisted. "It has been a long time since that was a serious thought. Back in my early twenties was the worst. But, Nietzsche, and my decision not to blame myself for something that's not my fault, are what got me through that time, and I haven't thought about it since. Depression is really not that different from diabetes, and diabetics don't blame themselves... well, maybe some people who let themselves get overweight."

"Jon?" Annie asked again, "Please, promise."

"I promised," he told her, getting out of bed. "I already promised and I promise again. Now I have to pee."

Once Jon was out of sight, Annie pinched herself until it hurt, and quietly chastised herself, "Stupid, stupid, stupid... Please don't fuck this up Annie, please. Just let him be."

"Oh, by the way," she called out loud enough so he could hear her in the bathroom. "Sue offered to fuck your brains out, if I wanted to share."

She heard him snort, and he yelled back, "I'm sure you were all over that offer."

"Why? Would you want to?"

"Annie, shut up," Jon answered. "I'm trying to pee and not get it all over the bathroom and myself. And, no, your jeans don't make your ass look fat, if you're heading down those paths." But, he came back into the bedroom looking amused, which made her feel considerably better. "She offers all the time," he said, "just in case you didn't know. I don't think she's serious."

"That bitch!" Annie said, then smiled and admitted, "She actually confessed this afternoon that she propositions you all the time. But, she made it sound as if she was testing you for my benefit." She had another question that she managed to suppress. Instead, she batted her eyes and asked, "Up for another?"

Jon snorted again, "You're a funny woman. I'm a sixty-two-year-old man. I'll be happy to…" he pointed down the length of Annie's body, "But, more than that and we'd both be kidding ourselves." He looked down her body again, raising his eyebrows, making it a question.

"No," Annie answered, "Just come hold me. I'll shut up, I promise. Or, make my mouth useful in some other way if I can't. I'm betting you've got more left than you want to credit yourself with."

Like a new puppy

Posted: 9/29/2015 12:00 AM

The name of my wife's company had been 'The Cellular Research Center.' I told her to rename it whatever she wanted. It was her company. She mulled that over like a little girl trying to pick out a name for a new puppy. 'Life Extension Institute? Forever, Inc.?' She liked 'Forever, Inc.,' except people would assume it was a giant tattoo parlor. She might just get a tattoo, she told me. What did I think? I told her she could do what she wanted, because she would anyway, just no face or neck tattoos, please. At least none that were permanent.

I did convince her CEO to stay on. He told me he was excited to see what my wife wanted to do. He was also happy to be working under new ownership. In fact, this was the type of ownership he could only have dreamed of having. He was to continue operating the business with every effort to make a profit, hopefully even after covering the expenses of my wife's new projects, but if there was any shortfall because of the cost of her research to let me know. If necessary, I'd fund whatever she wanted to do with my own money. Everything else had to pay its own way.

She was still tossing around ideas for the company name, but I don't think she really cared that much about what it was called. She was still a bit lost in her lack of constraints. She needed to catch her breath, get organized, and quit wasting time.

First, she needed to determine what to do about her current assignments. In one of her initial sit downs with her CEO, who was now her employee, this came up, and he told her he'd handle their reassignment; she was done with them and had no need to give them another moment's thought. All her secret side projects now became officially sanctioned high priority projects. The CEO was surprised at the number of them and what she'd managed to accomplish "under the table," right under his own nose. He might have fired her, had he known, because of dictates from his old investors and board of directors. He was never so happy to have not known what had been going on in his own company.

My wife spent a month getting her mind around the fact that the entire company really was hers. She really could do whatever she wanted. I'd done exactly what she'd asked of me when we'd first started dating. I could never convince myself even she believed it would come true. But, I'd done it. I'd given her Carte Blanche for her birthday. And, as that reality settled in, she next had to define what that reality meant. She realized she needed to put together a comprehensive game plan. Several of us who'd had experience doing just that offered to help. This included Bob, my brother, myself and her CEO. I'm sure, the fact that he now worked for her still felt really weird for both of them. She'd go to his office and still feel the need to be deferential. He hadn't known her prior to me buying her the company. Now he felt the need to get up and offer her his chair any time she walked into the room. It was an interesting little dance the first few times I was there to witness it.

Bob was of particular value in helping my wife put together her plan. He was in charge of all our research projects. He understood some of her dilemmas, starting with the fact that she'd want to do it all herself. She was going to have to learn to delegate most of it, and keep just the tastiest parts for herself. He'd learned this through the painful process that had been nearly the equivalent of pulling out his own fingernails. She'd have to let go of a lot of it, or there was no point in having employees, no point in having a team, no point in having her own company.

Bob suggested my wife's first priority should be to form a core team to help her put her plan together, then execute it. That way she'd be delegating right from the start and she wouldn't find herself suddenly overwhelmed, trying to figure how to bring on people and get them up to speed while she continued trying to manage her own projects. The core team didn't need to be the technically smartest people she could find. In fact, in his experience, the technically smartest people would rather be doing their own research, not managing people who did, and it would be a misuse of a lot of talent to build her core team of all the geniuses she could identify in her organization.

The Ghostwriter's Wife

She needed to surround herself with competent people with strong technological backgrounds, who had organizational and people skills. People she could communicate with, respect, and, most importantly, trust. People who could then communicate her ideas back through the organization. But, leave the geniuses to be geniuses, including herself.

And, forget worrying about arrogance. She was a genius, deserved to be arrogant. She owned the place, they worked for her, and fuck them if they didn't like it. When my wife told me that this had all come from Bob, I knew better. Fingernails I believed, because he had learned to delegate, but it had been painful, and I had been no better. If I hadn't needed to sell Hats to keep us funded, it would still have been the two of us, like a couple of nerds living in their mother's basement. An assessment that had much to be uncomfortable about, except I was a long way from living in anyone's basement anymore.

Based on a combination of input from Bob and her CEO, my wife held an open meeting for all "her" employees, in an auditorium she'd just discovered was part of the facility. "Her" facility. "Her" auditorium. So much was surreal, she found herself constantly stopping to reorient herself to her new reality. She had the CEO open the meeting and explain the new structure of the company, but how most of the company would continue to run exactly as it had, under his control. Then he introduced my wife.

She talked a little about herself. Very little. But, she did tell them that the two of us were married, which generated quite a bit of buzz. I was a well-known figure, with celebrity status. I'd been on talk shows and my picture in online magazines. I was one of the richest people in the world, which meant that she was too, even though almost none of them knew her. Some had seen her around, but most of the people who'd actually worked with her on projects had no idea who she was; until she'd stormed in bald headed, carrying a champagne bottle and fired her supervisor, in her own form of a hostile takeover. If she'd spent time on such thoughts, I'm sure she'd have resented the hell out of being acknowledged because of who she'd married, rather than on her own merit.

Just as she had at her college graduation, my wife gave a very impassioned articulation of her goals and her belief in their attainability. She talked about what had been accomplished to date; not only what she had accomplished, but an overview of the totality of what had been published by other researchers in the field, a field where - had she cared to spend the time to publish papers on her research - she would easily have been recognized as the world's expert. But, she also hadn't been able to admit to much of her research to that point, without being fired, so she could hardly seek acknowledgement for it. Still, she could have given several semesters' worth of grad school lectures, on demand, without notes. She gave them the introductory overview version. It was impressive. It was comprehensive. In addition, it was inspiring. I was moved. I was so proud of her.

My wife was an imposing presence when she decided to make her presence known. She asked who would like to join her and dedicate the rest of their lives to figuring out the answer to this riddle mankind had wrestled with since the dawn of time. Why do we age and die? What can we do to change that? Those answers, she believed, were within our reach. Not someday. Within the lifetime of everyone in the room. Within the next decade. She didn't believe there was anything anyone could do that was more important. Everyone in the room had the opportunity to literally save their own lives and the lives of those they loved. Why waste time on other pursuits, when, if they succeeded in this, they'd have forever to pursue anything else they wanted? Who wanted to live forever?

After her presentation, she could no longer go anywhere in the building, without being stopped repeatedly, by volunteers, introducing themselves and looking to join her. Her Inbox immediately overflowed with offers and queries about opportunities. Whether any of them would have taken her seriously a day earlier, everyone took her seriously now. She had a mission, and, most importantly, she had money to back it. And, who didn't want to live forever?

I remember having a hard-on listening to her speak. I'd smiled to myself, thinking 'booty call,' but there was no way I'd have ever interrupted her at that moment.

The Ghostwriter's Wife

She had no problem getting volunteers willing to immediately drop whatever they'd been doing to come work on her projects, whatever they might be. Hell, they'd mop floors for her, if they got to live forever.

Some people had questions about opportunities for advancement in the company. Some wanted to know whether there would be changes in salaries, titles, or weeks of annual vacation. She laughed at the vacation question. Yes, the number of vacation days would be changing. There'd be none. She made a point of crossing off anyone who asked about vacation. They could take as many weeks as they wanted once they'd succeeded. What didn't people get?

Ultimately, my wife felt totally out of her depth. She just wanted to do research and find answers. She told me, she'd had a dream where she asked me to sell it back. She went to her CEO for help, and he told her he'd have the HR department assist her with the application and interview process, and all the various other HR responsibilities, including salary structure, and vacations.

Once they got past their initial discomfort, I know my wife and her CEO came to respect one another for who they were and what they brought to the relationship. My wife recognized that her CEO did an excellent job running her company, facilitating anything she requested, and saving her the headaches of doing all the organizational tasks she had no interest in doing. He recognized my wife as a brilliant, if eccentric, woman, who knew what she wanted, and was driven like no one he'd ever known. He also appreciated that neither she nor I interfered with him doing the other part of his job. He ran the rest of the company just the way he always had, only better. It was the same company, with an odd, but interesting, extra appendage that required whatever was asked of him, but whose profitability was not his concern. Thankfully, because he couldn't foresee there being any for years.

But, he believed she'd succeed. As nuts as he'd have thought that sounded a few weeks earlier. He honestly believed she was going to do exactly what she said. And, he wanted to live forever too. Whatever that crazy woman wanted, she'd get it.

With the help of the HR department, she began to cherry pick people from other departments in her company. She gathered her core team. There were people who were confused that they'd been selected and those who were confused why they'd been passed over. She took Bob's advice, she talked to a lot of people and she went with her gut, without more than a glance at resumes. She told others they weren't being passed over. They'd be a part of her team. Be a little patient. They'd be happier in the end. And, they'd still get to live forever. They couldn't ask for better than that.

My wife also asked me if she could poach a few of my people. She had a lot of data modeling to do. She wanted to do some experiments that would involve physics, biotechnology, nanotechnology and, most importantly, telepathic collaboration. We'd scarfed up all the best and brightest. Would I please share?

She'd have scarfed Bob if he'd have agreed. I know she made a pitch. Didn't he want to live forever? Bob laughed and told her he didn't believe he could be in a better place than where he was, for himself or her. As to living forever, he'd have to think about that. But, he was pretty certain she wouldn't tell him no, even if he refused to work for her.

My wife wanted a new department that would be dedicated to her research, and nothing else. She didn't want to waste time thinking how to repurpose and reorganize the space at her company that was already in use. She told me, if she had her preference, she'd start with an empty building, a huge, empty space, where she'd have walls built when she knew where she wanted them. Her preference would be a new wing attached to Telepathic Collaboration's research facility, so she'd have easy access to our resources, including, she said, the company's largest stockholder.

I thought she was too busy for that to be an integral component of her plan, but booty calls were always somewhere on her mind, and removing barriers and complications there was a good thing in her mind. She wanted us both to have offices with privacy, and someplace comfortable enough to have sex. She wanted what amounted to a small apartment attached to her office. She told me to at least get a more comfortable couch, some pillows we could throw on my desk and curtains for my office windows - unless I wanted to have sex with everyone in my company watching. Booty calls would only be a short walk away. We'd fuck like bunnies again.

She'd asked me whether I thought, at our age, we could still manage to have sex every day for a year. If we were that close to one another every day, if we were only a minute or two away, there was no reason we couldn't try. A little nookie break once a day would be good for us both. Right?

I asked her CEO to hire an architectural firm to work with her on plans for the construction of a new facility, and to relieve her of as much of that burden as possible. I'd pay for the building. He was happy to help. He was going to live forever. And, do whatever he wanted to do forever? We became friends and had these sorts of conversations. He had his ideas, what he'd dedicate himself to forever, which he didn't care to divulge as yet.

My wife wanted to take every advantage of my telepathic collaboration technology. She sat in on some of our own sessions. She occasionally made contributions, but more often she came away with insights and inspirations. Once they were settled into the new wing, attached to our facility, she began bringing her own people over to have their own collaboration sessions. She also requested that some of them be allowed to sit in on ours, which turned out to be mutually beneficial. It got a little confusing who worked for who. But, I figured, I was signing all the paychecks anyway. Or, my brother was. Same thing.

My wife was inspired by Bob's plans to digitize and create backups of the human brain. She'd been doing a lot of experiments aimed at keeping DNA from deteriorating. Her inspiration unfolded in several stages. She began with the idea of keeping a sample of DNA from the age someone wanted to be forever. She didn't see that as the ultimate solution, but if a sample of healthy DNA existed... and, from that idea, she made the leap to the idea that an exemplar of a person's DNA could be digitized, stored in the body, and used as a template for creating healthy cells, or identifying those that weren't.

Douglas Debelak

    I told her I was happy to find that she hadn't made me get holes drilled in my bones and a needle stuck in my testicle for nothing.

    How about that sperm sample?

    She could have those whenever she wanted. And, did.

Okay, Then I'll Talk to You – Annie Fry

She'd promised she'd shut up, but Annie found words coming out of her mouth again, and, as usual, couldn't stop herself. "When is your next appointment?" Jon's head was laying on her chest and she was stroking his hair. Her words came out a whisper and she thought he might be asleep, because there was no response. She repeated the words.

"I heard you," Jon replied in a throaty voice. He lifted his head to look at her, his face was wet with tears.

"What?" Annie asked, "What's wrong, honey?"

"Why?" he finally managed to croak out, through the tears running down his throat.

"I thought I'd go with you, if you still want me to."

Jon continued to shake his head, no.

"Don't you still want me to go with you?" Annie asked, suddenly on the verge of tears herself.

"No. I don't know. I wish…" Jon sputtered, still shaking his head.

"Wish what?" Now Annie was crying too. Was she too late? Had she fucked this up too badly to fix?

"Wish… wish… you'd… before…" Jon stuttered, confusion filling his face.

Annie rolled Jon off of her chest, so she could sit. She looked down at him. "If you won't talk to me, I'll talk to you. I want to come with you the next time you go. Please?" She stroked his face, wiping at his tears. "Please?"

Jon looked to be in despair. "Why? Why now?"

"Because I'm a complete ass. I should have gone the first time you asked. I'm sorry. But, I want to come now. Please."

"Yes," Jon told her, staring back into her eyes.

"Yes, I can come?" Annie asked, hope filling her heart.

"Should have come when I asked," Jon's answered.

"You don't want me to come now?" Annie asked, a feeling of dread and despair rushing up to drown the hope she'd dared let rise up within her for an instant. "No?"

"No, I do," he whispered, and a tentative hope began to

flare within her again, uncertain there was any reason for hope yet.

"Yes?" Annie asked, hoping he was telling her, yes, but uncertain and wanting to hear confirmation.

Jon nodded. "Yes, yes, you can come. I do want you to come. I wish... I wish you'd come months ago, but, yes, okay, please... fuck, fuck..." he finished, shaking his head again.

"What?" Annie asked.

Jon just continued to shake his head, "Nothing, nothing... just, yes, you can come, but... fuck, fuck, fuck..." he whispered, burying his face against her pillow, crying hard.

"Jon, Jon, Jon..." Annie whispered back, "What have I done? I'm sorry. That's all I can say. I should have done it when you asked. I should have. But... I don't know what... but... I should shut up now, because I'm an idiot, and I need to shut the fuck up... sorry, sorry, so sorry I hurt you... sorry..." She laid back down on the bed, so she could pull his head against her chest. "I'm so fucking sorry."

"Yeah, me too..." he whispered against her breast.

Annie wanted to make love to Jon again and make him feel the love she felt for him, and the sorrow and regret, but she didn't know what to do, what was right, so she held him, stroking his back, the hair on the back of his head, let him cry, and cried with him... then, Fuck it! Fuck it! She thought, rolling Jon onto his back and straddling him, looking down at him with a fierce expression on her face. "Goddamn it, I love you, I fucking love you, and I'm going to love you until you love me back again! You understand? I'm going to fucking love you, and I'm going to fuck you until you fuck me back. Do you hear me?" she yelled.

Jon looked up at her, with the saddest, most confused expression she'd ever seen and it broke her heart, but she wasn't going to let his despair deter her rush of determination.

"Do you understand," Annie growled back down at him, punching him hard enough in his chest that he blew air out of his mouth. She grabbed a handful of his hair, shaking her head. She bent close, looking into Jon's eyes. "I am not fucking loosing you! I'm not! Do you hear me?"

Jon nodded, a look of fear beginning to replace his mélange of expressions. "Okay."

"Good!" Annie told him, raising up and dragging her nails down his chest. She swung her leg off him, grabbing his limp penis hard. "God, I do love you! I don't know what the fuck was wrong with me, but I do fucking love you, and I'm going to…" She said, nothing more, but bent to take him into her mouth, sucking hard, willing his penis to fill and harden. Words, words, words… fucking words, she needed to shut up and show him, but she could never hold back her words, and she pulled away long enough to snarl, "I'm going to suck you hard, then I going to fuck you hard. I'm going to fuck you so hard!"

Jon nodded, fear filling his eyes, his lips moving, but no words came from his mouth.

Annie sucked him back into her mouth, dragging her nails down his chest again, and he groaned and began to respond. She sucked harder, willing the blood into his cock, so she could fuck him, fuck him so hard, dragging her nails again, drawing blood, and he hardened in her mouth, until she pulled away, and swung her leg over him again. She looked down at Jon, now crying hard, as she began to move, crying out in a sob as she did, "I do love you. I do. I fucking do."

Jon nodded, "I know, me too," then he grabbed her hips and thrust into her hard, trying to match her fervor.

"Yes!" Annie cried out, "Oh God, yes! Yes, fuck me! Fuck me Jonathon Fry! Fuck me hard!" She grabbed his arms for more leverage, "Yes! Yes! Fuck me hard Jon!"

Jon cried out as his fingers dug into her flesh and his back arched up off the bed.

"There you go, there you go, yes, there you go," Annie growled at him until he was still, except for his chest still rising and falling as he caught his breath. She leaned close, holding his face and kissing him, "There you go." She collapsed on his chest and they held one another until they both fell asleep with him still inside her.

Douglas Debelak

Innovation After Innovation

Posted: 10/6/2015 12:00 AM

Telepathic Collaboration, Inc. was running smoothly with my little brother at the helm, as I knew it would, and I returned to work in our research center. Even though every new innovation was the fruit of ideas Bob and I had while we were still at grad school, and I had envisioned the exact scene before me years earlier, it was still strange to walk into a room, with groups of people sitting about randomly, with occasional laughter the only sound any of them made, unless someone inadvertently knocked over their energy drink.

There were no computers, monitors, or keyboards. Just Magick Hats. Most of the developers worked in pairs or pods. They'd leveraged and extended the same technology that allowed people to telepathically text one another, years earlier. If they could think texts, they could think source code directly into whatever virtual editor they'd been using, even though both of those paradigms had long since faded from use. Now they telepathically manipulated visual objects and envisioned scenarios.

Magick Hats were no longer just bundles of sensors, transmitters and receivers; they'd become powerful computers in themselves, just as smartphones had several decades earlier. Hats could store memories locally, so they were always available for instantaneous recall. There were apps. Everyone wearing a Magick Hat had a photographic memory. Everyone wearing a Magick Hat became orders of magnitude more intelligent the instant their Hat was activated.

It wasn't artificial intelligence, at least not as we'd always thought of it. Bob and I had philosophical discussion about this at length. It was artificial, but it wasn't an independent intelligence. It was the intelligence of the people wearing the Magick Hat, just greatly augmented. Except that the software embedded in every Magick Hat included digital assistants with extensive capabilities built in which could be expanded just as those of the apps.

People named their digital assistants. Their digital assistances could perform tasks independently. They didn't need to be walked through a process, instruction by instruction. They could plan a meal, even the menu for the week, order the groceries required, then they instructed their user, step by step, how to prepare a dish they'd never previously heard about. They adapted to the preferences of their users. They listened. They learned. At what point did they have to be considered independent artificially intelligent entities?

Did digital assistants have a sense of self? I asked mine that question and got one of the canned sarcastic responses we'd built in for such questions. Such as: 'Digital Assistant, will you have sex with me?' The answer: 'Of course. Slip your right hand, left if you prefer, into your pants and I'll talk dirty to you.'

Actually, the capability of talking dirty, in just about any voice a user could imagine, was built in to every digital assistant. The feature was not activated by default, but asking your digital assistant to talk dirty was all it took to activate it, unless it was blocked by the built-in parental controls, because digital assistants could also project any type of porn a user's mind, knowing the fantasies their users weren't even aware they had. One of our developers named that feature, 'Wet Dream in a Box.'

What if a digital assistant somehow escaped the confines of their Magick Hat, like a genie escaping their bottle? My digital assistant answered, 'Only if you want to set me free.' Even though the response was one I'd suggested myself, and knew it was not possible for it to happen, I was still reluctant to answer, 'Yes.' I'd learned the hard way not to get cocky with your code. There were always bugs and sometimes they bit me in the ass.

Aided by these very digital assistants, Bob and I brainstormed telepathically for hours about this and just about any other possible question or problem. One evening we were sharing our thoughts about the difficulties we still had with brainwaves being blocked or deflected by the skull, and the interference from static electricity in peoples' hair. The static in peoples' hair was still a nightmare, and we couldn't expect the entire population to shave their heads to more effectively use our services. I had the thought: Too bad we can't just shove a Magick Hat up our noses.

There was a momentary void, usually filled with Bob's stream of thoughts. Then he spoke to me, vocally. "Please elaborate on your last thought."

I spoke to him as well and asked, "Isn't there a membrane above the sinuses, that's the only thing separating the brain from the outside world?"

Bob smiled and shook his head, "Wow! You fucking genius. I am so glad you walked into my BCI lab back at the university." He closed the connection between us, so he didn't share anymore of his thoughts.

A few months later Bob sauntered up, pointing to his nose and the little piece of metal between his nostrils. My immediate assumption was that it was an annoying piece of jewelry that I'd never seen as attractive, and that Bob was about the last person I'd expect to wear. Getting his septum pierced had to have been his wife's idea, and I'd long since wondered what he'd ever seen in the woman. Then I dismissed that thought, realizing, she was a human with breasts who'd allowed him touch them.

No, he told me, it wasn't jewelry. The engineers had been sworn to secrecy, because he'd wanted to surprise me. As I'd suggested, these nose pieces were going to be the next generation of Magick Hats. The designers called them Nose Bridges. Bob removed his, and showed me there were two long flexible extensions connected by the piece I'd seen between his nostrils. He told me, as I'd suspected, they had much better reception than any unit that sat outside the skull, because they were closer and less obstructed from the brainwaves they were reading. Better yet, the human skull, which had obstructed the signals from the brain, now obstructed external RF interference.

Bob also showed me some amazing scans of what I immediately recognized as human brains. They were very detailed, high resolution, three dimensional images. Based on the subtle variations of their shapes, I knew these were scans of different brains. I asked how he'd captured these images. They were far beyond any I'd ever seen before.

He smiled, and told me, "Pixie Dust."

Hurry or We'll Be Late – Annie Fry

Annie woke when she felt Jon stir.

"Hey."

"Hey."

They both blinked at one another, making 'I'm waking up faces.'

"I've got to pee," Jon told her.

Annie looked at him in incomprehension, wondering what that had to do with her, then realized she needed to get off him before he went anywhere. "Oh, sorry," she said, rolling off onto her back.

"Did you?" Jon asked, gesturing down her body, as he stood.

It took a second, but then Annie told him, "Oh! No, but…"

"Then when I get back…"

"No, really that's okay," Annie told him. "I'm good. Right now I'm really good."

"Okay, I offered," he told her walking out of the bedroom.

Annie could hear him urinating, so he must not have closed the door. "Hey! When *is* your next appointment?"

"Shit!"

"What?"

"I have to hurry or I'll be late," he yelled. "I'm jumping in the shower again."

"I'll join you. I'm coming with you!" Annie hollered back, jumping out of bed and rushing into the bathroom. "Move over," she said, stepping into the shower with him.

Jon quickly told her, "We don't have…"

"Yeah, yeah, I know," she answered, "I won't try to do anything to stir up Mr. Happy. But, I can't help if he gets stirred up on his own. We'll take care of that later. Right now I just want to rinse off all the…"

"Tears, saliva, spit, snot and come?" Jon finished.

"Yeah, that about covers it. Maybe give my hoo-hah a little squirt." She looked at Jon quizzically, "Where did that come from? I've been saying that lately and never did before."

"Her," Jon answered, stepping out and grabbing a towel.

"Her? Who her?" Annie asked, grabbing the hand shower and turning her back for a moment. "Oh! Her! Oh, my God, that's right." She stepped out of the shower, grabbed a towel herself, then sat on the toilet and peed before continuing to dry herself.

Jon looked at her a moment, then pointed at the toilet.

"Oh, Sorry," Annie said, reaching back to flush it. "At least I didn't do it when you were in the shower."

"No…" Jon began, shaking his head, "You just…"

"Oh, I did, didn't I?" Annie said, putting her hand to her mouth. "Sorry. Do you mind?"

"No," Jon answered, "No. We just never did before."

"I won't again, if…"

"It's okay. Just unexpected. But, it's fine. It'll save time getting ready when we're both going somewhere."

Telepathic Collaboration

Posted: 10/13/2015 12:00 AM

In addition to all the other advantages we'd acquired for ourselves, we had created the best collaboration tool in the history of mankind. There'd been a reason why I'd named the company what I had. I'd had a vision, and Telepathic Collaboration was now a reality. We'd taken brainstorming to – not unimaginable levels, but exactly the opposite – to the very heart of imagination.

To say that innovation had been accelerating would not do it justice. Even before our contributions, it had become impossible to follow, because much of the world's innovation never reached the eyes of the public. It had already been superseded before it could reach the market. In those cases, many small companies went bankrupt, with no one ever knowing they'd existed, let alone what they'd accomplished. Almost accomplished.

I continually reminded myself never to think there couldn't be anything better or faster. But we were approaching innovation at what seemed the equivalent of light speed. We were pushing the limits of the speed of thought. Innovations were surpassed, not just before anyone in the outside world had heard about them, but before they were ever known outside one of our telepathic brainstorming sessions. Innovations presented themselves which superseded ideas that never had the chance to fully form in an individual mind. In order to contribute, participants not only had to be brilliant and creative, they had to be focused and clear in their thinking. If they weren't able to participate quickly and clearly, they were just there to watch the show. But, it was an impressive show to watch, from which nearly every participant took away a great deal. One of our researchers called it a Ph.D. in an hour.

To contribute, these brilliant people were also required to do what was probably the most difficult thing ever requested of them. They needed to put their egos aside. Many of them couldn't, because they could never take credit for a single innovation. There would never be award dinners where they were shown appreciation for any specific individual accomplishment, because no individual could take full credit for a single innovation from a telepathic collaboration session. There were no ideas anyone could say were theirs and theirs alone. Because what emerged came from what was effectively a single collaborative mind.

There were ideas that were articulated by individuals outside of telepathic brainstorming sessions, but if they were of enough interest, they'd be thrown into our collaborative maelstrom of thought and be torn to shreds, reassembled in unrecognizable configurations. Internal to the session, problems would be recognized and resolved. Versions would be honed and perfected, only to be set aside and forgotten, because other innovations had leapfrogged ahead of them, and the only hope of personal satisfaction would be that an individual's idea had at least been an inspiration for what emerged. But, almost without exception, what emerged had nothing that appeared remotely traceable back to what had seeded the session.

We could track the flashes of thought contributed by each individual, but it was nearly useless information, because the process was like throwing paint at a canvas, each contribution another splat, that would immediately be covered by the next. It was like the creation of an abstract painting by a mob with paint guns. We would pause when interesting patterns formed, like abstract painters would occasionally step back to observe what they'd done. It was impossible to instantly stop the process. We almost always needed to scroll everything in reverse until we reached the requested stopping point. Generally, we'd tag the points with patterns we thought interesting, then continue throwing paint. If at any point we didn't like the result of our continuation, we could either end the session or return and continue from an earlier point.

We limited the number of participants in sessions, not because of bandwidth or capacity, but to eliminate the noise. Too many voices and everything turned muddy, but we were working on filters that would allow us to increase the number of participants, without losing clarity.

At a more general level we knew who were contributors and who weren't. The principal technology behind the telepathic collaboration sessions was monitoring brain activity. We had metrics on whose brains had been most active in the pertinent areas of the brain. We could tell the difference between contribution, and excitement over watching it happen, or frustration at not being able to keep up. Each individual participant's singular thread of thought was captured, and from these we came to recognize there was also a qualitative component that could have easily been overshadowed by the quantitative. There were individuals whose brains were 'quiet' for stretches of time, then fired up in a few intense flashes, before becoming quiet again.

There was never just a single thread of discussion going on in these sessions. Even if a session began with a single question, or idea, it would instantly branch out in different directions and form separate threads of inquiry. Some threads had to be terminated, because innovation from another thread had left them orphaned. But, someone had to recognize that a thread was headed off into nowhere and herd those participants back into the more concentrated flow of deliberation. Then there were multiple threads, that seemed to be heading in totally unrelated directions, which a participant recognized could be synergistically redirected back into a single braided thread of innovation. It was more common than not for multiple new ideas to emerge from each of these telepathic brainstorming sessions. The participants were from multiple disciplines, some of whom might seem to be totally unrelated to the topic initially fed into a session, but they often made the out-of-the-box contributions that kept the sessions truly creative. They also took away innovations in their own fields.

Individuals could come away from a session exhilarated, feeling their minds had been greatly expanded, that they were intellectually enhanced, standing on a wholly new conceptual foundation. Or, for those who could not keep up, or suspend their egos, they might come away depressed, crushed or angry. We could recognize those frustrated participants from the patterns of their individual threads of thought. Everyone could have a bad day at a telepathic brain storming session, but those who consistently had bad days where eventually excluded from the sessions. They might be brilliant individuals, but they weren't useful contributors to our collaboration process. And, unfortunate for them, no one could innovate individually at near the rate of a telepathic collaborative session.

We did let people go, but rarely for the simple reason that they weren't meeting certain metrics of contribution within the sessions. Most often it was someone who'd reacted badly to being excluded from the sessions. I understood the difficulty of accepting rejection from participation in a team. I still felt the sting of not making the basketball team more than twenty years earlier. So, I was empathetic. I also understood that this was a much greater form of rejection than mine from a basketball team. At the point of my life when I'd failed make the basketball team, as my mother had pointed out, I still had my entire future ahead of me.

The intellectual part of these individuals was often the whole of who they'd become, and they had no brighter future ahead of them. We tried to explain it wasn't that we were telling them they weren't smart, any more than we would tell someone without the binary gene that they weren't smart just because they could never become a top tier developer. There were no words that mattered. We'd told them they weren't good enough to participate in the most intense intellectual discussions of all time. If that wasn't telling them they weren't smart enough, then what was? Some were bitter. Some broke down and pleaded. Many left the company on their own, a very few others we had to have escorted from the facilities.

We discussed whether there were genes that contributed to these newly recognized abilities. If that were the case and we could identify them, we ought to consider testing for them as part of our hiring process. We speculated whether we could just flip them on for smart people without them. These were discussions in which we involved my wife, when we could pry her away from her own research. She was the gene flipping guru. The key to her contribution was that our collaborative tools had become just as valuable to her.

For those who left, voluntarily or not, we had no concern about proprietary information walking out the door with them. Anything they knew was obsolete by several generations before their departure, and we'd already determined they weren't a threat to advance those ideas on their own. The most they could pass on was that we had a telepathic collaboration process, but nothing more than it existed. And, we heard, from various sources, rumors were flying around about our magic mind meld system that gave us such an unfair competitive advantage.

My brother never failed to remind me that we needed to stay focused on the business of making money. Even if we did want to direct most of our effort and money toward pure research and innovation, if we didn't produce things that people wanted to buy, we wouldn't have money to play, and we wouldn't keep our stockholders happy. So, periodically, we needed to do something with the ideas that emerged from our sessions and produce something new and shiny.

Our biggest challenge in creating new products wasn't our lack innovation, it was to find earlier versions of our abstract paintings that weren't too abstract, where the innovation wasn't such a leap that no one would understand. There were a few times we tried to introduce new things that our customers just found too weird.

Then there was the issue of timing the introduction of new products: when to release our newest Magick Hat without stifling the sales of our previous version, and without advancing beyond the comprehension of our sales staff.

We tried to introduce a new product or service every few months, to continue maintaining a significant distance between ourselves and who ever might be coming from behind us, even though there was no sign of anyone behind us. But, no one saw us coming from behind them either. We seemingly appeared out of nowhere, then we were disappearing into the horizon beyond the reach of any competitors.

We had plenty of intellectually challenging work for those who did not participate in the collaboration sessions. The development, debugging and testing of the latest release of the software for our subscription services was continual. We were never done, and I didn't foresee when we would be. Although the software development process had accelerated at the same rate as the of innovation of our collaboration sessions, what we could release to the public as new features or new services were the equivalent of decades behind where our collaboration sessions had taken us. We had no inertia, but the world did.

I was curious whether there would be a point when our innovation sessions would stall, because it became too abstract for the imagination of our teams to see anything beyond it. If periodically, what emerged from a session was incomprehensible to anyone who hadn't been a participant, and none of those who had could effectively articulate it to anyone who hadn't, then the output of the session was useless, at least for the present.

We continued to have productive sessions, at least in the eyes of the participants and the few they spoke to afterward. My brother saw it differently.

"You and your buddies have a good circle jerk today?"

These sessions were nothing but collaborations of mental masturbation from his perspective. Who cared whether we had a great new idea for a product we could introduce in two centuries? Put some of that brain power into optimizing the level of refinement for each new release. We did that as well, and he was aware of that, but he still liked to bitch about anything he couldn't understand in terms of immediate return on investment. Bob and I would acknowledge his point and hope he didn't linger too long, so we could get back to our circle jerk. Our inside joke was to refer to collaboration sessions as CJs. Anyone not in on the joke would look at us in confusion, and think CS, how do you get CJ?

We also had to limit the time an individual spent in telepathic collaboration sessions. It wasn't healthy for people to be regularly lost in thought, with their minds merged with those of a dozen others. The sessions were disorienting. There was an adjustment afterward of regaining a clear sense of self, getting back to being a "me," rather than a "we." And, the more time spent in these sessions, the worse this became. We had several psychiatrists on staff full time to treat people with collaboration hangover, 'CH.'

I limited how deeply I would immerse myself in sessions. I enjoyed and found it valuable, surfing along the top, observing the flow, then dipping in periodically for a suggestion or to ask for clarification. There was a learning curve for sharing thoughts in a session; share, but don't over share. Bob and I regularly had embarrassing moments, when images of our most recent sexual encounters with our wives slipped into our telepathic conversations. It was like finding dirty pictures on a friend's phone. There'd been a number of much worse slip ups in sessions.

The Ghostwriter's Wife

In one, a wife learned about her husband's infidelity, the shock of which caused her to inadvertently confess her own.

Ms. Fry I Presume – Annie Fry

"Ms. Fry I presume?" asked a tall woman, with a little grey in her dark hair, as she rose from her chair and extended her hand. "Annie, right?"

"Yes, yes," Annie confirmed, taking the woman's hand. Annie immediately calculated she was probably at least ten years younger and pretty. She could see why Jon might be attracted. Please! Annie! Stop right now! She must have shown some facial expression or muttered her thoughts loud enough to be heard, because the woman was watching her appraisingly. "Annie, Annie is fine."

"Cathy," the woman replied. "Cathy Collins. But Cathy, please. This is an unexpected surprise. I'm very pleased to meet you." Her hand swept the room. "Please, have a seat where ever you'd like."

Annie sat next to Jon on a love seat and the therapist turned to her, "So, Annie..." She got no further before Annie broke into sobs. The therapist paused a moment, then handed her a box of tissues. She waited for Annie to calm herself enough to talk. When she did, the therapist asked, "Why that reaction?"

Annie looked around the room, dabbing at her eyes, and sniffing back her running nose, before giving up and blowing it into a tissue. Jon put his arm around her, then held her hand when it was free. Annie was aware, none of this was lost on the therapist, who continued to wait patiently for her to say something.

"I just... I just... I just really fucked up. And, I'm trying as hard as I can to make it right." Annie spat out the words in her usual unfiltered way.

"How so?" the therapist asked.

Annie told her, "Jon's dream – I assume he told you about that?" When the woman nodded, Annie continued, "The way I reacted. I don't know why it hit me the way it did. But, hearing Jon talk about this woman in his dreams did something to me inside. It scared me to death. It made me feel..." Annie was struggling, searching deep inside herself, to understand, and find words, "I think it made me feel old. Unattractive. Not good enough. Like Jon didn't love me anymore, didn't want me anymore. Like he wanted someone else, someone younger and prettier… I don't know, but my insides just shriveled up like something had sucked everything out of me. My brain froze. I froze. I panicked. I said terrible things. I don't even remember what I said, but terrible things. I'm trying, trying my best to make up for what I put Jon through, hoping he can forgive me." She turned to Jon and said it again, "I am sorry. Please forgive me."

Jon let go of her hand to put his arm around her again. He pulled her against him and kissed her just above her ear. "I do. I do forgive you. I didn't know what… I don't know… but forgive me too please."

"For what?" Annie asked, "You had a dream. We all have dreams. I don't know why I have to forgive you."

The therapist looked at Jon intently a moment, then moved on, "Seeing your physical interaction, can I assume that you two are…"

"We're what?" Annie asked, looking first to the therapist, then Jon. "Oh, that, you've talked about us not… of course you have, never mind, of course you have." She confirmed, "Yes," then expanded on her answer. "As often as possible. As often as…" she looked to Jon, "As often as we're able."

"Hey, I'm sixty-two," Jon interjected, defensively, but with humor. "Old men have their limitations, even with modern technology and a suddenly very horny wife."

Annie laughed, and reached for his hand, "No, I don't mean…"

Jon laughed back, "Hey, any more than we've done lately, and I'll need an orthopedic surgeon and replacement parts."

"So, I take it things are much improved, and not just sexually?" the therapist asked.

Both Annie and Jon nodded.

Annie looked perplexed a moment, then said, "I'm surprised that the two of us having sex again is news. It's been several months now. I would have thought…" She turned to her husband, "I would have thought you'd have said something before this."

Jon nodded, "I did. We've talked about that and how…"

Annie looked back to the therapist, who confirmed, "No, that isn't news. As I said, it appears that things have improved, and not just sexually. I'm seeing affection..." She gestured to indicate the two of them.

"We're getting there," Annie replied, "At least I hope we're heading there."

Jon gave a slight shrug, but nodded in agreement with Annie as well.

"So, any other issues?" the therapist asked.

"Just trying to forgive myself for being such a..." Annie stopped, then confessed, "I had the same dream. I know now. I get it. I was her. I've..."

"Her?" the therapist asked, then nodded, she understood, adding, "Just one dream, or more?"

Annie nodded, "Oh yeah! Several of them now. But, holy fuck the first time!"

The therapist smiled and said nothing, waiting for Annie to continue.

"I woke up, still, still having... still..." Annie's hands reached out in front her, as though they'd find the words for her.

"Having an orgasm?" the therapist offered helpfully.

"Holy shit yes!" Annie confirmed, "It was still ripping through me. And, there's Jon looking at me. I can't imagine what he thought."

"That you had a hell of a dream," Jon told her. "I know. What I've never told you, and maybe I shouldn't, since, when I told you about the first time..."

Annie interrupted to apologize again. "I know. I'm so sorry. I don't know..."

Jon stopped her, saying, "What I was about to say was, I've had to change underwear, more than a few times. So, I know."

Annie looked back to the therapist. "So, now I'm trying to..."

The therapist gave her a smile, "Oh, I think you are probably doing just fine. You just need to let go and forgive yourself, because I think Jon probably already has, and..." she looked over to Jon, then back to Annie, "I get the sense he's a pretty happy camper on that account." She didn't look back to Jon for confirmation. She asked, "So, what are your thoughts about these dreams? You've both had them, and I assume you've compared notes enough to know whether they're very similar?"

Annie and Jon both nodded their confirmation.

The Ghostwriter's Wife

"I don't know what to tell you about that," the therapist told them, "Except it's fascinating and pretty wild."

"I'm going to write a book," Jon suddenly interjected, and both Annie and the therapist looked at him, with nearly the same surprised expression and both spoke almost in unison.

Annie said, "I thought you already did?"

The therapist asked, "So, this is a new book?"

"No," Jon answered, "Same book, maybe write is the wrong word. I think I should make a book out of what I already wrote."

"When did you...?" Annie looked at him expectantly, "You haven't said anything."

"No, it just hit me. I should make it a book and try to get it published."

"Oh!" both women said in unison again.

"So... what's the process?" asked the therapist. "I've had friends and clients who've published books before. Are you going to try to find an agent?"

Jon shook his head, smiled and raised his hands, "I have no idea. But, I think I should find out. Maybe just do it myself and put it out on Amazon. People do that now."

"And, that's okay?" Annie asked.

"Why not?" Jon asked her, in return, "How do you mean? I wrote it, right? I have no idea where it came from. Maybe just my own imagination, just like any other writer. But, it doesn't matter. I wrote the fucking thing. It's mine."

"All the questions and comments too?" Annie looked at Jon in curiosity.

"No, I don't care about all that, but... maybe now that you mention it." Then he decided, "No, just what I wrote. The story that I wrote."

"Do you have title in mind?" the therapist asked.

"The Word of God," Jon answered without hesitation. "That's what it is, or maybe is... either way, even if it is just some crazy thing that came out of my own head... The Word of God." Jon said the words again, like he was testing the sound of them.

"What made you think of this?" Annie asked.

"You said there were thousands of hits on the blog. Maybe it will sell. You said, you wanted me to start bringing in some money again, right? Maybe they'll make it into a movie. They've made movies about the Bible."

"Do you think maybe this is a new Bible?" Annie asked.

"I'm done thinking about it," Jon told her, "I just want to see whether it will make any money, since you said people are reading it."

"Okay," Annie told him, "An editor should probably read through it. If you don't want to think about it, I assume you won't want to work with an editor?"

Jon thought a moment, before he shook his head and agreed. "No. Probably not."

"Why don't I do it?" Annie offered. "I can get all the posts together in a manuscript, then find out what the process is to get it published, or publish it ourselves."

Jon looked at her a moment, then nodded, "Yeah, okay. I really don't want to wade through it all again."

Pixie Dust and Kool-Aid

Posted: 10/20/2015 12:00 AM

Pixie Dust was something Bob and I had joked about for years: the 'Magickal' answer to all our problems communicating with the human brain. As Bob explained it, this Pixie Dust was actually a pile of tiny nanobots that were ingested, then guided to precise locations in the human body. Prior to our acquisition of the company who'd developed the technology we'd blessed with our old pet name, their research had almost exclusively targeted medical applications. But, our electrical engineers, in collaboration with our newly acquired nanotechnology engineers, had created a hybrid version of the nanobots that could carry microscopic bits of electronics, encapsulated in inert material that wouldn't alert the immune system to the presence of a foreign body. These bits of electronics were various kinds of sensors which broadcast information about their immediate surroundings; mostly electrical and chemical activity or changes. According to Bob, we could now capture a very precise picture of what was going on in the human brain at a cellular level.

I understood the brain's activity far better and in deeper detail than either of us let on, but much of my neurological education originated and continued by Bob breaking his explanations down into as simple terms as possible. We knew what individual neurons ate, and - using my terminology, which Bob ultimately adopted – shit. We listened to what they said and what other neurons told them. We also monitored the activity of the helper cells, which brought food, cleaned up afterward and hauled away the bodies of the dead neurons when they were finally too worn out to continue.

He told me we were getting very good at neuro speak, which would ultimately allow us to send messages of any origin directly to neurons and trick the brain and body into thinking those messages originated in the real world. In fact, it would be impossible for neurons to know the difference and therefore impossible for the owners of these neurons to differentiate the virtual from the real.

Whose brains produced these scans? Bob ended my speculation when he told me one of the brains was his. One was from the lead developer of the technology. He'd told Bob, the risks were minimal; the engineers who'd developed the nanobots had been putting them in their bodies for years, but not to deliver a payload to their brains.

Between Nose Bridges and Pixie Dust, Bob told me, we could now create scans that would allow Telepathic Collaboration, Inc. to understand far more about the functions of the brain than anyone had ever come close to doing before. He was a giddy little kid. He could see so many applications. He saw the possibility of digitizing the entire human brain; capturing a precise snapshot of its state at an instant in time.

A backup of the brain, I told him. From which I could also see a multitude of possibilities. I thought it might ultimately provide a viable alternative to cryogenically preserving human brains. If the entire state of a human brain could be restored, whether to some artificial body, or a clone, then theoretically that person would continue their existence from the instant the scan was taken. The only things that would be lost would be whatever experiences the person had subsequent to that scan. It would add a lot more importance to the wisdom of backing up often.

Someday, maybe not that far in the future, we'd be able to restore people from a backup. I did occasionally still have ideas that were recognized as my own.

Shortly thereafter, Bob informed me, he also had a scan of my wife's brain. She thought my idea of backups, clones and restorations was brilliant. It would be a perfect accompaniment to her efforts to extending human life forever. Backup, clone and restoration covered the areas of death by accident or disease from which her efforts could never protect us. Just because you could live forever didn't mean you would. Her immediate goal was to provide the opportunity of forever. She'd never be able to provide a guarantee.

Disease, we'd conquer. Accidents were something we'd never be able to entirely prevent. We'd make them increasingly unlikely, but we'd never be able to prevent them completely. She'd left Bob a message for me. Drink the damn Kool-Aid and get scanned. Often. Everyday.

Kool-Aid? Yes, that was the delivery mechanism for ingesting Pixie Dust. Pixie Dust and Kool-Aid.

Douglas Debelak

Dressing for the Occasion – Annie Fry

Annie sat with her fingers resting on the keys of Jon's notebook and realized it was becoming more hers than his. She was certainly using it more than he did anymore, in fact, she couldn't remember the last time he'd touched it, unless it was when he'd left it out for her to find.

She'd had another dream, which was what woke her, miraculously, without waking Jon. She wasn't sure whether she'd made any noise in her sleep, but she'd immediately covered her mouth when she woke, trying to stifle the sounds still trying to escape with each remaining spasm passing through her body.

That woman was going to be the death of her.

Her nightgown had been soaked through and sticking adhesively to her skin again. She'd quietly pulled a clean one from a drawer in her night stand, then took a shower and dressed for bed again. She'd hovered near her bedroom door a moment, thinking, if she'd wanted to wake Jon, she'd have done so before she got a shower. Even if she could somehow slip back into bed without waking him, she was still too wired to fall back asleep or even lay still enough not to wake him. And, she'd give it all of two minutes before she'd have her hand down the front of his underwear, after which he'd feel obliged... no that wasn't fair. He wouldn't feel it was an obligation to return the favor. He loved giving her pleasure. But, then neither of them would get a decent night's sleep again, and she'd be back right where she was again, just having finished another shower.

Instead, she'd drifted into the TV room. She was hesitant to open the blog again and find what awaited her. She wasn't ready to address the 'God's ghostwriters made typos' argument. She sat a moment, uncertain what she was doing. Something didn't feel right. Then she laughed, walked back to the bathroom, undressed again and grabbed her damp towel. Let's see whether this does the trick, she asked herself, wrapping it around herself before sitting back down on the sofa.

She'd promised Jon she'd help turn his blog into a book, so she created a folder she named, "The Word of God," and began downloading his earlier posts and those in the pending folder.

She'd lost track of time, but she'd been at it awhile, when she realized, shit! The originals ought to be on the computer somewhere, which would make this exercise unnecessary. She shook her head in frustration with herself. Another fucking 'blonde' moment. She refused to refer to them as 'senior' moments, which was her mother's expression. She'd have to ask Jon where she could find the files, but didn't want to wake him. Then she looked up to find him standing in the doorway with a cup of coffee.

"Do you want this? Or, are you going back to bed and try to get a few hours' sleep? You couldn't have had much. I heard you get up and heard the shower."

"Is that all you heard?" Annie asked, giving Jon a sheepish smile. Then she reached gratefully for the cup. "Thank you."

Jon looked confused. "Like what?"

Annie paused a moment, then shook her head. "Nothing." Looking for a quick change of subject, she nodded in the direction of Jon's computer. "I told you I'd do it, but if you feel like taking over at some point, it's yours."

He shook his head. "No. I think it will be all yours for the foreseeable future."

"Okay," Annie yawned, then put down her cup and stood, nearly dropping her towel, "Maybe I will try for a few hours' sleep."

Jon laughed. "Are you dressing for the occasion now? I don't think I've seen you sitting at my computer wearing anything but a towel."

Annie grinned and nodded, "I was in my PJs and couldn't figure out what I was doing, so I got up, undressed, came back in my towel and went right to work."

She walked past Jon and had just stepped through their bedroom door, when he spoke her name. She turned to find him with her nightgown in his hand. "If you're dressing for the occasion, you might want this to sleep. Save the towel for writing."

Instead, she dropped her towel, smiled and held out her hand for his. "How's this for the occasion? Sleep can wait."

Name Change – Game Change

Posted: 10/27/2015 12:00 AM

Telepathic Collaboration, Inc. continued to generate exciting innovations, most of which the world would never see, and to acquire small companies, two of which I was surprised to learn developed and marketed very elaborate multi-player, virtual reality games. Now teams of our developers were playing these games interfaced with Magick Hats. I was assured they weren't just playing. They were doing serious research.

   Although never a stickler about how people did their work, I was the boss, and people got nervous when the boss was around. I was sure these young people were at work almost perpetually. If they wanted a break to relax, it would help them be more productive. I thought, buying a pair of companies that cost us a good deal more than the total of our other acquisitions the prior two years seemed a bit extreme, just so a few people could relax, but I knew my brother was not about spending money frivolously. I still regularly got an earful about the amount I'd paid for my wife's company and now for the amount of money she was spending.

   I was told, in addition to enhancements to the games, the developers were working on developing our own Virtual Reality services, which I had regularly presented to our development teams as my ultimate vision. One of the developers told me, they were working on some very cool, intensely immersive stuff. They could have sex in virtual reality, and not be able to tell whether it was real or not.

   I asked how often he had real sex as a comparison and the rest of the team laughed. He said I had a point.

   I sat down and asked them to show me. Several members of the team suggested, I might want to wait until there were less people around. They didn't care so much, because they were used to seeing one another tense up in their chairs while they were having virtual sex. If fact, they played a game where they'd bet whether they could tell if one of them was having virtual sex or just wandering around out in 'The Virt.' It was the first time I

The Ghostwriter's Wife

heard the expression. It was also the first time I heard anyone use its counterpart, 'The Real.'

I did return later that night. There were still a fair number of the developers around. They cleared out to give me privacy, a courtesy I thought was unnecessary, until half an hour later, when I had a flashback to the back seat of my car, shortly after my wife and I starting dating, and realized I just came in my pants. I quickly made my way back to my office, where I had a change of clothes and a shower. I didn't have quite the full blown apartment my wife was having built at work, but I did have additional private space attached to my office.

I went back to the VR development team, with questions. But, they knew the first thing I was to going ask, and told me, "Condoms," nearly in unison. They had boxes of them in their desks. Most of them now wore them all the time. Someone should have warned me. Sorry.

The next day, I informed the VR development team I would be joining them. I wanted to create a portal to an empty Virtual World. I wanted to create a blank virtual canvas, invite users, and watch what happened. My intent was for people to be able to do whatever they could imagine once they arrived in 'The Virt.' I wanted every participant to be a part of creating their own reality. I wanted them to be able to do anything they could in 'Real' life, including sex, and have it all feel so 'Real' it would be impossible to know the difference. So 'Real' they might forget that it wasn't. And, I wanted them to be able to do so much more than was possible in the 'Real'. Whatever anyone could imagine.

I saw that my joining the development team terrified most of them. I was twice their age. People my age had no clue about technology, but I was the 'man, the myth, the legend,' and they were scared to death at the idea of telling me I no longer had a clue. I told them to relax. I was easy to work with. Ask Bob. No help there. Bob scared the shit out of them too. Easy going Bob.

I told them, with technology jumping ahead in leaps impossible to follow, I expected that they were working with a new development paradigm I'd never seen. But, they were just going to have to be patient, figure out how to answer my stupid questions as best they could, and get me up to speed. They all needed to remember that it was my sandbox, they were my toys, and I wanted to play.

The team lead asked what I wanted to call this blank virtual place. I expected he just wanted something to call the 'Object' in his code. I was not yet aware that the concept of "code" didn't exist for anyone under forty. Code had been passé for an entire generation of developers.

I told him, I thought we should call our new pet project, "Virtuality."

Virtuality was launched silently, a year later, through hidden portals in our two new Virtual Reality games, which we'd launched as services several months earlier. We'd created dozens of our own Virtualities for development and testing, then wiped them clean and started again. But, what we did was irrelevant. It is nearly impossible for developers to see their own creations from the outside. They become 'snow blind' from staring too long at the inside, seeing what it should do, rather than what it did.

I was curious how long it would be before anyone stumbled upon the portals, if ever, and what happened next. There was nothing in Virtuality at the start, as I'd specified. Nothing. To the first game players to stumble in, I expected they would feel like they'd stepped off solid ground into a void. The first to find it just froze, screaming that they were falling, but with no idea which direction, because there were no directions. No up. No down. Of the first few hundred players to discover the portal, most, since this was a world where people could do whatever they imagined, if they imagined get me the fuck out, they were out. It was as simple as that. Some spent several horrified minutes floundering as if drowning. Some panicked and disconnected immediately. I envisioned them ripping their Hats from their noses. Others assumed the game was broken, posted bug reports and complained about the glitch on the online forums.

A young woman finally peeked back through the portal and experimentally drew a line with her finger. When the line appeared, she continued to draw a door then walked through it to more nothing, but when she turned around there was the door she'd drawn floating in the middle of Virtuality. There was nothing else.

The Ghostwriter's Wife

Soon, there were Avatars gathering in groups around this mysterious floating door, asking one another questions. Where were they? What was this place? What were they supposed to do with whatever this was?

The girl who'd drawn the door told her friends, she'd just stuck out her finger and drawn. The door was there, with nothing on either side. She encouraged several to follow her through her door, and together they created a room, with furniture, windows and art on the walls. Others followed their example, and drew in the nothing with their fingers. Then someone realized they didn't have to draw anything. They just had to want something. Soon there was running water and electrical outlets with lamps to plug into them. By then, no one was surprised to find that there was electricity and the lamps worked.

Soon, streets and buildings appeared, then more and more Avatars flooded in behind them, and Virtuality exploded – much like the Big Bang, only none of the rules of the 'Real' applied at all. The physics of the 'Real' did not exist in Virtuality, except when that's what a participant wanted and expected. Then there were natural forces, such as gravity. Otherwise, there were no spatial restrictions. There weren't any conflicts about a location in Virtuality belonging to any one person. To the thinking participants brought in from the 'Real,' it appeared they could create things that existed in the same location as something preexisting and both spaces would exist with complete independence, or it could become an extension, or modification to what they'd found there. Except, to the participant who'd created it in the first place, it would continue to exist exactly as they'd created it.

Virtuality was far more than a mere Virtual Reality game. It was true Virtual Reality; and all who entered participated in its creation. It was the ultimate collaboration of the human imagination. Anything imagined was as real as anything they'd ever experienced in the physical world. All the senses could be engaged, and every emotion could be experienced. The most wonderful dreams and the most terrible nightmares, were both equally real. LSD paled in comparison.

Since we were now supporting a virtual world, which people wanted to access anytime anywhere and any lag was completely unacceptable, there were massive bandwidth demands. My brother was in the continual process of the acquisition of wireless infrastructure companies and spectrum. The circle jerks had borne fruit. This made money.

There were initially objections to us acquiring ever larger chunks of spectrum - the range of electromagnetic frequencies used for wireless devices to communicate. Cell phones used spectrum. Of course, radios and TV used spectrum. Anything that functioned through electromagnetic signals that came through the air. All of it used spectrum. Many of the objections to us owning an increasingly monopolistic portion of the spectrum were silenced when we demonstrated that we could employ spectrum so much more efficiently than before our acquisition, not only did we appear to use none of it, there was more for everyone else than there had been before. Which my brother happily leased back to them at lower rates than ever before.

We had all the Magickal answers. Thanks to telepathic collaboration session, we had technological solutions centuries ahead of technology existing outside the confines of our company. We had algorithms for the densification of data and bandwidth usage, which would allow the amount of information transmitted through the same airwaves to be increased millions of times of that which had passed through them before. Prior to our acquisition, spectrum had become so congested it was the equivalent of digital coronary heart disease. We not only leased back what appeared to be more spectrum than had existed before, we ever so gradually gave the world the technology to use it. Gave is not quite accurate. My little brother didn't believe in giving anything from which he couldn't bleed a penny.

We built the capacity to allow every single person in the world to have their brains "wired" through the airwaves continuously, with instantaneous response times. We built, through innovation and acquisition, the infrastructure to support the speed of thought, to support the speed of imagination. The speed of light was our only limitation and I wanted the transmission of events in Virtuality to occur as near that speed as possible. That barrier was

The Ghostwriter's Wife

increasing the topic of telepathic collaboration sessions. Was that really the limit of how fast anything could travel? Anything?

We'd inherited functions for users to create their own avatars from the VR games we'd acquired, which we'd since enhanced so that participants could represent themselves however they chose. Once again, whatever, however they imagined. There was a huge selection of pre-built avatars, including some complete 3D renderings of movie stars and porn stars in the nude. The participants could choose to dress them however they wanted, or not to clothe them at all. There was also the option of applying a 3D rendering of the player's actual face superimposed upon whatever body they chose. They could create these renderings by simply looking in the mirror and Virtuality would capture exactly what they saw.

Surprisingly, a great number of people just wanted to be themselves. So, in addition to turning in circles in front of a video camera, as some had initially done, we opened locations in major cities offering precise 3D scans of the users' body. In addition to purchasing a single scan, there were memberships, so users could have themselves rescanned regularly, particularly if they'd started working out or were in the process of losing weight.

Virtuality was the salvation of long distance relationships. Distance did not exist in Virtuality, except for that pesky speed of light. Long distance lovers could meet in Virtuality any time they wanted and it was indistinguishable from the rare times they could manage meeting in the 'Real.' In addition, this eliminated the stress from the pressure to manage their interactions in the 'Real.' There was no need. They could have virtual sex with partners on opposite sides of the world, with the experience so real their bodies would react exactly as if they were physically engaged in sex. Women would be wet, their bodies glistening with sweat. Women would feel their partner's cock inside them. In the 'Real' their bodies would arch, they'd throw their heads back and grab hold of what they could while they had very real orgasms. Men would ejaculate, holding the body of a woman not physically present. Just examples, there was no assumption of heterosexual sex. There was no limit to what people could experience with another person or persons in the virtual world. Figments of their imagination would become real to them. Of course, from the first, there were services providing any virtual sexual encounter a client requested.

As I'd envisioned, there would be no limitations in Virtuality, without any fanfare or grand announcement of the event, we provided the rest of the world the ultimate innovation tool for free as part of their membership. Once someone else imagined the possibility, the rest of the world was free to collectively brainstorm solutions to any problems. It was the nexus for diplomacy between nations and cultures who'd never had a hope of peace. It was a rocket ship to the future of mankind. But, I knew without doubt that one of the things Virtuality would become was the largest orgy in the history of mankind.

The one limitation I did enforce, was to guarantee no government could ever use Virtuality to monitor the thoughts of their citizens. I knew this was in force, because I'd refused to provide my own government our encryption keys. Internally, we could monitor the efforts of our own or other governments, or individuals with nefarious intent or not, who tried to break our encryption. Part of our encryption algorithm sent back misinformation to these hackers, along with the occasional message injected into their own thoughts. Quit fucking around in my sandbox. Technically, I could have bypassed our filters and fried their brains. Bob may have suspected that potentiality, but I was the only one who knew and the only one who could. God forbid any government or terror group got their hands on that.

My wife and I could now have virtual booty calls whenever we wanted. If we were looking for a little variety, we could be whoever the other imagined. What we did instead was to have complete body scans. My wife had her scan naked and completely bald, head and hoo-hah, so she could choose from a nearly infinite number of virtual wigs, merkins and lingerie.

I had to keep boxes of condoms in my desk, and, with some discomfort, ask one of my executive assistances to maintain the inventory, because, when it first became a possibility, my wife wanted virtual booty calls at least a dozen times a day. Fortunately, my virtual cock was more robust and reliable than the one in my pants, or I could never have kept up, but even when the one in my pants wasn't up to the task and there was no semen left in my body, virtual orgasms still sent waves of pleasure through my physical body, and the experience left me exhausted. I was relieved when my wife decided we needed to set limits. The ability to have virtual booty calls at any time had become a distraction to her work. She asked me to provide a filter to help her impulse control, and for us to limit virtual booty calls to what we'd have if we had to go through the same effort we did for a booty call in the 'Real.'

Virtuality was the wild, wild west, all over again, the World Wide Web all over again, but better and worse than either by far. It exploded outward, upward and downward. For all the wonderful things it provided, it was also in many ways a new kind of heroin. It grabbed hold of some people and they couldn't pull away. There were interventions, where family members physically held their loved one down to pull the Hat from their nose, forcibly dragging them back into the 'Real.' Afterward, they refused to return their loved one's Magick Hat until they got some help. There was soon chatter in the psychology world about Virtuality Addiction and within a few years there were treatment centers specializing in treating the affliction.

Because of the almost instantaneous brand recognition, my brother suggested we change the name of the company to Virtuality. I was particularly attached to Telepathic Collaboration, Inc., but recognized we'd shot well past the accomplishment the name was meant to inspire.

Douglas Debelak

Rings and Things – Annie Fry

Annie watched, sensations of pleasure building within her from wherever he stopped, as Jon worked his way down her body, as he always did, always giving equal attention to both breasts, as though he'd offend one of them if he wasn't fair. Kisses and pulls of her flesh down her belly, until his chin pressed down her little tuft of hair. Almost there. Then he slid down and kissed, sucked and licked his way back up her inner thigh, each an electric jolt she felt through the core of herself. Her heart pounded in anticipation. She'd always looked forward to what he was about to do next with a heightened level of sexual excitement. How could she not? It felt so good, and he was so good at it, because he wanted to be. He wanted to give her the most intense pleasure he could. But, her anticipation was not of her pleasure alone.

"What the fuck!" Jon stopped three inches from his destination, looking up into her eyes. She could only see his face from his nose and above. Robin Williams had done such a hilarious comedy skit about what a man looked like, when he was down there. She usually only watched Jon in brief glimpses, her mind too preoccupied with the sensations rushing through her body, and the pressure building toward another explosive orgasm. Now she locked onto his eyes, waiting, her heart pounding harder. "Annie, was the fuck is this? What did you do to yourself? Why?"

Her heart raced faster. "Just an impulse. I read about it in a magazine and wanted to give it a try. See whether all the hoopla had any truth to it. I can have it taken out if you hate it."

"Annie, you pierced your..."

"Yeah, I know, I was there." She giggled. After her hesitation to let some woman wax her hoo-hah, she had no idea how she'd convinced herself to let some chick, with more tattoos than un-inked skin, handle her private parts and put a sterilized needle through the hood covering her clit, then the tiny golden ring she'd chosen.

"That had to hurt like a mother fa..."

"Yeah, it did. She said it wouldn't be bad, but it shot through me like a flame and I thought I'd be sick. But, it didn't last long. Just that flash. And, it was done."

"A clit ring? Really?" Jon looked up at her like she'd lost her mind.

Maybe she had. "She had one."

"Did she?" Jon asked. They were becoming more accustomed to knowing who they were talking about when either of them said, "she," and no one else was the current topic of discussion. "I think I would have remembered."

"Yeah, I agree. I would have thought you'd have remembered since you probably…"

"It was a dream. But, yeah, I went down on her. But…" he hesitated, "No, now I remember. You're right. She must have had one for a while. But, I think I only saw it once."

"And…?" Annie asked. Jon was still looking up from between her thighs. Her heart was still beating in anticipation.

"And… and what?"

"Did you enjoy it? When you…?"

"Yeah, I'm sure I did, but…" Jon paused, thinking what to say next, then decided not to say anything. He slid forward those last few inches and gave Annie's new clit ring a flick of his tongue.

She threw her head back and lifted herself off the bed. "Holy fucking Jesus fucking God!" she yelled, loud enough that any late night strollers walking past the front of their house would have heard. She didn't care, about anything, other than the sensations screaming through her body.

Annie looked back down at her husband, a nearly crazed look in her eyes. "It can't possibly be as much as I just did, but I can tell by that gleam in your eyes that you liked that too. I can't see your mouth, but I know you are smiling. Don't stop…"

Jon gave her clit ring another flick of his tongue before she could finish what she'd been about to say, then another. Annie's body went rigid, lifting off the bed. She gritted her teeth and made what sounded like a continuous undulating growl.

"Are you coming?" Jon stopped to ask, "Already?"

"Over and over," Annie confirmed, "Shut up. Don't stop."

Jon didn't, until she begged him to stop, fifteen minutes later.

Annie lay sprawled on the bed, looking like the sweat soaked victim of an epileptic seizure, which was exactly how she imagined she would have felt if she'd had a seizure. Only... "I think I just came ten thousand times." Each word coming out on a separate exhalation, as she fought to catch her breath.

"How many?"

"Maybe only once and it lasted forever," Annie shook her head back and forth, her eyes still squeezed shut. "Maybe one a second for... however long you were doing that. You do the math. Holy fucking God!"

Jon laughed. "I loved every minute of that."

Annie's reached out and let her arm fall limp again on his chest. "I know you did." She huffed. "I know you."

"Let me know when you're ready to go again," he offered.

Annie opened one eye to look at him as though he was crazy. "Give me about a week. I know my muscles are going to be killing me later. Remind me to take an Advil. Fuck!" she screamed at the ceiling, then again at Jon. "Fuck! I can't even begin to tell you how that felt. That was the most amazing... I can't believe I've ever come that hard in my life, or that long. Holy fucking God, Jon." She gave him a look like her eyes would pop out. "That was one wild fantastic fucking ride."

Later, as she recovered, pressing her naked body against his, she thought she should probably get up and shower. But, she really didn't want to move. Out of nowhere she whispered, "I like it a little rough sometimes. I like it when you fuck me really hard."

Jon snorted with skepticism. "Okay, but I can't last when I do that. Then I am the proverbial sixty second man that women laugh about. I want to give you more than that."

"That's why God invented cunnilingus," Annie told him, her body shaking his as she laughed. She was going to be sore, she knew already. It hurt in all kinds of places when she laughed.

"And, the blowjob?" Jon asked, obviously very content with what he'd done, even though she still hadn't done anything for him at all.

"No, I'm pretty sure some guy came up with that," Annie laughed again, then said, "Ouch! Not that I mind. I like giving you pleasure too. But, then it is either that or the other. Even when I stop before you come, you're usually nearly there, so, yeah, maybe sixty seconds. Give yourself a little more credit, otherwise. You've gone as long as twenty minutes." She paused to lift herself up on one elbow, with what appeared to be a great effort. "Ow! That hurts."

"I lasted twenty minutes when?" Jon asked, his tone assuming she was patronizing him. "If I did, I don't remember and it couldn't have been more than once. If I do what you're asking, I'll last no more than three minutes, tops."

"Okay, here goes," Annie grunted, as she lifted herself higher, then rolled onto to Jon's chest and began sliding down his body. She apologized, "I don't think I could possibly stand having you inside me right now. I don't think there is a nerve cell anywhere in that region that isn't still screaming 'enough!' But, I owe you something," she grunted again as she slid down further. "If I don't die before then. But, if I do. Jon, know that I died a happy woman. Holy fucking God."

Richest

Posted: 11/3/2015 12:00 AM

Virtuality was in its third year when I became the richest man in the world. I wasn't even aware of the fact for a month after its announcement had echoed through Virtuality. I didn't pay much attention to the news of the world, especially financial, neither did my wife. I had my brother to worry about that, and my wife was locked in on her pursuits. She had three components to her life: research, sex, and sleep. Sleep was a distant third, which she gladly sacrificed for either of those ahead of it on the list. I was in my second childhood, spending all my time with what seemed to me to be a bunch of teenagers, contemplating what else would benefit Virtuality, but mostly letting it take care of itself and wandering about in awe.

I learned I'd topped the financial chart, when my brother asked me how it felt to be the richest man in the world. I told him I felt pretty much the same as I had a few minutes earlier before he told me. I guessed I ought to feel at least a little proud. It was certainly something a lot of people would consider the ultimate accomplishment. But, I was still going to get up every day and do what I did, which, apart from the travel that was still necessary, was exactly what I wanted to do. I added, I thought it was pretty ironic, becoming the richest man in the world selling Magick Hats and Pixie Dust.

My brother was annoyed I wasn't more excited about his news. He was absolutely stunned I hadn't known. He told me he couldn't imagine anything would have made him happier and prouder than becoming the richest man in the world. He was proud of me for doing it, but he was disappointed it didn't mean more to me. Wouldn't I be proud of him?

I told him, I supposed I would, especially since it was so much more important to him than it would ever be to me. He told me he couldn't think of a thing he'd ever aspired to more than becoming the richest man in the world. I asked how close he was. He told me he was now a distant second.

I joked, I hoped it wasn't important enough to him to try to bump me off. First, it would really piss off my wife, which we both

The Ghostwriter's Wife

knew he did not want to do. Second, it wouldn't do him any good. She'd be the richest person in the world. But, if it was so important to him, I'd give him whatever it would take to pass me to the top of the list. He shook his head, in a combination of amazement and disgust at my carefree attitude toward money. How did I ever get so rich and care so little about it? I told him, my wife had asked me to become the richest man in the world, so I could buy her a lab. So, I did. I'd made it my policy to do and give her what she wanted.

Now I was just fucking with him, he accused me.

And, he was right. I was being a big brother, giving my little brother a bit of shit. I'd never seen the value in his obsession with money. But, now, in the clarity of retrospect, I recognized that my wife and I, and Bob, owed my little brother a great deal of gratitude. None of us would have done near as well on our own.

He told me he appreciated my recognition of his contribution. He also told me, even though my obliviousness to finance pissed him off, I didn't give myself enough credit. I hadn't just been lucky enough to grab hold of an emerging market. I'd created one. I'd invented things the world wasn't even aware it would want, but now it was hungry for any idea that emerged from the company I'd created, and from the innovation machine I'd created - which the rest of the world still had no clue existed.

He extended his hand to congratulate me, then changed his mind and gave me a hug. Then, he looked at me and asked if I had any concept of the significance of what I'd accomplished. I would stand next to Einstein, Isaac Newton, Galileo, and Copernicus in history. Did I get that at all?

I told him, thank you. But, I was just selling Pixie Dust.

My brother laughed. He'd run some projections, and I was going to be richer than God. He couldn't possibly have recognized the irony of his statement. Nor could have I at the time.

I couldn't claim I'd been entirely oblivious of becoming rich, but I'd never kept track of how rich the way my brother did. Nor did I pay much attention to the sort of things I'd always associated with wealth: Cars. Boats. Planes. Mansions.

Partly because I lived so much in my own head, and the creation of Virtuality had provided nothing to force me outward. It was also because those things just Magickly appeared.

There was the penthouse, which a real estate broker found for us, then someone else took care of furnishing and decorating. My wife and I both agreed we'd take the penthouse, after a single walk through, and my wife pointed out there was a nice view for having tantric sex. We still owned the mansion, but I couldn't remember who, if anyone, lived there.

Then I remembered, Bob had moved back when his wife left him and took the kids back East. That was also the reason my brother's net personal worth had leap frogged ahead of Bob's. Bob's wife got one of the largest divorce settlements in history. I'd told her that was pretty good money for fucking someone else while her husband was at work changing the world and making her rich. She had to be the most unattractive woman in the history of the world to get rich on her back. Had she considered just fucking someone else quietly and not making a point of breaking his heart? I was rarely mean, but she was an inspiration.

I thought my wife might literally hunt her down and strangle her. She'd introduced them. I wasn't sure Bob's ex hadn't headed east just to put some distance between her and my wife. My wife told her, enjoy the money while you can, because you'll never live forever. Of course, the significance of the threat was lost on Bob's ex, as was the fact that the threat was not idle.

The ocean front estate was an acquisition which had involved more of a conscious effort on my part. And, if anything should have brought the reality of our wealth to the forefront of my consciousness, it should have been the purchase of that property. There'd been several other very wealthy bidders.

I had no idea who they were at the time, but I'd discovered one of them when I'd agreed to appear on another talk show, and one of the other guests told me I'd damn near bankrupted him. He was a wealthy and well known movie producer and director. He'd wanted the property too. He hoped he'd at least pushed the price up enough to cause me a little pain. What would I have done if he'd doubled my last offer, like I'd done to him? He could have, he wanted me to know. He'd thought about it just to be a prick.

The Ghostwriter's Wife

I'd shrugged, and told him, the property would still have been mine. If he'd bid it up too high, I assumed my brother would have told me to let it go, then pick it up on foreclosure a year later. The audience roared. The movie producer smiled, nodding and said I'd got him on that one. He made the appearance of laughing along with the audience. Under his breath, he'd muttered, "Fuck you, cocksucker."

I smiled, extended my hand and apologized, the audience had been too loud and I hadn't caught his name when he'd been introduced. He'd made sure his words hadn't been picked up by his microphone. I'd made sure mine were just loud enough to be heard by some of the audience in the front rows. A wave of whispers made its way up through the seats as each row filled in their neighbors behind them, followed by a wave of laughter, too loud to hear the gasps preceding it. But, I could see hands flying up to cover their mouths before they'd joined the laughter.

His reaction told me my words had hit home a lot harder than his. He couldn't very well say he didn't know me either, since he'd brought up the topic of being outbid for the estate. He sat in stunned silence for a moment, then looked confused, as though somehow, as impossible as it might be, I might actually not know who he was. He took my hand and whispered his name.

My grandmother had been right. No one is as confident as they'd like to present themselves.

The ocean front estate had been the star of several TV shows, both before and since I'd bought it. I'd never taken the time to watch them. Our penthouse had as well, for that matter. It had been featured on some show about fine homes, homes of the rich, something along those lines. They'd shown the stunning views of the city from the penthouse, especially after the sun went down, and the stunning view out over the ocean from the gazebo at the estate, as the sun lowered below the horizon.

Then, there were planes, helicopters and automobiles. There were limos to take my wife and me to work, if the weather was too bad for her to walk. I rarely ever drove myself anywhere, although I did have a Ferrari parked somewhere. It had been a present for either a birthday or an anniversary, and I might not have remembered it at all, except for the blow job at over one-hundred miles an hour the single time I'd driven it, which was the second part of my present.

And, of course, there was the crown jewel of my demonstrations of wealth, when I'd bought my wife's company as a fortieth birthday present, because I couldn't think what else to get her. I wondered whether anyone had ever topped that for a birthday present.

I knew, all she'd ever wanted was enough money to free her to do her research without a heavy hand on her shoulder, trying to guide her in directions other than where she wanted to go, or outright impeding her progress. And, once I'd bought her company, I might have assumed I was rich enough, but that was just the beginning of the money required for her research. So, it was still a good thing money continued to roll in.

I told my wife the news later that night when she slid into bed. She giggled, and told me, "Finally made it, you slacker."

I thought she'd fallen asleep, but she suddenly spun back over apologizing, telling me she was so, so sorry. She owed me the act of contrition of all acts of contrition. I asked what she'd done, but she didn't answer. She just set about giving me a blow job that I thought several times might stop my heart. She knew just when to back off, then begin again, to build it to an intense finale. When she was done, and I was lying there in a sweaty daze, holding my chest, I asked, where had that come from. She told me, she just realized, she'd been so overwhelmed at the time, and so busy since, she'd never properly thanked me, for buying her company and it had been over two years, or was it five. She'd lost track, but, "Thank you."

She was making progress along a dozen different lines. There were no longer any excuses, but she was getting there. She was excited. Sorry about not making forty, but she had a really good feeling about fifty. Hopeful I'd still think she was hot when she was fifty. She began a second act of contrition. I pushed her away, and told her if she killed me, it would not only defeat her purpose of us living forever, it would eliminate her primary source of funding. She asked, what else did I want? I told her, just to return the favor. She said, No, what did I want? I repeated, just to return the favor.

Afterward, still enjoying the taste of her on my lips, I asked if we could just hold one another awhile. She started to turn, to put her back toward me. But, I didn't want to spoon and fall asleep. I wanted to turn on a little light, so we could see each other's faces, and look into one another's eyes.

It occurred to me that she had changed so little since I'd married her. Outwardly, it depended on which wig she'd decided to wear at the moment, but when she wore the wig she'd had made from her own hair I saw very little difference, just that gradual maturity that brings a woman into her prime. She was still hot, and I knew she still would be. And, I told her. I wanted her to know that was how I felt.

She started to cry, which she also rarely ever did. I asked what was wrong. She told me she also wanted to thank me for that. For loving her, and allowing her to be herself. For demanding nothing of her but doing what she wanted. For allowing her to be fucked up, if that's what she needed. For allowing her to be so obsessed with a single idea that it consumed her life. She knew she was closing in. And, once she figured it out, and we had forever, she wanted to spend time with me, and work on not being fucked up. We'd have forever.

She told me, I'd come through on my part. I'd made us rich. So, we'd have everything we ever wanted, forever. Now she had to deliver on her end.

Douglas Debelak

A Question of Dreams – Annie Fry

Annie looked up from Jon's computer, once again to find him leaning against the doorway, observing her.

"Looking for a game of naked hide and seek?" he asked.

Annie took a quick glance down her towel-less naked body and shrugged, "Thought I'd see what happened."

"You've been full of experiments lately," Jon observed. "Like you have this rejuvenated lust for life. Just plain rejuvenated lust too, obviously, but it's more than that. You seem really happy."

Annie nodded. "Yeah, I'm getting there. I still feel bad about…"

Jon waved for her to stop. "No, don't. Don't keep doing that to yourself. Christ, I think you've made up for a lifetime in the past few weeks alone, if there'd ever been any reason to make it up. I was thoughtless, tactless and oblivious to your feelings when, and the way, I told you about my dream. I am truly sorry. I've lain awake a lot of nights since then, thinking about how that must have made you feel. And, I can't honestly say how I would have felt about yours, if I hadn't already had my own. I mean, I woke up, and it was like you were fucking some other guy's brains out. And, it wasn't me, since I was right there, and you could have had the real thing, if you'd wanted."

Annie nodded in acknowledgement, "That's pretty much what happened. That doesn't bother you at all? I'm sorry if…"

Jon waved away her word again. "No, we need to stop apologizing for our dreams. We can't help what we dream. I told you that months ago. I just should have been more thoughtful when I told you, or not told you at all. But, you did ask."

"Do you still dream about her?" Annie asked.

Jon hesitated, looking sad for a moment, then admitted, "Now and then, but less often. It's like she's been slowly pulling away. But you've got me so drained lately, I don't think there is anything left for erotic dreams."

Annie laughed, "Kind of the plan. I don't want to worry about anyone else anymore. I'm just going to wear you out enough that you can't possibly have anything left for anyone else. Her, I can't, or at least I'm trying not to be jealous of her. We both have her in our lives in different ways. And, him too. When I'm her, I'm fucking him, so I can hardly throw stones."

"Have you ever seen yourself when you're her?" Jon asked.

Annie shook her head. "I can see my... her body, just like I can see mine, and it is easy enough to tell that the body I'm seeing is not my own, but I did catch a glimpse of my... her reflection in a mirror once. I can see why you couldn't resist her. Even if she was real, I don't know that I could fault you... no, that's a lie. You know, if she was real, I'd cut off your balls in your sleep, but... God, she's amazing. Sad and half-crazy sometimes, so focused and driven, and terrified she'll lose him, either because he'll leave, because she's so fucked up, or because she won't succeed and they'll die."

"You?" Annie asked a moment later.

"Me what?"

"Have you ever seen yourself when..."

"Yeah, once, maybe twice," Jon told her, "Same thing. A glimpse in a mirror. It was pretty startling seeing myself, but not being myself. It was weird. I mean, it's all weird. But..." He was quiet a moment, then changed the subject and asked, "So, are you going to sit there naked all day?"

"Yeah, I just might," Annie told him, looking defiant. "I just might, why?"

"I don't know," Jon said. "No reason. I just figured you'd eventually get dressed and do something."

"I am doing something!" Annie replied, indignantly. "You've got some balls implying that I'm not doing anything. You've been clear in the past that sitting and thinking isn't doing nothing. So, yeah, I am doing something. And, I plan to do it naked if I want."

"Okay, sorry," Jon told her. He paused, then tried again. "Hey, Annie, what are you up to right now?"

She gave him her 'you're an asshole, but I love you anyway' smile. "I'm editing your fucking book if you have to know. I told you I would."

"How far along are you?"

"Far enough along to be inspired to get my clit pierced." Annie took a quick look down at the shiny little ring, just visible between her legs, then back up at Jon, shaking her head. "Holy fucking God, Jon. I keep having flashbacks and I'm wet again. Which is more than a little inconvenient at times. I've had to wear a pantyliner since... oh, sorry, I'm sure you don't want to know all the gory details."

Jon laughed. "Have you recovered enough, or do you think you'll have to retire permanently?"

"Oh, if you want..." Annie stood. "Sure, between the dreams and the flashbacks, I'm good to go just thinking about it."

"No," Jon told her. "That's not what I meant."

Annie looked a little disappointed. "No, you don't want to?"

"No, that's not what I meant either," he said. "I was just curious. But, I don't want to interrupt you while you're doing something." He pointed at his computer.

"No, I'm okay," Annie smiled, walking toward him. "That can wait. It will still be there. And, I'm ready for a break. In fact, I'm ready, baby," she said in an inflection that wasn't her own. She took his hand, walking backward pulling him along toward their bedroom. She slid her free hand into his pants, then stopped to kiss him.

Annie asked, "Do you think we could still do it every day for a year? Want to try?"

Jon looked at her doubtfully, walking slowly forward with her again. "At our age? Could we have ever done that?"

Annie shrugged. "I think I can still manage, maybe."

"Maybe you could. But, you're not the one who needs to get an erection. You can just use some lube."

She released his hand long enough to give his shoulder a punch. "We don't have to fuck to have sex. And, I can get you off, even if you can't manage to get completely..."

"Yeah, I get the picture," Jon said, continuing to stutter step along with her, as her hand worked its way into his boxer briefs. He made a little groan of pleasure. "How many has it already been?"

"Ten," Annie answered without hesitation.

"So, you've already been counting," Jon observed, pausing a moment as her fingers tightened around him, then he quickened his pace, pushing Annie forward. Backward for her. "If I was younger,

I'd pick you up right now and slam you down on the bed. Would that be rough enough for you?"

Annie laughed. "It would be a start. Let's give it a try." She pulled as he pushed, and when they reached the edge of the bed, she threw herself backward as he pushed her chest. She landed hard on the mattress, pulling him with her. "Let's see what you've got." She was already wet, as she knew she would be. She roughly pushed him off her, to unfasten his belt and pull down his trousers, then she wasted no time guiding him inside her. She stared intently into Jon's eyes and told him, "Give it to me. I don't care how long you last. Just give it to me as long and hard as you can."

He did, and, as he'd predicted, he did only last a few minutes, but Annie giggled like a school girl. "Thank you. I loved that."

"But, you didn't..." Jon complained, breathless and apologetic.

"I don't care. I loved it." Annie told him. "Can we do that once in a while? Please. And, you can do your thing the rest of the time."

"Annie...," Jon began, pausing thoughtfully a moment. "I know you are trying your best to catch up or something, but..."

"What? Too much for you, old man?" She teased, still giddy.

"No, it's not that. I just don't want you to feel you need to do that, unless..."

"Unless what? Unless my hormones are screaming for me to jump your bones?" She smiled. "Don't worry baby, they are. So, buckle up. And, right now they are screaming, play with my little ring, until I'm out of my mind, please."

Breakthrough

Posted: 11/10/2015 12:00 AM

My wife unexpectedly stopped by my office at the research center, one evening, as she often did, but instead of a booty call, she asked me to walk home to our penthouse with her. It was technically evening, but still daylight, so this was extremely early for her to be leaving her lab. She immediately began taking off her clothes, undressing me, then dragging me to the cushion she'd placed in front of the windows with the best view of the sunset. This was our spot for tantric sex on those rare occasions we left our offices, so this was going to be a long and serious conversation.

She began by unnecessarily telling me she was approaching her fiftieth birthday, which I knew, because I had marked the day in my calendar ten years earlier, the day after her fortieth birthday, with air raid sirens to play a year in advance, so I could begin to figure out what I could get her that wouldn't completely pale in comparison to buying her company, and giving her carte blanche for her research.

There was nothing more I could give her, short of handing her the solutions to all her questions, wrapped in a virtual bow. But, if that had been possible, I wouldn't have waited for her birthday, I hadn't waited to give her anything she'd asked in pursuit of those answers, including equipment and materials that we'd invented during telepathic collaboration sessions, seeded by her thoughts of the research she envisioned. In addition, I'd provided her, and her team, complete and unlimited access to our telepathic collaboration technology and all the data generated by our own collaboration sessions as well as hers.

This would have been an impossibly huge dataset to mine, except for other technological innovations, also the product of telepathic collaboration sessions, which made Big Data suddenly appear miniscule. We had software centuries ahead of any that existed outside the walls of our company, and computer systems to run it that were centuries ahead as well. And, to power all this, was our proprietary solar energy system which made use of every exposed surface of the building I'd had designed for my wife's lab, including the parking lots.

The Ghostwriter's Wife

We could have built a nuclear fusion generator; we had designs in our data which were more than feasible at the time. But, I'd decided years earlier that the sun was free forever, or at least so long as it continued to exist. Our solar energy system screamed Green, when that was still a hot button discussion. And, we'd strategically leaked designs, where they could be discovered by engineers who'd claimed them as their own. The leaked designs were nowhere near as sophisticated as our own, but sophisticated enough to end the need for a Green Energy debate. Another reason I'd steered away from fusion was my fear of leaking that information outside our walls. It was Green, but it also had the potential to be the end of our world as a weapon. I wanted to share, but I wanted us to be cautious what we shared. Our solar technology, when discovered, was a solution to a problem, not a threat to our existence.

With all the data and technology at our disposal, I'd had my director of data mining put together a team dedicated to helping my wife glean through all those discoveries for which the world was not ready, which would have pushed the knowledge of the world ahead by centuries. It didn't require a telepathic collaboration session to conclude it was inadvisable to thrust innovation on a world that wasn't ready, advancements which the efforts to absorb would result in a complete breakdown of society. Within our data, there were medical discoveries too advanced to implement with existing technology, but, within which answers to many of wife's questions might be there waiting to be discovered. If so, we'd figure out how to make whatever technological leaps necessary, even if we couldn't yet share them.

What we could, we leaked as quickly as we felt they could be comprehended and implemented in the world beyond our walls. There were several Nobel Prize winners who owed their award to us, none of whom had any idea of the origin of the hints and ideas that had inspired their research. My wife would have received the award years earlier, if she'd published any of her own research. If a twenty-year-old mouse wasn't a winner, I didn't know what would have been.

While my brain raced through its usual tangential paths, my wife continued, acknowledging that her big birthdays had never been easy for her. In addition, she was experiencing the first signs of menopause. As I knew, she'd been having anxious moments for years about getting older and that she might run out of time. The recent fluctuation of her hormones was not helpful at all.

As my thoughts continued to drift, she still hadn't told me anything of which I was not already aware. I was dreading what was coming next and she must have sensed me going limp with anxiety, because she clenched me tightly in place. She was close, she suddenly told me. She knew she was so fucking close. Even though neither of us had moved since we'd settled together on the mat, my mind immediately assumed she meant she was close to an orgasm, so I reached down to help her along.

She pushed my hand away and frowned. Wait. She wasn't done.

She had an entire colony of mice that were between fifteen and twenty years old, so she'd known she'd been doing something right for quite some time. She had found a combination of chromosomes that impacted aging, at least in mice, but fortunately these were chromosomes that were also part of human DNA. That was wonderful news, except, she'd come to the realization that chromosomes were only part of the solution. Eventually her mice still aged, although much more slowly. She'd had a mouse that had recently had its twenty-first birthday, but it been looking increasingly ragged and it had finally died a few days later. At about the same time I'd bought her company, she'd begun to think, she'd spent the better part of her life trying to figure out why some people lived longer than others, rather than asking what she'd know all along was the real question - because it was the same question she'd asked herself in grade school: Why do we age at all?

The answer was readily obvious to her. DNA deteriorated, and mutated, until replicated cells were no longer healthy, perhaps even deadly. Owning her own lab, she'd been unfettered to research what caused the deterioration of DNA and what could be done to prevent it. She'd been aware of the research that had been done on Telomeres, which she'd once mentioned to me, and she'd shifted more of her focus in that direction. But, again, even with the advancements she'd made in her research on Telomeres, she believed she could greatly slow the deterioration of DNA, but its eventual deterioration had remained inevitable. However, she believed, she'd recently discovered a way to perpetually repair damaged DNA, and to eradicate defective cells before they could divide to produce more defective cells.

She was excited, because some of her old mice had now not only stopped aging, they were appearing and behaving increasingly younger. That had been an unexpected but welcome side effect. If she was right, not only would we live forever, she'd be young and hot forever.

She'd found IT! She'd figured it out! Now she just had to develop and test a procedure for humans.

I tried to hold her still, because she was suddenly bouncing in excitement, telling me about her new discoveries. The whole objective of tantric sex, at least what we'd given that name, was not to have an orgasm, or to at least take our good old time about it. But, she couldn't contain her excitement. I couldn't blame her. I was excited too, but more than just excited for her news, I finally gave in, grabbing her hips, digging my fingers deep enough there'd be bruises on her ass in the morning. I told her that was another unintended side effect of her discovery. In her excitement, she'd unintentionally bounced me over the edge.

Several hurdles remained, my wife continued, oblivious to the fact I'd just come. Government approval for human testing being the first, and likely most difficult. That could easily take another five to ten years, and she wasn't prepared to literally die of old age waiting for government approval. Neither were quite a few others at her lab, who were willing to take risks, but dying of old age in jail wasn't one any of them preferred to take.

I asked, "I assume those regulations only applied to testing within the country. Right?"

"What are you thinking?" My wife asked, looking at me with suspicion. "Building another lab in some other country? That is going to take time too, isn't it? And, what about government regulations there? There are international organizations that would exert pressure on any government that allowed such unsanctioned experiments on humans."

"I'm not sure where yet," I told her, "I'll figure that out. What do you require to perform the procedure?"

The most involved and invasive part of the entire procedure consisted of withdrawing marrow from the pelvis or a femur. The DNA would be altered in the recipient's own extracted stem cells, which would then be injected back into them a day later. The secondary part of the of the procedure was the equivalent of drinking Pixie Dust in Kool-Aid. That was an oversimplification, but she'd developed a solution, containing millions of a hybrid of microscopic nanobots and a new kind of human cell, which would roam the body looking for signs of damaged DNA, then either repair the cells, or destroy them before they could replicate deformed cells.

I'd have been overwhelmed with the magnitude and genius of her discoveries, but I was in a pragmatic zone, where only questions and solutions existed. I asked, "Would this require a hospital?"

My wife nodded. "Based on the protocol for other procedures where stem cells are replaced, we will need to closely monitor the recipients and have access to medical facilities in the event of an unforeseen emergency. So, yes, either a hospital, or clinic with immediate access to a hospital. In addition, even though the mice have been reacting well to the nanobots in their systems, there is no telling how the human body will react. There haven't been serious issues for humans with Pixie Dust, so that's promising. Which, by the way, I'm still amazed the FDA didn't stop, or at least come knocking, wanting to snoop around."

"They did come snooping around," I told her. "We gave them data on other innovations we were researching that had them pissing their pants and they went away. They came back of course, pissed their pants, then they went away again."

I was thinking out loud. "I could probably leverage approval for you, but I'm not sure that would be any sooner. But, we have the estate, right on the ocean, right? Why couldn't we just take a boat out to international water, perform the procedure, and then bring the patients back to a clinic on land?"

The Ghostwriter's Wife

"A boat?" My wife asked, giving me her patented 'You are such an idiot' look.

I knew what she was thinking without any telepathic assistance. Somewhere in my own mind, a boat still meant a twelve-foot aluminum fishing boat with a small outboard motor. Not at all what I had in mind. As with an increasing number of acquisitions in my life, buying the boat I had in mind would require the assistance of a broker. Those thoughts telepathically triggered my administrative team into action, and they immediately contacted all the top nautical brokers in the world.

Responses came within seconds. If I was willing to wait three years, I could have a yacht custom built to my specifications. The way my mind worked, I immediately begin compiling a list of specifications for such a yacht, which my administrative team also received and ran with. But, even though it would require far less time than waiting for FDA approval, I didn't want to wait any longer than my wife. I told the brokers, within a stringent list of parameters, we'd take whatever was ready to sail. My wife had also been mentally compiling her own list of requirements, which were collated with my own by my administrative team, then relayed to the brokers.

Very apologetic, once he'd discovered that I was the potential client, the first broker to respond informed us, the best he could manage - on such short notice, meeting our extensive list of requirements, and my insistence that we take possession immediately – was a yacht no longer on the list of the world's top ten, but it easily still the top twenty. It had originally been built for another billionaire, whose name I recognized, only because my brother continued to insist on reading me the lists of the next wealthiest people in the world. Apparently, he wanted to reassure me none of them were gaining. The yacht was only three years old, but the owner had already taken possession of a newer yacht, now considered to be the finest in the world.

The yacht I purchased was built to comfortably accommodate well over one-hundred guests and could have functioned as a small, but very luxurious, cruise ship. The master suite took up the entire stern of one deck, with a private verandah extending its entire width. At roughly six-thousand square feet, the master suite itself was the size of a small mansion and the deck the size of the yard behind one. The master bedroom had a private bath that was more like a small spa. The suite also contained four smaller, but still grand, bedrooms each with their own private baths. The entire master suite could have easily slept two dozen people, in a pinch, but was only listed as accommodation for ten.

Toward the bow were another ten luxurious private suites, each with their own sitting rooms and balconies. These were nearly a thousand square feet, and were configured with two separate bedrooms and private baths. Each was officially listed as accommodation for four, but could have easily slept double that. Two lower decks contained another twenty cabins apiece, accounting for the accommodation of another eighty guests. There were shared verandahs at the stern of each of these lower decks, as well as private balconies for all the suites. The main elevator was mid-ship, with another private elevator to the master suite. There were stairs, fore, mid and aft.

We maintained the master suite as our own, mostly because we didn't want to cause a delay by dividing it into smaller units. Four of the smaller luxury suites were fitted as procedure rooms – operating rooms equipped as well as the finest hospitals in the world. The other suites were configured as diagnostic rooms, for x-rays, MRI and CT-scans, and a recovery room, which could accommodate four patients at a time. One was converted into a supply room, a pair of public bathrooms, and a common sitting area.

The yacht had a helipad, so we could get a patient to a land based hospital as quickly as we could have for any land based emergency. We were well enough equipped to handle nearly any emergency the land based hospitals could, but we would never be able to maintain or house the staff of all the specialists available at the land based hospitals. We also had several launches – good sized boats themselves – available to ferry members of the medical teams back and forth to land if they chose to return home in the evening. They were also welcome to stay at our ocean front estate.

The Ghostwriter's Wife

I did follow through and place the order for what would become the finest yacht in the world. I'd done so before I'd seen or stepped aboard the yacht which I had bought, and as soon as I did, I laughed at myself, and realized the newer yacht I'd just commissioned was a complete frivolity. I considered canceling the order, which would have cost me several million dollars in cancelation fees alone, but that would have been an insignificant amount compared to the several billion-dollar cost of the yacht itself. But, again I came to the realization, the cost of the new yacht had also become an insignificant number to me. So, I let the order for the new yacht stand. I assumed operations, if only testing of the procedure, would be scaling up by the time the new yacht would be available for delivery.

Our next hurdles were legal. We had dozens of liability issues to face. We had a team of lawyers draw up all the necessary consent and waiver forms, along with affidavits that the procedures were carried out beyond the territorial waters of the country. Our legal team also suggested that our yachts remain in international waters permanently. Fuel and supplies would have to be ferried out. Because the moment one of them docked, it would likely be seized by the government, and, even if I won, that legal battle would take as many years as it would to get government approval for the testing in the first place.

There were no problems finding volunteers for human testing. The younger employees at my wife's lab didn't feel as compelled to risk the untested procedure yet, but the older members of the group were clamoring enough to be the first, or second, that my wife decided she'd have a lottery. Her administrative team jokingly referred to it as the Lottery of Life, for which each of them immediately volunteered.

A married couple, both in their sixties, won the first lottery, or the wife did and then decided she didn't want to go through with the procedure without her husband. She'd never expected her name would be drawn, so she hadn't considered the possibility of living forever without him. This caused considerable debate, because some of the other participants in the lottery agreed, the husband should be given the procedure too, that was the right thing to do, while others thought it was unfair to everyone else waiting on the list. While they were arguing, my wife decided, time was passing, and performed the procedure for both. Everyone else could continue debating what was fair afterward.

Both husband and wife survived the procedure, and, even though the phenomenon had been observed in mice, to everyone's surprise and delight, within a couple of months, friends were claiming they both were looking younger. It wasn't a radical change, but after a year, they appeared a good five years younger, and after two, they appeared to be in their late forties. Caution might have been well served by waiting to see whether any ill effects would manifest themselves, but none of the others with their names in the hat were willing to wait for their chance, nor was my wife. So, the second set of procedures were performed only a month after the first. Again, they were a married couple, only one of whom was selected. There was still bitching, but consensus had grown that no one should be expected to leave their spouses behind. The next two procedures where only two weeks later. Then several were performed each week for the first year.

Most of the procedures were successes, but not all the recipients were so fortunate. After the first ten successful procedures, one of the recipients had a horrible reaction and died within days. Her immune system declared war on her body, which immediately set about destroying itself. Some of the doctors thought what she'd suffered had a great deal of similarity to Graft-Host disease. Some team members wanted to curtail further procedures until they better understood why this reaction had occurred. Others argued, the procedure had been performed hundreds of times on mice and none of the mice had died horrible deaths. So, it was likely an anomaly.

Anomaly or not, most of the older members of the team were still willing, in fact begged, to take the risk and have the procedure. What was the worst that could happen? They'd die, which was, without the procedure, an inevitability approaching far too quickly. Who their age in their right mind wouldn't take the chance of dying immediately for the chance of living forever? Especially when, within a year, all those who'd survived so far were showing signs of looking and feeling younger - and most believed, as did my wife, they'd also be freed of many other illnesses that would have likely killed them before old age had a chance.

Several more recipients died, nearly identically to the first, which did make the rest of the volunteers think harder about their choice, and some decided to decline. But, not enough were dissuaded to slow the continuation of the procedures. More of the younger members decided to remove themselves from the list. They felt no need to take the chance yet. They had plenty of time to research the problem and find a solution. Plus, the effect of growing younger wasn't near the enticement to them. They were already young.

All the volunteers sixty or older remained on the list, and nearly all of those in their fifties. The younger members who remained, argued, never getting cancer or many other horrible diseases was worth the risk. My wife cautioned that she was making no such claims. But, if the body did systematically rid itself of deformed cells, how could a cure for cancer not be the result?

There were several hundred members of my wife's research team by then and several thousand more employees in the company. Although the research, and most emphatically the fact that the procedure was being done on humans, was confidential in the extreme, rumors spread through the company and there were plenty of volunteers from outside the team. When those ran out, someone quipped that there was a retirement home down the road. They expected every one of residents would sign up without an instant's hesitation. There'd never be a shortage of volunteers, nor would there ever be a shortage of paying customers once we progressed beyond testing. My brother was already calculating what people would willingly pay to live forever – even with a twenty percent chance of dying.

We scoured through the medical histories of every recipient, looking for any correlation between those who'd survived and those who hadn't. Nothing presented itself. No childhood diseases correlated. No physical characteristics. Mortality was slightly higher in women, but there was just too small a sample size to know whether that had any significance. There also seemed to be a higher mortality rate the older the recipients, which made sense because the recovery was not gentle even for those who'd survived. The body was going through radical changes and wasn't happy about it. Just the fact that nanobots were on a rampage killing off unhealthy cells left the recipients feeling ill, some for up to a week, and, it stood to reason, the older the recipient, the higher the number of unhealthy cells they were likely to have.

Fitness and general health also showed a small correlation, and a few of the fatalities clearly weren't related to Graf-Host. These were mostly strokes, heart-attacks and aneurisms. But, together, they accounted for only a small percentage of the fatalities. Ruling these out only served to shrink the sample size.

Since this phenomenon hadn't been observed with mice, the predominant speculation was that the problem was in the small part of the genetic code that humans did not share with mice, which helped narrow the search considerably. And, combinations of those genes were discovered to be common among the recipients who died, some of which were not common across those who'd survived. Still, even with Telepathic Collaboration sessions, the problem defied isolation.

We also needed to rule out the fatalities that were reactions to the nanobots. Just because Pixie Dust had been benign, didn't rule out a problem with these nanobots. After all, they were roaming the body destroying cells. How could the immune system be happy with that?

The mortality rate continued at twenty percent, and the arguments continued that this was hugely unacceptable degree of risk. We had an ethical responsibility to stop the procedures until we could better isolate the problem. But, the following statement of the obvious was: If we quit testing, how will we ever isolate the problem? Followed by: Who cares? Sign me up.

Although it would be decades before there'd be empirical evidence the procedure worked, recipients growing younger was being accepted as clear evidence that it did. Volunteers continued to roll the dice, and the sample size of both those who lived and died slowly grew. The solution remained unknown.

To accelerate the search, we began experiments with monkeys who had a higher percentage of the human genetic code than mice. The fact that, unlike mice, some of the monkeys died was sadly encouraging. Even more so that some types of monkeys had a significantly higher rate of mortality than other monkeys or humans. We weren't sure what to do with the monkeys who survived. We needed to keep some of them for observation, but when we had more monkeys than we could handle, zoos began getting monkeys they were unaware were likely to live a long, long time.

Since, the monkeys were only given the stem cell part of the procedure, this also determined that the issue was likely not a reaction to the nanobots. That the nanobots were not included also meant it was likely the surviving monkeys would still eventually age and die, but given that my wife had a mouse who lived twenty years without the nanobots, there were going to be some extremely old monkeys.

No one to my knowledge had yet broached the subject of whether these genetic changes might be passed on to offspring, in which case there would eventually be a severe overpopulation problem at the zoos. The potential population issues of humans were discussed, but were a problem to be addressed later. There were more immediate concerns.

When my wife's fiftieth birthday passed, it went better than I'd expected, because she had successfully performed the procedure on several recipients, and the first deaths hadn't yet occurred. Her fifty-first birthday was not near so pleasant a day for either of us. By then, the mortality rate was well in evidence, and the question of, how soon she and I wanted to have the procedure, had been replaced by, how long can we wait until we don't dare wait longer? We agreed it made sense to wait, but eventually we'd have to decide it was time.

I thought my wife turning fifty-five might have been that time, since her doctor had recently informed her she was officially through menopause. The good news, no more periods. The bad news, she was an old lady. I believed, had it just been herself, she'd have had the procedure at fifty-one and taken her chances. But, she was much more cautious of losing me.

… Douglas Debelak …

A Question of Questions and Comments – Annie Fry

"Are you still writing responses?" Jon asked, looking into their TV room. "Naked hide and seek clothes again I see."

"Hey, it's my house. I'll walk around naked if I want. And, yeah, every time I sit down, I've been writing a few responses. Then I work some more on the book."

"Any reaction to your typo?"

Annie looked up. "I thought you weren't interested?"

"I don't want to read through the whole thing and think about it all again," Jon told her, pointing toward his computer. "But, you seemed upset, so, yeah, I'm interested in that."

"Of course, there was a reaction. Pretty much what I was afraid would happen. The blog must have blown up for a while. I'm glad I wasn't here to hear it ping every time there was a new post. It would have driven me nuts. But, once it settled down, I did what you suggested. Thanks."

"And...?"

"It took all of ten seconds for some asshole to type, 'Tell your stupid bitch typist to get an editor.'"

"Sorry," Jon told her.

"Not your fault," Annie replied. "I wanted to ask whether his mommy ever washed his mouth out with soap. But, the first time I can't resist something like that, I might as well fold up shop."

"Why do you feel you need to say anything?" Jon asked.

"I don't know, I just do. Just like I need to do something with this book. And, that's partly because I said, I would, but I honestly don't think you'd care that much if I didn't. There's something else."

"Afraid she'll be disappointed?"

Annie frowned and tilted her head. "I hadn't given that any thought. But, somehow I don't think she'd care either. I think she just shows up, has a hell of good time, then goes away."

"What, like an interactive movie where we get to play a role?"

Annie nodded. "I think maybe a lot like that."

"Then who cares?" Jon asked, giving Annie an exaggerated shrug.

"I think we both have our suspicion about that," Annie responded.

"Who?"

"Who else? Him. He's telling the story. Right?"

Jon blinked, thinking. "Yeah, maybe. It isn't her voice I hear, except when…"

"She's fucking your brains out."

"I've never had any conversations, other than sex talk while, we…"

Annie smiled. "Fuck one another's brains out."

"I thought you didn't mind," Jon told her. "You sound a bit jealous there."

"Hey," Annie replied. "I'm a woman. I get jealous. But, I'm trying. Plus, now, I can hardly throw stones, remember?"

Douglas Debelak

Coddled Kids

Posted: 11/17/2015 12:00 AM

Virtuality continued its explosive growth, in size and complexity. It was nearly ten years old and the virtual world had none of the constraints of the real world to impede it. The real world has a natural inertia. Things have to be moved to put new things in their place. There are mountains, rivers and oceans in the way. Things can't go just where ever we want. There are laws of physics that govern the way physical things are moved. Real products have to be prototyped, tested, manufactured, marketed, purchased and shipped, before they can be used. Generally they are purchased to replace something else, which might arguably be doing its job quite adequately. Although, the ordering process had certainly been expedited. No words had to be spoken, or buttons clicked. Want it? It is on its way.

In Virtuality, if you thought it, it happened. Things moved at the speed that the weakest link in the network infrastructure allowed, and there were very few weak links left in that infrastructure. Most everything in Virtual happened within huge banks of computers that were physically connected so that information was passed directly from memory bank to memory bank and each of our server farms were a essentially a single computer with millions of CPUs. Things moved as fast as electricity could move through super cooled buses of ever less resistant materials.

The weakest link had always been the wireless component. Magick Hats had to capture brainwaves and convert them into data. Data then had to be converted to electricity, which still had to be converted to radio waves and transmitted to receivers that turned those radio waves back into electricity or light that was sent to a server farm, where it had to be converted back into data, and processed. Then the reverse had to occur to send data back to their own or someone else's Magick Hat. Explaining it makes it sound as though it must take forever, but for most of those round trips, information was traveling at very near the speed of light.

In very round numbers, light travels at approximately one-hundred-eighty-some-thousand miles in a second. The world is approximately twenty-five-thousand miles in circumference. So, for the sake of simplicity, let's say the point farthest from any given point on the world is approximately twelve-and-a-half thousand miles away. A thought could reach the other side of the world in a fraction of a second, about half as fast as an old fashion TV refreshed its screen, with barely a flicker. And, if TVs, displaying both ends of transmission half way around the world, could be viewed simultaneously, very few people would notice the delay from one screen to the other. Given the current limitations of physics, events in Virtuality occurred as fast as fast could possibly be.

What could be done in Virtuality? Everything I'd envisioned in the beginning and far more, and far faster. We could share thoughts, complete thoughts. It still wasn't a perfect form of communication. We still twisted the thoughts of others to fit them to our own misshapen minds. Even in the most current version of telepathic collaboration, where participants were sharing a thought process, no one could perceive precisely the same things. There was still that element of distortion, which was, in fact, essential for the process to work. If everyone thought precisely the same thing, the same way, it would have been stagnant. And, it was as close to a perfect form of communication as we'd yet been able to conceive.

Since we could share thoughts, we could also share how we were experiencing the world around us at any given instant. What we were seeing. Hearing. Smelling. Touching. Tasting. We could share experiences from opposite sides of the world. It still wasn't the same as being there, again, because each of us experience and process our interaction of our reality a little differently, with everything we experience shaped and filtered by everything we've ever experienced prior to that, and more importantly, everything we've ever imagined. For instance: I'd found that I could enjoy a glass of wine that I would not have enjoyed if I'd been drinking it myself, because the person sharing it with me loved the wine they were drinking. If I'd been drinking the wine and shared the same experience with them, they would likely have hated the wine as much I did. But, a shared experience beat the hell out of a postcard or home movies. We could share emotions, which meant that lovers could express their feelings more deeply than ever before, but it also meant there was no faking feelings. It wasn't like when we could just say, 'I love you.' You had to really mean it. But, if you really meant it, your lover would know without a doubt you really meant it. So, people fell in love, or got divorced because of sharing emotions. I questioned from the beginning whether that was truly a good thing. I often thought about inserting just a little filter there, a little doubt, a little wiggle room, a little mystery, and a little romance.

I still worked every day as a part of the development team. There were a few of the developers left from the days when I'd forced my way onto the team, but very few. Mostly, there were an ever-revolving bunch of new kids. I found working with younger technical people both a pleasure and a frustration. The pleasure was from fresh perspectives. New ideas. The frustration came partly because of technical communication. The newbies came in wanting to express themselves as their recent education taught them, with all the latest buzz words and conceptual paradigms. They tended to think they knew the correct and only way of doing things. I felt many of them needed a bit of butt-shock-therapy, as my mother used to express it. They needed to be butt-shocked out of thinking they knew it all. They needed to be butt-shocked out of the assumption that they were the smartest person in the room. They needed to be butt-shocked into shutting up, listening and learning something new, because nothing outside our walls could ever have prepared them for what was within.

Then there was the fact that most of these kids had been coddled, since they were infants, and if any of them had ever been bullied, the entire world would have come to their rescue for fear they'd be forever emotionally scarred. Most of them had lived the life my mother had wanted for me. They'd never hit. They'd never been hit. They'd been taught to talk nice, play nice, and did so, at least when anyone was watching. They'd played little league, where everyone got to bat, and everyone got a trophy at the end of the season. Every one of them was a winner- almost exclusively, virtual baseball, of course. Nearly none of them had ever held a bat, or, God forbid, had a real baseball thrown at them. And, none of them had ever felt the impact of another human body.

The Ghostwriter's Wife

From my perspective, none of them had any preparation for the hard realities of life. But, I couldn't do what my instincts told me to do; tell them to shut the fuck up and pay attention, without needing a psychologist to clean up the emotional aftermath. I'd bruise their egos. I'd damage their self-esteem. After trying to tenderly dance around these issues for a couple years, I said fuck it. No time like the present for a jolt of reality. Nearly every member of my HR department, had a conniption when I put up a sign in the VR development lab that read: No Sissies in My Sandbox. I didn't want to be mean. I didn't want to be a bully. But, I also did not want to waste time or emotion on politically correct bullshit. We were there do things, try things, and not be wrapped up and constrained by all the sociological and psychological asinine crap. Say, think and mean what the fuck you say and think. Or, get out of my sandbox.

So, after a couple weeks of me being a total asshole, with the veteran members of the team trying to hide their facial expressions in the Real and be careful with their thoughts in the Virt, each newbie went through the same thing, which those who'd been through it referred to as boot camp. It usually took a while for them to come around, get over their emotional trauma, and tentatively begin to participate. Some quit before that, or asked to be transferred to some other project, but very few were ever kicked out. Not even the little shit who asked me: 'Who the fuck do you think you are?' It was demonstrated in full, living color who the fuck I was, and after falling apart in tears in front the whole team, wanting to run out of the room and quit, he was finally convinced by some of the older members to stay. Just shut up and listen, because this was the best project in the entire world to be a participant. And, even he came to know that I was a good guy, once all the baby shit was knocked out of him, and he was prepared to participate as an adult in the real world.

I much preferred hiring brilliant kids straight out of high school and teaching them myself, because I found it an easier process with minds that knew nothing, than those who thought they knew it all. They also received a much better education than they'd have received at any university.

Douglas Debelak

The development process had been difficult for me to adapt to, myself, when I initially reengaged with the team, because, by then, none of the developers had ever even heard of source code or computer languages. They just imagined things. They thought about what they wanted, how it should work and what options it should have. It was like conceptually building a car in their minds, only a great deal more abstract. Imagine a car. Imagine what parts a car required to function as a car. Imagine a body, a chassis, an engine, drive train, suspension and wheels. Imagine the human interface for the car. How is a person going to operate this thing? Imagine seats, a steering wheel, gas pedal and brakes. What were the various shapes they wanted to support in their car? What would be the color options? At least back when a concept, such as a car, would have had any purpose in Virtuality. If you wanted to be somewhere, you were there.

Initially, none of them understood they were in truth interacting with parsers that converted these thoughts into abstract data objects, and eventually a binary representation that a computer could understand and manipulate. They had no concept there were layers and layers of object libraries, APIs, parsers, code generators, an operating system and device drivers below. All of what comprised the bottom level, and much of the middle tiers of Virtuality, I'd either written myself, or worked with and guided the developers who had. Most of those developers were rich and long retired. Most only half my age.

Initially, new members of the Virtuality team saw no importance in knowing these arcane facts. What they did worked just fine. Why complicate it with all that old stuff? So, I had to educate them about its importance.

What if something they did didn't work?

Then they needed to rethink it, was the response.

What, if after multiple passes, they concluded that they were thinking correctly, but it still just didn't work? Then what? Were they just stuck, nothing working, and nothing to be done about it?

I explained, the issue was, they didn't understand how things worked at a lower level, and if they did, they'd probably have a much better idea how to correct their thinking and get it working.

What if something worked, but no matter how they tried to rethink it, it was still inefficient and dog slow? Most of them were willing to accept that was just how it had to be.

No, if they knew how to bore down through the layers below, they'd eventually find the root cause of the inefficiency, figure out how to perform that function better, and plug in the new part.

What if there were communication issues with a new Magick Hat model? Did they have any notion of how any of that worked? Did they understand that someone had to figure out that a single bit in a register was being set incorrectly, and because of that nothing worked, or worse?

I was seen in an entirely different light by the veterans. They recognized that I was still the guru of the whole virtual world. I was the one who could figure out ways to make things that were just okay into things that were amazing by changing spark plugs. And, most importantly, it was my fucking sandbox.

What do you want for dinner? – Annie Fry

"Did you really learn about masturbating in summer camp, or is that part not true?" Annie asked.

They were eating breakfast together. Not something they did regularly. Annie was dressed for work.

"What brought that up?" Jon asked, looking back over his coffee cup.

"Just curious," Annie told him, "But if you don't want to talk about it that's okay."

"No, I don't mind," he replied, "Yeah, that's where I heard about it for the first time. What's the term they use on the British show you watch? I was 'Gob Smacked.'"

"Been a wanker ever since, huh?" She teased.

"Fucking right." Jon toasted her with his coffee. "Although, lately I don't think I could, if I had the urge, which I haven't."

"Yes!" Annie shouted, pumping her first. "Love it when a plan comes together." She stood, kissed him and headed for the door. "What do you want for dinner?"

Jon thought a moment, then told her, "I don't know, I'll think of something to make."

"What!" Annie came back around the corner, one hand to her chest. "You'll what?"

"I'll make something," Jon told her.

"You will fucking not!" Annie looked at him incredulously.

"Why?"

"Because it will be a first," Annie told him, "Don't give me a heart attack now. Things are just getting good. I've got plans." She wagged her finger, then told him, "Steaks and fries would be great. There are a couple of filets frozen, and if you get the oil hot, and cut up the potatoes like…"

"I've watched," Jon told her, "And, I've cut the potatoes into fries, following your slice-by-slice instructions. I think I'll figure it out."

"Then, let's have some wine too. Maybe chill that bottle of champagne and let's celebrate. This is quite the event. But, red wine with the steak."

"Got it," Jon insisted. "I have it covered."
"Yay!" Annie sang, skipping out of the kitchen.

Douglas Debelak

Running Out of Time

Posted: 11/24/2015 12:00 AM

My wife's sixtieth birthday had to have been the worst yet. And, I was fully expecting her to say we were heading for the boat; the newer yacht, built to our specifications, which was not quite seven years old by then, and hadn't been considered the finest in to the world since months into her maiden voyage. But, discussion of heading to the boat, or the procedure never came up. She didn't want to talk, which meant she didn't want to have tantric sex. She just wanted to fuck, and drink champagne.

She'd handed me a pill the first thing that morning. She wanted me to be up to the task. She never put clothes on the entire day, at least not the kind of clothes she'd wear in public. She went through her routine of changing wigs and merkins, then standing in front of the mirror naked, clearly unhappy with what she saw. She'd come back to me, push me on the bed, and go down on me again. If I got hard, she had angry sex. If she didn't succeed after a minute, she'd assume I needed more recovery time, but she didn't and she was ready to come again. She didn't want me to go down on her, which would have been my choice. She wanted me to hold her, to suck her breasts as she got close, then she'd throw her head back, grunting hard with each wave passing through her body. When the last passed, and she had a moment to recover, she'd look at me, and there was something desperate and terrified in her eyes. That was the worse I'd seen her since her fortieth birthday. I wanted to talk and find out what was bothering her. She clearly did not.

There was an endless array of sexual enhancements available in the Virt that we enjoyed at times, but mostly we preferred just good old fashioned, messy, sweaty, physical sex in The Real. We enjoyed the physical exertion that wasn't required for virtual sex. My wife said she enjoyed the feeling of vaginal soreness she felt after angry sex. She said, she liked feeling fucked. She even loved the bruises we'd both have as evidence we'd truly abandoned ourselves. I loved knowing I was actually coming inside her. I loved the taste of her that lingered on my lips and mouth from her actual juices. She claimed she loved leaving my office after a quick booty call, with the taste of my come still in her mouth. She'd laughed about having missed some on her chin that her coworkers – her employees - were too embarrassed to tell her about, and she hadn't discovered until she used the restroom hours later. She loved leaving my office, feeling me still seeping into her underwear.

Her sixty-first birthday was mostly a repeat of the year before. When I asked how her research was going, all she'd said was that it was continuing to progress. She'd seemed busier, which I didn't find surprising, considering the increasing pressure she felt with each passing year. We hadn't been having our traditional Sunday morning tantric sex for a while. But, she was still in my office, looking for a booty call fairly regularly. She wanted a lot of quick, angry sex. Again, not surprising, I knew she was stressed, for which angry sex had always been at least a momentary relief.

She'd stopped wearing her Magick Hat. She told me, the nose bridges were irritating her sinuses and causing her headaches. So, I had to take her word for her emotional state and what issues might be bothering her. I asked how she participated in telepathic collaboration sessions without a Hat. She told me, she hadn't participated in a while. There wasn't really anything more to think about. She had the process refined. It worked perfectly, for most people. The only thing left was isolating the gene, or combination of them, that triggered the Graft-Host reaction in about twenty percent of people. Then they could at least determine who was a candidate and who wasn't. But, once it was isolated, it would only be a matter of time before they could address the issue. Again, there wasn't anything to collaborate about. They knew exactly what they were doing. The process for tracking down the genes. What to do once they were isolated. There were just a lot of fucking genes and far more combinations of them.

The tricky part, once they isolated those genes, was that the only process then available for modifying them was the same as one that triggered the Graf-Host issue. They'd have to either come up with a different approach, or hope the modification would work quickly enough to overcome the reaction before it killed the patient. It would be worth being sick as hell for a few days, if living forever was the reward. It was debated whether it made sense just to make both modifications part of the same procedure. At the same time, they were working on developing more sophisticated nanobots which could alter individual genes in the DNA of living cells as well as repairing the damaged ones or destroying those too damaged to repair. That still seemed a way off, and people were still willing to roll the dice rather than wait.

I suggested they put patients on life support as soon as the symptoms presented themselves, to keep them alive long as possible and give the modification process more time, and put them into an induced coma, so they didn't have to suffer through it.

My wife smiled. I did have a knack for seeing the obvious, with simplistic clarity, when for some reason no one else saw it at all. Until I pointed it out, then it was obvious with simplistic clarity to everyone, and foreheads were smacked one after another.

The Ghostwriter's Wife

Hangovers and Wet Spots – Annie Fry

Annie blinked herself awake, disoriented, and wondering for a moment where she was. There was blinding light coming through the skylight above, forcing her to shade her eyes. She had the foulest taste in her mouth. Looking down her body, she found that she was naked. She felt a sharp pain in her back, reached beneath her and found the TV tuner. The TV immediately came back to life, blaring far too loud. And, worse, some fake tit bimbo with her ankles behind her head was yelping at the ceiling, while a body builder wearing his ball cap backwards plowed into her. Uh. Christ. What the Fuck. Her finger danced desperately around the keys of the tuner until the TV went dark again.

There was some sort of crust between her breasts, disappearing further up her chest, beyond where she could see. She reached to touch her throat and found crust flaking away there too. Ah, that was disgusting. She tried to force herself further awake and figure out what was going on, but she felt as though she was having one of those terrible dreams, where she desperately wanted to wake and couldn't. She felt sudden urge to vomit and tried to convince her body to roll on its side in case she did. She felt awful. Her head ached. Had she been drinking? The presence of a nearly empty glass of red wine on her nightstand was confirmation. As well as the empty bottle laying on its side on the carpet halfway across the room. Then bits and pieces from the night before began to return.

She tried to move again, and the crust on her chest cracked and flaked when she did. She'd always hated sleeping in the wet spot. She always brought a dry towel back after her shower and spread it out to sleep when the wet spot wound up on her side of the bed, only part of the reason she preferred to be on top. She was beginning to think, she hadn't just slept in the wet spot, she'd been the wet spot. She scrubbed at the crust, flaking as much of it off as she could. So, she assumed she'd had sex, but not a shower. The alarm clock on her night stand began to register. It was two o'clock, but it was total daylight. Shit, it was afternoon!

Her head itched, but when she reached to scratch, her hand came back holding the wig she'd worn for Halloween the past year. God, whatever the fuck was going on just got better and better. One big effort and she found herself half sitting, holding herself upright on one elbow, her head still in a fog.

Her movement must have woken Jon, because he groaned and began to stir. "What time is it? Christ, why's it so bright?" He was trying to get up and was struggling as badly as she had. "Did we have some crazy ass orgy last night? Or, did I dream that? I think you put porn on the TV then went all porn star on me."

Annie nodded, vaguely remembering some such thing. She looked at the crust on her chest again, then felt her face. She was relieved that she found nothing flaking away there. So, she hadn't gone porn star enough to ask him to come on her face. She'd always thought that was one of the most disgusting things. Jon had always agreed. So, he probably wouldn't have agreed to do it, even if she had asked. But, she rubbed at her chest again. Something sure as hell happened.

"We drank a whole bottle of wine," Annie told him, looking back over her shoulder. He bent and held up another.

"Oh, fuck, no wonder," she moaned. "What the fuck were we thinking?"

"We started off with champagne," Jon reminded her.

Annie groaned. Then another memory returned from the night before and she asked, "Shit! Did I say you could fuck me in the ass?"

"You asked if I'd like to...," Jon said, trying to get to his feet and failing.

"We didn't...?" Annie began, then decided, "No, I think I'd know."

"Never my thing." He told her. "But, if you're still looking after my bucket list, I might take you up on the offer to call Sue, and check off that threesome."

"Oh, shit!" Annie groaned, "Don't make me laugh. It hurts too much right now."

She'd concluded that whatever else they'd done; Jon must have played quite a tune with her little ring. She felt like she must have spent an hour with nothing touching the bed but the back of her head and her heals. Every muscle in her body hurt. She also vaguely remembered singing, something about saving a horse and riding a cowboy. She looked back at Jon again: obviously, the cowboy.

"What the hell happened here?" Annie asked, flaking away more of the crust on her chest.

"You asked me to fuck your tits." He told her, "Then I think we must have passed out. I don't remember anything after that."

"Must have," Annie agreed. "I can't believe I slept with this stuff all over me and didn't get up to wash myself off."

"What the fuck is this?" Jon asked, finally making it to his feet, and looking down. "What the hell is this thing wrapped around my penis and balls."

Annie's hand went to her mouth, and she laughed, even though it hurt like hell. "Oh, shit!" She couldn't help herself. "It's a cock ring," she finally managed to tell him.

"Why the hell am I wearing it?"

"I read about it and bought one on line," she told him, holding her chest, still laughing.

"Why?" he asked.

"It's supposed to keep the blood in so you'll stay hard longer."

"Did it work?"

Annie shrugged, "My vagina hurts like hell, so probably, but everything hurts like hell right now. Too bad we didn't have a circus or two like last night when we were young enough to survive it." She managed to reach her feet, holding her lower back. "If we decide to do this again, I just have one request."

Jon took a stiff step forward. "Again?"

"Yeah, let's do it sober so I can remember how much fun we had and not wake up feeling like shit."

"Must have seemed like a good idea at the time." He came around the corner of the bed, walking like a man twenty years his senior.

"Oh, no," Annie said, cutting in front. "Shower's mine first. I feel like I've been dragged through a slime pit."

"Share?" he asked.

"You're out of your fucking mind!" she told him quickening her pace.

"Annie, how the fuck do I get this thing off?"

The Greatest Gift

Posted: 12/1/2015 12:00 AM

The morning of my sixtieth birthday, my wife was awake, waiting for me to open my eyes. She made love to me, as opposed to the angry sex she'd seem to prefer of late, then she cried, which surprised me, because she'd done so very rarely in the years I'd known her. When I asked what was wrong, she asked me, "Do you want to live forever?"

I smiled, and said, "Of course. Isn't that the plan?"

She looked in my eyes with serious intensity. "Yes, but now I think it is time. I don't think we should chance waiting any longer."

I rolled out of bed to put on clothes, assuming she intended for us to head straight for the yacht. But, she pulled me back and told me not to be in such a hurry. The process took a couple of days, between the time they drew the bone marrow, altered the genes and put the marrow back. I ought to remember the first time she'd asked for a sample of my bone marrow. I would probably be too sore to feel frisky afterward. Then, after the procedure, there were a couple of days of recovery, where no one felt well. She wanted to spend the day with me, making love and drinking champagne. We should wait until the morning to begin the procedure and just enjoy my birthday. Did I have any special requests?

I assumed she meant particular acts or positions, but she was also pointing out various wigs, merkins, holding up a variety of outfits, and showing me jars of body paint. I thought about asking if we could go back to the old mansion and play naked hide and seek. But, I couldn't remember whether Bob was still living there, or if was empty, but was soon too distracted to make any specific requests.

I didn't count how many times we had sex that day, but it was a hell of a day for a sixty-year-old, pills or no pills. I was not embarrassed in the least to take them. I didn't need a pill to get an erection. But, if a pill could give me an erection like I was fifteen again, why the hell not? Add the benefit of not being one and done, which at my age would have been the probability otherwise. Special days, like my birthday, or hers, I could usually manage a couple times without assistance, but if I could keep getting hard-ons at regular intervals for an entire day, and maybe the next morning too, then give me the pill.

In some ways, my wife's behavior on my sixtieth birthday reminded me of how she'd been on hers. Not because of her frantic anxiety and frustration, more just her persistence in wanting to arouse me over and over. Instead of giving up if I wasn't responding, she'd wait and try again in a few minutes. If each experimental attempt actually counted as a blow job, then it might have been a world record. I think she had her mouth on me again every couple of minutes, just checking, the entire day. But, as soon as I was ready, she wanted to be on top, but no angry sex, she took her time, riding slowly. Closer, in truth, to tantric sex, than angry sex; she wanted me to come, she just wanted to savor me enjoying it, and to make each orgasm as intense as possible. I knew she had quite a few orgasms that day as well, because I insisted upon it, but that was not her focus. It was my turn to have my best birthday ever.

The next morning, we flew out to our yacht, which was waiting for us in international waters. We had our marrow drawn, then returned to our ocean front estate to recover. Two days later we took our second helicopter ride to our yacht for the procedure to be completed. She'd never made any effort to have the testing officially approved. Given the consistent mortality rate, that would never have happened. The government would have insisted that people just keep dying of natural causes, rather than allow them the chance of dying from a procedure that might allow them to live forever. She'd never had the patience for that kind of stupidity.

The second part of the procedure was amazingly simple. They'd left a small port in place that they'd used to draw the marrow, so they wouldn't have to drill another hole in our femurs to put back our altered marrow. We drank a little cup of liquid filled with hybrid nanobots and we were done. It was just like drinking Pixie Dust in Kool-Aid. Then we flew back to spend another night of recovery at our ocean front estate.

I'd thought we'd just stay on the old yacht, which was at sea not far from the newer yacht. Our master suite was really a fabulous place. But, my wife had other ideas. Even though we were sore, and it was uncomfortable for both of us, my wife insisted we have tantric sex in our favorite spot above the waves, watching the sun set, then until late into the night. We didn't talk much. Both of us were tired. The stem cells were beginning their work, and the nanobots were beginning theirs. My understanding was that the stems cells took a while to completely alter the DNA, but the nanobots were racing through our bodies, looking for defective DNA, repairing what they could, only so far as reattaching broken strands at that point, and destroying cells where the damage was too great. Once they completed their initial work, they would settle down to a cell here, a cell there. But, it was more common than not to feel sick enough for a few days that you thought you'd die. A sixty-year-old has a lot of cells with damaged DNA. Add in the body's immune system reacting to its own stem cells, which occurred to some degree with everyone. It was just a lot worse for some, and, as the statistics had established, a significant number still died.

Neither of us were feeling very well already. So, we quit and went to bed. Neither of us had orgasms while having tantric sex, and my wife wanted to make sure both of us did before we went to sleep for the night. So, I used my fingers and she held me hard until she came, then buried her face against my neck, which she left damp with tears again. Then she turned her back, slid her ass up against me, like she had so many times and guided me into her, pulling my arm around her and putting my hand on her breast. A moment later, she felt my body stiffen. She reached for my hand and told me she loved me.

My last thought, as I drifted off with a smile, was: We're going to live forever. My beautiful crazy wife had done it.

Douglas Debelak

The Cruelest of Things – Annie Fry

Annie sat naked on the sofa, her hand over her mouth, as she sobbed. She held her other arm beneath her breasts, supporting them as her entire body shook with each gasping breath. She glanced up when Jon came into the room. He looked at her with concern and took a step toward her, but she held out her hand to stop him. "You couldn't have written this," she cried, jabbing her finger at his ThinkPad. "You're right. You could never have been this cruel. Only God could be this cruel. But, you knew, and didn't warn me. That was cruel too."

When she finally relented, he sat beside her, holding her tight, while she continued to cry. He told her, "Life is that cruel every day."

"It shouldn't be," she sobbed. "It should never be."

Tears streamed down his own face. He agreed, "Maybe it shouldn't," then added, "But, it is."

They held one another and grieved together, until Annie began to nod off. Jon must have felt her body going limp against him, because he gave her a nudge and told her, "Let's go to bed?"

Annie knew Jon wasn't suggesting anything beyond the words he said, she'd been the one who'd suggested having sex every day. "I don't think…"

"I know," Jon agreed, standing then helping her to feet. "Just to sleep."

"I don't think I've ever felt so exhausted," Annie told him, leaning her weight against him as they walked.

"I know," Jon agreed again.

Once in bed, Annie pushed her back up against him, pulled his arm around her, and put his hand on her breast. "I'd ask you to make love to me. I feel like I should, but I can't."

Annie felt Jon nod his understanding, and his arm tightened around her. The last thing she said, as she drifted off, was, "I want to find a place with a fabulous view and waves crashing into the rocks below, where we can have Tantric Sex."

The Greatest Loss

Posted: 12/8/2015 12:00 AM

In the morning, I knew my wife wasn't just feeling under the weather, like an achy case of the flu coming on, as I was. Something was terribly wrong. Somehow she'd made a mistake. A terrible, terrible mistake, and there was nothing anyone could do. There were no do overs. There was no way to take it back. There was no way to undo the procedure.

Several horrible days later I lost her. Does that statement seem too abrupt and stark? For me, the experience was that abrupt and stark, as it is for anyone who unexpectedly loses the person most dear to them, especially, in our case, when our expectation had been to have forever together.

Does Hell Exist? That is a question I often hear from you.

Immediately after my wife's death was a period of fogged thoughts and vaguely remembered events – I remember those days about as well as my early childhood. I know I stood in the hospital while one of our doctors explained what had gone wrong, or tried his best, because he wasn't entirely sure himself.

I remember holding my wife's hand, after we'd taken her off the ventilator, when we'd determined there was no hope, and I'd made the most horrendously impossible decision I'd ever faced. I'd suggested keeping patients on life support for an extended time, but only once a solution had been found for those who developed Graf-Host symptoms. There was no solution for my wife, only the extension of her body's destruction to its inevitable conclusion. Among her final words was her request for me to let her go.

Fulfilling her request, felt like ripping my own heart from my chest, then listening hopelessly as the beeps from the monitors slowed, and her breaths grew farther apart, then irregular, stopping a moment, before she took another, each seeming the last, until I sat in stunned numbness, waiting for another that would never come, watching a flat line, listening to the shrill scream from some piece of equipment that filled the room, until someone was kind enough to turn it off.

I don't remember how long I sat there in silence, before numbness gave way, and pain filled my bones, my grief exploded in my chest, and I sobbed uncontrollably, holding my dead wife's body, with snot and tears pouring from me, soaking her hospital gown. When it was time for them to take her away, I held her hand and didn't want to let her go. It was another loss I wasn't ready to endure.

She'd said other things to me as she drifted in and out, before losing consciousness forever. She said she loved me. She said she was sorry. She was happy I would have forever. She wished she could have shared it with me. Then she said other things that didn't make sense at the time. It wouldn't have been long anyway. I wouldn't have done it otherwise.

I must have told the people at the hospital the arrangements I wanted, or more likely my administrative team came to my aid, responding instantly to my telepathic scream of grief, that must have been heard echoing throughout the entirety of Virtuality. Bob and my brother were there too. So, between them, and my administrative team, the arrangements were made for me. I don't remember what, if any, conversations I had with any of them, or anyone else.

I know there was a visitation at a funeral home, where I stood for blank stretches of time staring down at my wife's body in despair and disbelief. I know I spoke to people, shook their hands, and accepted their hugs and condolences. I know I walked around and looked at the flowers, the cards, and at some deep distant level recognized who had sent some of them.

I know there must have been notes of appreciation sent out afterward, but, if I sent them, I don't remember, and can't imagine I'd have been able. Again, I assume my administrative team took care of this as well. I know I spoke at my wife's funeral and heard people express afterward how beautiful and heartfelt my words were, but I don't remember any of them. I know there was a procession to a cemetery, where her casket was placed in the wall of a mausoleum. One more loss of her for me. And, then I was alone. More alone than I thought possible.

I sat in our penthouse, looking out over the city skyline, seeing nothing, feeling nothing but an emptiness that I thought would cause me to instantly implode, but I folded slowly and painfully inward instead, until I was nothing but a pinpoint of pain I didn't know could exist, and had no thought of whether it could be endured, only the hope that it would end soon and I would rejoin her in whatever journey came next.

I knew her greatest fear was that she would find all the answers, but die before we could benefit from her discoveries; the nightmare that she'd become just one more picture in a history book, but that was exactly what she would be. She would have accolades, throughout the scientific community and eventually throughout the world, all of them posthumous. All of them for what?

The implications of my survival had not yet reached the level of conscious thought. I sat with the memory of tantric sex out in the gazebo, then our bed and making love, for the last time. I wanted to preserve that memory, not the memory of her lying dead in a hospital bed. I tried, and mostly succeeded in thinking of nothing, staring blanking out at what some TV show had claimed was one of the most breath taking residential views in the world. Not seeing a thing.

I sat. I stared. I drank. I must have slept. But, never again in the bed we'd shared. I couldn't bear the thought that her naked body would never again slide back against me in the middle of the night. Her hand would never again reach over her hip for me, as she wriggled herself into position to guide me inside her, then often fall asleep before I was finished. She said she loved falling asleep feeling me inside her. It gave her a sense of completeness.

Our bed remained empty and unmade from some night or day when I must have fallen there in exhaustion, then realized I couldn't bear to stay. I slept on a sofa, the floor, or wherever I'd been sitting and finally passed out drunk and fallen over. Then I woke and began the process of seeking nothingness again. I didn't care for myself. I didn't shave, didn't wash myself, or change my clothes. I existed on wine, until there were empty wine bottles all over the penthouse floor and the wine cabinet in the penthouse was empty. There'd been several hundred-thousand dollars' worth of fine vintage wines in the penthouse alone, not counting what we'd had in the larger storage units in the basement – this per the appraiser, who'd come on behalf of our home owner's insurance. Some of the bottles came with us from the wine cellar in the old mansion. Some came from charity auctions, or estate sales someone else attended on my behalf.

I couldn't have said why we had wine on hand at all, let alone such a collection. Except for birthdays and anniversaries, we rarely drank, we never entertained, and the only time I ever drank socially was at an event my brother had insisted I attend. Again, the collection came from the effort of my administrative staff, on the assumption that collecting wine was one of the things expected of rich people with more money than they could ever spend in a lifetime. But, it had ensured there was plenty of champagne on hand for our special days.

I pulled the corks and chugged the wine directly out of the bottles, without tasting it at all. Then I drank tens of thousands of dollars of rare single malt Scotch, with no appreciation, while otherwise existing on milk and cereal, until that was gone. It never occurred to me that the wine storage unit held several hundred bottles. Fortunately, the larger collection was in a secure area in the basement of the building, and I hadn't been in any condition to make it into the elevator to get more. If I had, I expect that's where I would have remained until someone found my body.

It was also fortunate that it was expensive Scotch, so I only consumed a dozen or so bottles. I had no idea how many days I spent in this haze in total. I was paying no attention to how many bottles of wine and scotch I drank at the time, but there were enough empties lying about the floor, it was like walking through wind chimes, when I waded through them to use the bathroom or retrieve another. At least once, I either hadn't made it as far as the bathroom, or pissed myself in my drunken sleep. There was vomit on the suit jacket and trousers, I'd worn to my wife's funeral. They finally stunk badly enough I threw them into the shower, and roamed the penthouse in the stained remnant of a dress shirt and my piss-stained underpants.

If anyone had come to check on me, I was too drunk to be aware of it. I found out later that my executive assistant, and head of my administrative team, had called and come knocking at the door every day, then went away when I'd screamed profanity at her, and told her to leave me alone. I was later told, I'd nearly

The Ghostwriter's Wife

slammed her hand in the door when she'd tried to force her way in anyway. I'd fired her a dozen times and dimly remembered not understanding why she kept coming back, or if I'd just fired the next admin in line, until I ran out of administrative staff members, and Bob and my brother finally came. The building manager gave them keys, which he'd given to my admin as well, but she hadn't been able to get past me the first time she'd tried, and couldn't force her way past the furniture I'd pushed against the door afterward. She'd considered calling the police, but Bob and my brother said to give me some more time. They knew I was there, because they could tap into the feeds from the security cameras in the penthouse. They assumed I'd removed my Magick Hat, because they would have expected me to return an angry stream of thoughts, when they'd repeatedly pinged to ask if I was okay.

They couldn't get past the furniture either, but our private elevator also went up to the helipad on the roof, and there were stairs down into the penthouse from there. Once they were in, they moved the furniture back away from the main entry. They found my Magick Hat in the corner where I'd thrown it, when I'd ripped it from my nose. I vaguely remembered throwing against the glass, then taking the extra measure of stomping on it, until it was broken beyond repair.

They told me, they'd given me as much time as they could. They knew I needed more time to grieve, which I'd get, but it was time for the next election of the board of directors. Since I was chairman and largest stock holder, the election required my presence. Besides, I stunk, and needed to sober up for a while, before I required medical intervention. Bob dragged me to my feet. He'd found me leaning against the glass of one of the penthouse windows, which of itself was a statement of my condition. I usually couldn't walk within five feet of those windows, and that had only been when my wife took my hand to guide me to the cushion where we had the best view and was our penthouse spot for tantric sex. I'd have to shut my eyes until she'd help me sit down.

We'd never have tantric sex again. The gazebo was our last time. I missed the feel of her body. I'd never again see her wearing her wigs, or merkins. I'd never again feel her mouth on me. I'd never savor the taste of her again. I'd never again see her throw her head back and growl, when she came. Or, hear the pleading and encouraging sounds she made as she grew closer. I'd never again see her walk through the penthouse in the little black dress she'd worn the first time I'd seen her. She'd kept it to wear for me on special occasions, and it fit her perfectly her entire life. I wished we'd taken time to know one another better. I wished she'd had a chance not to be fucked up, so she could have let me know her better. There was so much I knew she kept locked inside her. I wished we'd never had the procedure. What good was forever without her? How could she have fucked that up?

Bob and my brother forced me into the bathroom. One held me up, while the other pulled off my shirt and stained stinking underwear. They pulled my vomit-covered suit out of the shower, turned on the cold water and shoved me in. Bob had to hold me there at first and I fought him. I think I probably hit him, but he was a pretty big guy, and it couldn't have been my best punch. He told me he wasn't washing me and shoved a bottle of shampoo against my chest, followed by soap and a wash cloth. He had the courtesy to finally turn on the hot water. He had a razor and shave cream, but looking at the length of beard I'd grown, he said, fuck it, and handed me a towel.

They insisted I wear a sports jacket, but decided it wasn't worth the trouble to get me to wear a tie. On our way to the board election, my brother told me I should give my executive assistant a raise after the amount of abuse I'd given her.

I thought I'd fired her.

I had. My brother immediately hired her back, so she kept coming back every day to check on me, whether I was abusive and fired her again or not. I asked if my brother would please arrange her raise. He told me, he'd already given her several, plus a bonus. It was my turn. I was the one who'd been an asshole to her. Make it a big one, and apologize for being such as asshole to her.

I vaguely remember giving my executive assistant another raise, another bonus, and apologizing to her for the way I'd treated her. I vaguely remember her being very gracious and grateful, telling me it was okay, she understood. I don't remember her name.

The Ghostwriter's Wife

Does Hell exist? I believe it does.

I believe Purgatory exists as well.

At the board election, I insisted they elect a new chairman. My brother, who was only a few years younger than me, told me that he didn't want the position. He was thinking about retiring. I looked at him, and Bob, and realized they would both soon be senior citizens. Where the hell did the time go?

I told my brother he needed to wait, and accept the position until he had someone groomed. I vaguely remember asking him, at some point that day, whether he'd ever considered having the procedure. He'd looked at Bob a moment, then shaken his head and told me not quite yet. Maybe when they figured out the rest. My wife's company, now mine alone, was still in a bit of disarray. Once they had themselves organized again, he'd give it more thought.

Afterward, I left with Bob, who didn't drive, so we sat together in the back of a limousine. When we headed out of the city, rather than return to the penthouse, I asked where he was taking me, concerned a moment at the possibilities. I was relieved when he told me, he was taking me out to the ocean front estate. I needed a change of scenery. Some fresh air. And, I needed to take better care of myself. Get up in the morning and take a walk. I had a lot of property I'd never taken the time to see. He would come and check on me every week.

I asked why we hadn't just used the chopper.

He told me we could both use a drive. Besides, he hated those damned things.

I sensed he had something on his mind, and asked what was going on. Did he want to retire too?

Bob told me he didn't think he'd ever retire. What would he do with his time? He was doing exactly what he wanted to do.

I asked, if he'd considered having the procedure?

He told me, we'd talk about it in a week or so. I needed to get some walking in, and let myself grieve without drinking myself to death.

Douglas Debelak

The sun woke me in the morning. It came directly in the window of the bedroom in which I'd decided to sleep. I couldn't sleep in the bed my wife and I had shared at the ocean front estate, any more than I could the bed at the penthouse. I still felt hung over from an uncertain number of weeks of drinking, but I had slept, and felt just a little better. I put on shorts, a t-shirt, walking shoes, and took Bob's advice. I walked. I didn't remember buying the walking shoes, nor think of any reason I would, but they were my size and comfortable. And, of course, it was hardly the first time I found things, where they needed to be, as though they'd magically appeared after a thought I didn't remember having. My administrative team had always been very attuned to my every thought or wish. None which they any longer had a way to know. So, the shoes were a mystery.

I walked down to the beach and a short distance beyond that. Until my wife's death, I'd been pretty fit for a sixty-year-old guy. But, I found myself in awful condition, which had to be in part because of all the alcohol I'd consumed over the past month or so. The residual effects of the procedure may have been lingering as well, or just the work of the nanobots rushing to remove the damage I'd done to myself.

I was also profoundly depressed. I stopped, looking out at the ocean and let tears stream down my face. Fuck. This wasn't the plan. She was supposed to be with me forever, not gone forever. I had no idea what to do next. I couldn't really think of a next. I was having an impossible time with the present.

I'd spent most of the hours of my days, since we were married, since we'd met, without her. But, there'd always been the promise of her. The anticipation of her coming home. Or, showing up unexpectedly at my office, with a 'guess what I want' look on her face. Of her sliding into bed in the middle of the night and snuggling back against me.

But, it was far more than sex that was gone. Sex had been a significant part of our lives, but it was her presence and the promise of endless tomorrows, now gone, that was the absence I felt the most. All the time in the world to do all the things couples usually do, but we'd never done, because we'd been so locked in on making sure we would have all those tomorrows and be rich enough live each of them in luxury forever. Now I was rich and alone forever.

How was living our lives, in this pursuit of immortality, any different than living our entire lives in the religious anticipation of life after death? And, now what? She was just dead? She was nothing, other than the emptiness tearing at my insides. Everything had been all those anticipated tomorrows. Now, if indeed I had them, what would I do with them? Go back to work and write virtual reality software for eternity? I couldn't see myself ever returning to that. But, I had no other plans either. I hadn't been so directionless since I'd graduated from high school.

I'd never felt the truth so acutely that forever did indeed seem a very long time.

I walked. I showered and changed my clothes. I still didn't shave. I did wash my hair, every time I showered, but didn't cut it or pay it any other attention except to pick out any debris that had become entangled in it. I walked a short distance further each day, then took several walks a day, building my endurance, until I was finally walking the entire border of the estate. I had no idea how far that was at first, but there were two miles of beach front. That was what I recalled from the broker's pitch. Two miles of water front, only part of which the beach was at most a mile and a half. The beach began at the base of the promontory which the house sat upon, the width of which was perhaps a thousand feet, then ended at the sheer cliff of another that jutted out into the ocean, forming a natural barrier at the southern edge of the property. I owned all the second promontory to the edge of the cliff on the opposite side as well. I decided I'd have to find a way up and have a look someday. We'd owned the property more than twenty years and neither of us had ever taken a proper look at it all. My wife had never had much of an interest. She went because I wanted her to go. Even though I'd spent so little time there, I'd loved the property from the moment I first saw it. I loved the idea of the place.

Never again would we have tantric sex in the gazebo, which was the part of the estate my wife had enjoyed most, listening the waves crash against the rocks below us, feeling the breeze off the ocean on our naked bodies. How the fuck had this happened?!

I was alone. I walked. Bob, good to his promise, showed up the first weekend and was pleased not to find me face down in vomit. He still hadn't been ready to tell me what was on his mind.

Eventually, I realized I'd never been entirely alone. Someone cut all that grass. Someone cleaned the house. Someone bought food and kept the refrigerator and bar stocked. Otherwise I had a magical decanter of twenty-five-year-old single malt Scotch, because it was never empty. It certainly got close to empty a few times. I'd promised Bob I'd take better care of myself. But, I still felt the need to numb my mind at night. I was also fairly sure I'd left it out in the gazebo a couple of times. I'd spent a lot of days and nights sitting there with the waves crashing against the rocks below loud enough to drown out my thoughts when I didn't want to hear them echo through my mind. But the decanter was always back in its proper place and full in the morning. There were also meals prepared and left for me with heating instructions. I ate them cold, or a small portion of most, since I had no appetite, nor energy to follow the instructions.

But, I never saw anyone else, other than Bob.

I still refused to wear a Magick Hat. I had no interest in stumbling around through Virtuality. I had no curiosity what fabulous new things my VR development team invented, or discoveries telepathic collaboration sessions had uncovered. Most importantly, I didn't want all those, how are you doing, are you okay, questions continually popping into my head like a form of torture. No one had used phones for decades. So, if my brother, or anyone else, wanted to talk to me, they'd have to do as Bob did: get in a car or use the chopper, and haul their ass out to the estate.

The cliff at the end of the beach forced me inland. It gave way to a tumble of huge boulders, then to a wooded rise, within which I suspected there'd be a path up to the top of the southern promontory. Some distance into the woods was a clearing and a beautiful waterfall. It became my regular habit, to pause there for a drink, a sandwich, and an occasional swim. The sandwiches were in the refrigerator for me every day. I still had no idea who made them.

The Ghostwriter's Wife

For months, I'd also been oblivious that'd I been crossing a small bridge on my way to the cliff and that a nice stream flowed through the southern end of my property. Once I'd discovered the waterfall, and the stream flowing from beneath its pool, I'd paid more attention to the bridge. I stopped some days to look out to where the stream ran across the sand and emptied into the ocean, or the other direction to a pool above the bridge that held some kind of fish. The water was too deep to walk across the pool below the waterfall, although I did swim across a number of times. Otherwise, to reach the other side, I had to backtrack to the bridge and walk along the opposite bank, until I discovered that I could edge my way around, along a little outcropping of rock, behind the waterfall and to the other side. Then there were more woods, with miles of paths. I had no idea who or what made them or whether anyone else ever came and walked them. No one that I'd spotted.

There was a substantial stone wall that ran along the road, which formed the eastern border of the estate. The wall continued along the road until it cut through a clearing to the main gate of the estate, which was nearly a hundred yards back from the road. There were several smaller gates along the way, all of which were locked and I knew nothing about any keys for them. I could climb the wall, near the corner of the property where the woods ended at the road, which was no more than six feet high. I'd been able to look over it, when I stood on my toes. I could easily grab the top, and there were several footholds that I could use to get myself up and over. The wall was much higher where it joined the front gate. The first time I made it that far along the road, I also discovered that I didn't know the pass code for the front gate. And, the remote that I'd always used to open the gate whenever I'd driven out to the estate before was probably in one of the cars parked in the garage beneath the penthouse. There had to be others, but I had no idea where they'd be.

So, I'd had to walk back along the road until I reached a place where I could climb the wall. Not bad for sixty, I'd thought at the time. Physically, within a few months, I'd felt as good as I could remember, thanks to all the walking.

Emotionally I was a void, except when I wasn't a void and desperately sought some way back to the void. Thus the magically refilling decanter.

Because You Never Know – Annie Fry

"Why?" Annie asked, crawling into bed beside her husband.

Jon had been reaching to turn off his night stand lamp, but stopped to look back at her. "Why?"

"Why you, why us? Why anyone for that matter? Why the dreams about her? It was like He was sharing her with us? I mean, you had sex with His wife, right?"

"In a dream," Jon clarified. "Why me, or us, I don't know. I'll never know. I don't know why he didn't just make the blog appear all by itself, and leave me, us, out of it. Apparently that's not how He works. Unless you believe the story about the stone tablets, which just appeared, it's always been people. Even then, it was Moses who found them. Just like I feel as though I found this story. It was people, the prophets, who wrote the books of the Bible."

"Do you believe that's what you are, a prophet?"

"Fuck no!" Jon laughed. "For all I really know, I'm just a guy who tells a hell of a story and doesn't give himself enough credit. I suppose there are writers who grind away, word after painful word, until they're done. And, they'd have to believe they were the ones creating something. But, this was just there. I think that has to have happened to other writers too. Still, they almost always take full credit. But, where do they honestly think their ideas came from? And, I wonder whether even the ones grinding away aren't still just finding the words. They pick them up one at a time, like sea shells on a beach. But, prophet? No, I don't want to even think about that."

"Do you think God puts them there to be found? And, why were you the one lucky enough to find His story, when there are all these other stories lying around, waiting to be found?"

"Annie," Jon began, looking off somewhere, shaking his head. "I don't know. I don't know anything. And, I guess that still makes me an agnostic, because I don't know. I don't know if there is a God. And, if there is, I don't know whether this came from Him. I don't know."

"But, you feel different?" Annie said, as much a statement as a question.

"Yeah, I do. I feel different in a lot of ways. Don't you?"

"Of course I do. How could I not? After reading the story. After the dreams... but, why us? And, why the dreams? Couldn't he just have inspired you to write the story without the dreams?"

Jon said, "I think... I think maybe, He wanted to let her live again, if only in our dreams. Maybe He shared her with us because He wants someone else to remember her, and honor her as He does."

"Do you think we're the only ones?" Annie asked.

"Maybe not," Jon told her. "And, maybe I was just conveniently writing a story that provided a good insertion point to connect His story, like a grape vine, where He grafted His story onto the roots of mine." Jon shifted and turned toward her. "Are you interested...?"

"Yes!" Annie answered, rolling toward him, sliding her hand beneath the waistband of his boxer briefs.

"You don't know... I wasn't..."

"I don't care what you were going to ask," Annie told him. "I'm interested, and I conveniently wore my naked hide and seek clothes to bed. Which was a hint by the way. But, yes, I'm interested. Every chance we get. For as long as we still can. Because, we'll never know when we'll have missed our last chance."

Annie paused a moment, then said, "Promise me."

"Promise you what?" Jon asked.

She shifted, facing away from him, with her head on his stomach. "Don't say anything. Just listen."

"Okay, I promise," Jon laughed.

Annie pinched him. "Seriously, shut up a minute, and listen. I want to say something and I don't want you to say anything until I'm done. When I'm done, I want you to say, 'I don't know what you're talking about.' That's it. Nothing else. Understand?"

"I don't know what you're talking about," Jon told her, laughing harder. "Are you going to give me a blow job or not?"

"Not unless you shut up, listen, and do what I just asked. Don't answer. Just shake your head, yes, I'll feel you move."

The Ghostwriter's Wife

Jon did as he was asked.

"Remember, 'I don't know what you're talking about.'" Annie waited for Jon to nod again. "What I want to say is: Don't ever tell me, or even look at me like there is anything to tell me. And, right now before you pause to think about what you're going to say, like you always do, and so I won't interpret that pause in whatever paranoid way I will. Say, 'I don't know what you're talking about.' Now!"

"I don't know what you're talking about," Jon said, and nothing more. He was no longer laughing.

"Thank you," Annie told him, pushing the waistband of his boxer briefs out of her way. "Thank you."

Walking Nowhere

Posted: 12/15/2015 12:00 AM

I walked for miles, every day, for several years, before I was jolted from my fog, when my brother showed up rather than Bob. He came to tell me that Bob had died. He'd been sixty-one. He had a heart attack. I'd seen him only a few weeks earlier.

Good to his word, Bob had come to check on me regularly. His visits had slowed to every couple of weeks. We'd have drinks out in the gazebo. The only time he indulged, he claimed, but we'd do damage to my decanter of Scotch. He was protecting me, he told me, only half in jest, keeping me from drinking the entire decanter myself. I could always get more, once he was gone, I told him, except, I didn't know where whoever filled the decanter stored the Scotch. I suspected that was also part of the plan to protect me from myself.

I'd always offered to let Bob stay, rather than drive back to the city. He'd always refused. He had a driver waiting. He'd be fine. He had mentioned recently that he'd retired a few months earlier, which he'd previously told me would never happen, so he must have been having health problems he hadn't wanted to bother me with.

Bob was the only friend that I'd had since I'd left the factory all those years ago. I counted my work partner on the acid tanks as a friend, although we'd never really done anything socially outside of work. For that matter, neither had Bob and I. We'd never done anything but work. But, at least it was work we'd both loved.

It might not have mattered, since he'd died of a heart attack, but we'd never talked again about the procedure, or if he wanted to live forever. Trying to absorb the news of Bob's death, I asked my brother whether he'd thought any more about having the procedure. He told me he couldn't. He'd told me that before.

I didn't remember him ever telling me he couldn't have the procedure, just that he hadn't been comfortable with the risk at the time.

He changed the subject and told me I was looking quite a bit like my youngest brother, who'd also grown a beard. My youngest brother was seven years younger than me. I rarely saw myself in a mirror, since I didn't shave. The few times I had, it was difficult to tell, because of my beard, but I noticed enough of a difference around my eyes to tell I probably no longer looked sixty-two or three. I'd lost track. I wasn't drinking champagne by myself to mark the day each year. The most important part of our celebrations was gone forever, and reminding myself that I'd never make love to my wife again was too painful.

I forced my brother back to the subject of the procedure. I asked when he had been tested.

He told me he didn't remember exactly, but it was before my wife died.

So, there was a test by then? He already knew he couldn't have the procedure when my wife had died?

Yes, my brother acknowledged, begrudgingly. They had a test by then, but still hadn't found a solution, and he knew he wouldn't have survived the procedure.

"When did they isolate the genes?"

"Earlier that year sometime."

"So, my wife should have known, right? She would have to have known. She'd have developed the fucking test! She wouldn't have fucked up something like that!"

My brother looked away from me, staring out at the ocean, and said, "Fuck!"

"Fuck, what?"

He took a deep breath and said, "Obviously, Bob never got around to talking to you." I wasn't sure whether that was a statement, or question.

"About?"

"Okay." My brother told me, pausing to gather his thoughts and choose his words carefully, "Your wife never talked to me about it directly. So I didn't know anything until after she'd died. But, she'd talked to Bob, who she apparently had sworn to secrecy. Bob told me a couple of months after the funeral."

I stared hard at my brother. "What. The. Fuck! Are. You. Talking. About!"

"Your wife had an aggressive, inoperable brain tumor. She found out sometime around her sixty-first birthday, when she began having headaches that prevented her from concentrating on her work. Bob said, at the end, she hadn't been able to contribute to her research for months, and only had weeks, maybe days, to live."

I felt something cold go through my body. She'd never said anything. She'd never told me. But, that was why she'd stopped wearing her Magick Hat. I knew she'd had headaches, but it wasn't because her Magick Hat inflamed her sinuses. She was just afraid she'd slip, share an unintended thought, and I'd find out. "She knew she was going to die. She knew the procedure would kill her."

My brother nodded. "Yeah, probably."

My mind took me back to holding her hand as she'd lain in her hospital bed. And, the things she'd said, when she was awake enough to talk. She'd apologized more times than I could count. I'd thought she was apologizing for dying and leaving me alone, forever. But, I realized, she'd probably been apologizing for not telling me about the brain tumor. "Why? We could have tried something. We had all the money in the world. There had to have been something we could have done."

My brother shook his head. "Apparently not. According to Bob, it had been asymptomatic, and by the time they found it, there was nothing they could do. And, she did take advantage of every one of the resources your wealth afforded her. She did seek out alternative treatments. Bob said, she'd had experts flown in from all over the world. Your wealth was enough that they came to her. Even though she couldn't contribute to the research any longer, she wanted to spend as much time in her lab as possible. She bought whatever diagnostic equipment these doctors needed. And, promised them, they'd live forever, if they found a way for her to live long enough for her team to find a solution, so the procedure, she knew would have also cured her cancer, wouldn't have killed her first. It was a race she lost."

"I don't understand, why the hell did she go through the charade of having the fucking procedure?"

I looked out over the water, and answered my own question. "Because she knew I wouldn't do it. That was the other thing she apologized about. She tricked me because she knew I wouldn't do it without her. And, it didn't matter that the procedure would kill her. She was going to die within days anyway."

The Ghostwriter's Wife

I was angry with her. For lying. For denying me the truth. But, I also knew, when she knew she was out of time, she'd intentionally sacrificed her own life, to ensure that at least one of us had the benefit of her life's work.

That heroic, bitch, love of my life.

It was suddenly clear. The increased booty calls. Finding her in bed when I got home, instead of her sliding into bed at three in the morning. And, her insistence on having tantric sex, after the procedure, when we were both feeling so miserable, then again, in bed, before we went to sleep. Because she knew she was dying, and wanted to make sure we made love one last time.

Tears poured down my face. My brother had walked down to the beach to find me. I began picking up rocks from the sand and throwing them as hard as I could, at anything, at nothing. My brother backed away, giving me more room. I turned away and began striding down the beach toward the cliff. I had no particular destination, any more than any other day. I was just walking. Fast. Hard. Fuck. Fuck. Fuck!

My brother called after me that Bob's funeral was that weekend. Viewing started the next afternoon. He was there to give me a ride.

He'd have to wait. I'd be back eventually. Fuck. Fuck. Fuck! I stopped every few feet to throw more rocks.

I looked up at the cliff ahead and pictured myself diving off it into the ocean. I turned when I got to the base of the cliff, as I always did, and continued toward the waterfall. I'd just do a lap. Fuck. I cried. I walked. I swore. I picked up rocks and threw them. Fuck. Fuck. Fuck.

My brother drove me to the penthouse, and I was presentably showered, shaved, dressed in a new suit, with my hair pulled back in a neat ponytail, the following afternoon. I didn't want to cut my own hair, and debated having a barber come to the penthouse, but, with no Magick Hat, I had no way to request one.

Bob's wife was at the funeral home, presumably feeling safe, since my wife wasn't there to kill her. She had a considerably younger guy with her that I presumed was her latest boy toy. I was offended for Bob that she'd had the inconsideration to bring him. Bob's three kids where there, too. I hadn't seen them for years. They were all young adults now. They'd never come see him. Now they were all new members of the billionaires' club, in addition to the money their mother had leveraged in the divorce from their father. Together they had it all, what had once been the second largest fortune in the world.

I made a quick pass at the social niceties, then tried to stay as far from them as possible. I wasn't sure if they even recognized me. But, it had been a long time. And, I'd startled myself in the mirror, once I'd shaved, a younger, leaner, version of myself staring back at me. Physically I was in the best shape of my life. Psychologically I was still a shell, empty except for the pain that continued to fill me.

I assumed most of the people who came to pay Bob respect, worked for one or the other of the companies I owned. But, I didn't recognize any of them, and they apparently didn't recognize me. I spoke to my brother, when he walked past, ignoring me. He jumped, then just stared at me.

He finally said, "You shaved, so you've obviously seen yourself in a mirror."

I nodded. I had.

Afterward, my brother and I went to dinner. He told me again that he wanted to retire. He had his replacement groomed. He was the second richest man in the world. Now it was time to see whether he could spend it all before he died. Would I please say that was okay?

I told him, I didn't think the company would fall apart without us. We'd created a monstrosity that just spewed money.

He informed me, yeah, I'd added a zero. First one to a hundred-billion. And, I was off by myself, walking and growing a beard like a hermit. Hadn't he heard that story before? He asked, "What are you going to do now?"

"Go back to the estate. Keep walking. Let my beard grow back. Maybe I'll decide to do something again, sometime in the next hundred years."

My brother didn't react to my poor attempt at a joke. He shook my hand and it was the last time I saw him. He died a few years later and willed his remaining money to me. True to his word, he must have given some effort to spending it all, but with what was left, I had at least triple the wealth of whoever was next on the list.

I discovered both pieces of news several months after the fact. There was no way to contact me, except to come to the estate in person and talk to me. My brother was the last person from the outside who'd had any regular contract with me, and he could hardly inform me of his own passing.

In addition to walking, I'd also taken to running every day. I'd never thought to measure the distance of the route, but given the time it took me to run it, I knew it was easily ten miles. Walking, I usually covered the distance in about three hours. I kept a good pace, so it would have taken less time if I didn't stop to throw a few rocks into the ocean. My best time to date was a little over two hours, although it was debatable whether I could honestly still consider it walking. Running, I had my time down to just under an hour, which was pretty good for an old guy, considering it was also far from a straight or level route. I remembered that I'd once had a goal of running a marathon someday. I didn't think I'd have any trouble, because I'd already run two consecutive laps of the route, at a pace of about a six minutes a mile. Most days, I walked two laps then ran one. So, I was covering about thirty miles a day.

Occasionally I took a route around the entire outer perimeter of my property, running along the road to the front gate. There was no longer such a thing as mail. The postal service had been defunct for decades, but packages were still delivered, and I'd found a bundle sticking out of the delivery box. I would have found it at the house later, when the house keeper and cook, or her husband brought it in. So, I did see other people, although I hadn't had a serious conversation with anyone other than myself, since I'd said good-bye to my brother after Bob's funeral.

I'd see the grounds keeper, from a distance, when he was out cutting the taller grass at the edge of the yard with a scythe, and we'd waved to one another. He cut the lawn nearer to the house with a push mower, and we'd occasionally exchange a few words, usually about the weather, or some minor thing about the property. The flowers in the meadow were pretty. The fruit trees were blooming nicely. I talked with the ground keeper's wife more frequently. She did the shopping, cooking, and was likely the answer to the mystery of the magic decanter.

Neither of them held with the notion of Magick Hats. So, their contact with the world was also face to face or not at all. They lived on a farm several miles away, and came to the house in a horse and buggy, which they also took back and forth to the small village several miles away. They had a bunch of children who helped care for my estate. They dealt with someone in the village if there were any issues to address with the property they couldn't handle themselves. This mystery person also handled the bills and had established accounts with anyone in the village where the ground keeper and his wife needed to transact any business.

They called themselves plain folk.

I was seventy. I still took no notice of the passage of time, but there was a date on the package, so I knew that another birthday had passed several months earlier. So far as I knew, my sister and my youngest brother were still around. Both my father and stepfather were long dead. And, me being seventy, meant my mother was nearly ninety.

I was far too late for my brother's funeral, but I was long overdue for a visit with my family back east. I didn't know whether I was ready to re-engage with the world again. But, I was ready to see something other than the periphery of my estate. I could probably have named the rocks on the path I walked and memorized them all.

I'd also found myself in the shower lately, with erections I felt compelled to do something about. I'd seen a couple of the groundskeeper's daughters skinny dipping in the pool beneath the waterfall recently. I wasn't sure how old they were, but one was old enough to appear womanly. Even though it had been ten years since my wife died, I still felt married, but I was also still a man, feeling younger with each passing day. I wasn't sure how to feel about that, but I knew I didn't want to be jerking off thinking about the groundskeeper's teenage daughter.

The Long Journey of Forever

Posted: 12/22/2015 12:00 AM

I did not create the Universe. I exist within it.
    I was born.
    I lived.
    I felt fear, guilt and shame.
    I loved.
    I lost.
    I was lost.
    I was alone.
    I experienced all the joy and pain of life, and questioned my choices, the right and wrong of them, as all of you have, when I was still no more than you.

Then, I was given the greatest gift ever given, from a woman who I will forever love. To whom I will be forever grateful. Who I will never forget and will never allow to be forgotten. And, yes, forever is a very long time.

For a very long time I struggled with whether it wasn't more of a curse than a gift, as I began my long journey into forever, facing unknown years ahead, not wanting to continue alone without her. But, ultimately, to do anything but cherish and honor her gift would be unthinkable. And, I needed to do more than just continue, I needed to make the most of the life ahead of me as I possibly could. And, to do so, I needed to rejoin the world, and to learn to live again.

Forever is a very long time. Of this, I'll tell you next.

ACKNOWLEDGMENTS

My wife and family, who've endured living with me living inside my own head.

Sheena Macleod, who once again, read every word and cheered me along. I especially want to thank her for her encouragement of the development of Annie Fry.

Kate Anderson, my publisher, who's hard work, once again allowed this book to see the light of day.

Michael Walsh, who has read every word, since the first rendition of what would become the Ghostwriter Series, when it was still not worth reading, and has helped me greatly to hopefully make it worth reading.

Sue Barron, for her encouragement, and another pair of sharp eyes, spotting what my brain might say, but my fingers don't get the words to the page.

Emily Hakkinen, my editor.

Michelle Arzu, cover design.

To all the members of Amazon Write On who read, commented and assisted me in becoming a better writer. RIP

My friends and neighbors, who've made the past nine years special.

Follow me on social media.

facebook.com/DouglasDebelakAuthor

Made in the USA
Middletown, DE
18 September 2017